BOOK ONE OF THE TROJAN HORSE IN THE
BELLY OF THE BEAST TRILOGY

# THOUGH THEY COME FROM THE
# ENDS *of the* EARTH

I0526422

A Novel of the Iran Nuclear Weapons
Interdiction Project

A Novel by

## CARL DOUGLASS

Former Neurosurgeon Turned Author
Who Writes with Gripping Realism

PO Box 221974 Anchorage, Alaska 99522-1974
books@publicationconsultants.com—www.publicationconsultants.com

ISBN 978-1-59433-458-0
eISBN 978-1-59433-459-7
Library of Congress Catalog Card Number: 2014936143

Manufactured in the United States of America.

# DEDICATION

To Vera and all the other good women.

# DISCLAIMER

*T*hough *They Come from the Ends of the Earth* is a work of fiction and any resemblance to any person living or dead or to any actual event is unintended or coincidental. The premise of the story is just that, a story. Considerable fictional latitude and invention was employed to create a "reality" of persons, places, dialogue, and actions. But, remember, this is a novel, a creation of the author and not reality.

# BOOK ONE

# *Though They Come from the Ends of the Earth*

Oh, East is East and West is West, and never the twain shall meet, Till Earth and Sky stand presently at God's great Judgment Seat; But there is neither East nor West, Border, nor Breed, nor Birth, When two strong men stand face to face, though they come from the ends of the earth!

*-The Ballad of East and West*
by Rudyard Kipling-

# CHAPTER ONE

"I know you've grown up. You will marry. But to me you are the same little angels who carried the kiss of Ahoora and innocence on your forehead, and it will always be visible. Who knows if you were not the angels born out of poverty and suffering, if you were not petitioning for a women's rights campaign, or if you were not born in this corner of the land that God has forgotten, then maybe you would not be forced, at thirteen, with eyes full of tears and envy under the white bridal veil, to say goodbye to school for the last time and experience completely the bitter experience of being the second sex."

-Farzad Kamangar, Iranian Kurdish teacher, poet, journalist, human and women's rights, and environmental activist from the city of Kamyaran who was executed on May 9, 2010. This is an excerpt from a talk he gave to his grade school girl students.

## Qushchu Village, Kurdestan County, West Azerbaijan Province, Iran, November 22, 1980

The screaming coming from inside the rust colored birthing tent ceased after forty-eight hours because little Nawsheen was exhausted. The last sound the women outside the tent heard was a low agonal moan, and then there was five minutes of silence. They knew that the thirteen-year-old primiparous child—the fourth wife, trying to deliver her first infant—was dead. They shared knowing looks and the long, deep sadness of women. After the short quiet pause, the tent emitted a lusty cry from a strong baby protesting its entry into the barren world of Kurdestan, Iran. The midwife looked out through the tent flap and motioned for Fereshten—the first wife—to come to her. They spoke for a moment and shook their heads at the double tragedy that had occurred in the tent that morning.

"Is it a slave?" asked Ahriman Shakibaie, Nawsheen's fifty-two-year-old husband of two years, when he came to the tent an hour later.

Fereshten bowed her head and admitted that the new baby was a girl. They were speaking Kurdish.

"Is it dead?" he asked, speaking of the thin little girl who was until then his wife.

"She is. She suffered to death. Her pelvis was too narrow. The midwife had to cut the slave out of the little womb," Fereshten replied matter-of-factly.

"Worthless," Shakibaie said.

No one called him by his given name.

"Put the slave on the mountain."

He turned and walked back to the goat pens, his interest in the matter completed.

Azedeh—the third wife—turned her head in her chador and hid her tears. *"Not even the women have pity in Iran,"* she said to herself.

"Azedeh, take the baby to the top of the Mount of Thorns," Fereshten ordered the third wife.

Fereshten disliked Azedeh because she was younger and had a softer and more rounded face that her husband preferred. She never missed an opportunity to take out her annoyance on Azedeh or the other wives. Nawsheen was a child whose breasts had hardly formed, and why her old husband bothered to take her to wife was a small mystery to Fereshten. The girl was lazy and awkward. Nothing but a pretty face.

As always, Azedeh obeyed with alacrity to avoid a slap from Fereshten or worse, a few strokes of her husband's camel quirt. Her name meant "free"; however, she was anything but that; and had she taken a moment to contemplate the irony, she would have had a small chuckle. She took the new baby girl—naked, squalling, and still coated with blood, amniotic fluid, and cheese-like vernix caseosa from the delivery—slowly up to a bare spot on the rocks half a kilometer away from the cluster of the clan's tents.

"Poor little thing," she said softly. "But it is better this way than to be a woman of Islam."

She laid the shivering little girl baby on the hard rock and took note of where the baby was located so that she could return the next morning to pick up the corpse before the wolves could get to it. She hiked up the skirts of her chador—the enveloping cloak worn by post pubescent women that covered females from the top of the head to the ground to protect men from their own lust. In accordance with local custom, Azedeh wore hers without a face veil and unfastened in the front. She was careful not to let any hint of her shapely young legs show, even though she was the only member of the clan outside away from the warmth of the fireplaces.

She made her way back down the rocky hillside trail. She was barefoot but did not notice the impact of the sharp rocks or the occasional thorn on the soles of her feet that were hardened by her fifteen years of walking without shoes. Only Fereshten had sandals since she was the privileged first wife, and she had nothing but disdain for the other three wives—now only two. It would not be long before the master of the clan found another wife or concubine. He needed the workers.

"*Inshallah*," Azedeh muttered.

The next morning was especially cold, and Azedeh comforted herself that the girl child would have died quickly during the freezing night and would not have suffered long. Shivering and hungry because she had been punished for grumbling about having to clean up the birthing tent the night before, she made her way back to where the baby—now blue and stiff—was lying. It was a human being, after all, Azedeh reasoned; so, she picked it up gently and held it close to her chest. As she carried her cold little bundle down the trail, it seemed to her as if some of her own body heat was passing into the baby. She was astounded when the girl began to move. At first, the movement was barely discernible and then it gathered strength. By the time Azedeh was down at the bottom and making her way to the tents, the child was crying vigorously and clutching at Azedeh's covered breasts.

"*It is a miracle, a gift from Allah, the merciful*," Azedeh said to herself and wondered who she should tell about the little miracle.

She knew not to tell her husband. He would kill the slave and whip Azedeh for having returned with a live baby. Fereshten would never countermand an order from Shakibaie, and would probably take a knife to the baby herself. That left Astera—beautiful Astera—the star. She was the third wife, the girl with the shimmering light brown hair, the woman with the shapely young figure, and Shakibaie's favorite; but still, she had a trace of regard for the other women and even for girl children.

Astera was perplexed to see the living baby, but made an immediate decision to keep the fact quiet and to find a wet nurse among the women of the clan. She wrapped the little one in a warm sheepskin blanket and put her finger in the tiny infant's mouth. The baby sucked with remarkable vigor for one who had come back from the dead.

Once she had placed the baby in the arms of the wet nurse—an older woman of forty-five named Yasmin—she and the older woman talked about what to do with the new addition to the clan.

"Shall we enter her name in the *shenas nameh*?" Astera asked Yasmin.

Throughout modern Iran, when a child is born, an official document that serves as identification for the rest of the person's life is issued. Events such as marriages or the birth of children are recorded in the document. The document is required to be presented to any official; and without it, one is regarded as not being a citizen of the country, or worse, not even a person.

"Husband will be angry if we do," Astera said. "It's better that we don't. This one will suffer enough without Shakibaie taking out all of his anger on it for having become another mouth to feed, let alone having to pay the filing fee."

"What shall we call her?" Astera wondered out loud.

"How about Afsoon? She was born under a charm—a spell and a bewitchment—so let that be her name.

Yasmin had grey hair and a wrinkled face, both of which spoke of wisdom and experience. It was settled. Afsoon started life as a nonperson.

# CHAPTER TWO

Sweet dreams, form a shade O'er my lovely infant's head; Sweet dreams of pleasant streams By happy, silent, moony beams.

Sweet sleep, with soft down Weave thy brows an infant crown. Sweep sleep, Angel mild, Hover o'er my happy child.

-William Blake (*1757-1827*)
A *Cradle Song* from
*Songs of Innocence*

## 28314 Terrace Drive, Saint Francis Wood nabe, San Francisco, California, November 30, 1980

Gideon Emmanuel Rothsberger III had the delivery of his son planned down to the smallest detail. The baby was due to arrive in the world in two weeks exactly. He would be a boy because banker Rothsberger III had decreed that it would be so. Rothsberger III's firstborn—as scion and heir to the Rothsberger fortune started by Rothsberger I—would one day succeed to the pair of thrones occupied by his grandfather and father—Rothsbergers II and III. The two most powerful men in the influential and rich family now sat in the two top seats in the family business. Beginning with great grandfather, Rothsberger I, each man magnified his office and holdings and would pass that office on better and richer than he had found and received it. Rothsberger I was ninety-three, fully retired, and was cared for in a hospice section of the family home.

When he was in San Francisco, Rothsberger II occupied the upper two floors of the mansion, described by the rest of the family as the rooms with the views. Rothsberger III and his wife occupied the bottom two floors of the mansion, and he was the current president of Rothsberger & Company Bankers. Rothsberger II—the as yet unborn Rothsberger IV's grandfather—was still very much alive and active and was CEO—head of the parent company, the global conglomerate Gideon Products Universal. The succession in the company was so set in stone that it was as if the finger of Yahweh, Himself, had written it there. Rothsberger II had become bank president when the company expanded globally. His father, Rothsberger I, created the new position CEO of the global company for himself in 1951. Rothsberger II moved up to the CEO position when Rothsberger I became too frail and demented to carry on; and his son, Rothsberger III, moved up from his seat on the bank board to become its president. God was in His heaven, and all was right with the world of the Rothsbergers. The new child would be named Gideon Emmanuel Rothsberger IV, and he would one day be on the board of the bank. His grandfather would die, and his father would become CEO, and he would become bank president. His father would someday die, and he would become CEO. He would have a son who would succeed him when he, too, died, and so *ad infinitum*. Therefore, it is easy to understand why the expected child would be a boy—it could not be otherwise—and why it was the perfectly sensible thing to name him the fourth in the line—Gideon Emmanuel Rothsberger IV.

It was unthinkable, and therefore, could not happen, that the first child of Rothsberger III and nineteen-year-old Chava (pronounced k'hava) Dayan-Hershowitz Rothsberger would be a girl. Gideon had nothing against girls—he loved his diminutive beautiful wife dearly—but it was unthinkable that a woman would ascend to the head of Gideon Products Universal. There was very little that the forceful man had ever failed as he passed from boyhood to his Bar Mitzvah, and on to his highly successful university career and finally into the bank. As dictated by his august father, Gideon II, young Gideon III had climbed the corporate ladder from the basement—as a copy boy and courier—to the cashiers' desk, and finally to the board room. He did not speak of it—even to his wife—but he got his key to the executive washroom six months earlier than his father.

Once each new Gideon Emmanuel Rothsberger had his Bar Mitzvah, he became known by his number. So, it had been G.R. I, G.R. II, G.R. III, and would soon the G.R. IV. Each man had taken to signing his name in a nearly unreadable flourish, but the G.R. and the Roman numeral were always somewhat discernible. It was as much an affectation of the Rothsbergers as the Queen of England signing her official documents, E.R. II. The hubris of the affectation was not lost on any of the family members, and it was a standing joke to pretend confusion at the number system. There was no joking about the proud names outside the family circle.

Chava—beautiful raven-haired Chava—was proud of her dynamic and very wealthy husband; and it never occurred to her to question that the child filling her abdomen so heavily would be anything but a Rothsberger boy. There would be no question about the boy's name either; he would be Gideon Emmanuel Rothsberger IV. The family succession was by strict primogeniture. Second or third sons were given important positions, just not the top two seats. The Roman numerals after each successive scion's name were as important as if they had been M.D., D.D.S., M.B.A., or Ph.D. Every Rothsberger male—twenty-two of them—had gone into the family business. Although each had graduated with honors from one or another prestigious university, none of them included a B.A., or a B.S. after his name; and none of them had ever gotten a postgraduate degree. The Rothsberger name was sufficient. There were a few other men who had Roman numerals after the Rothsberger, but from other lines, and there were no other Gideons or Emmanuels. Only brothers and their sons of G.R. I ever sat on a Rothsberger board. Every board member of Rothsberger & Company Bankers bore the same last name. The Gideon Products Universal board was composed of fifty percent Rothsberger men—all Orthodox and no women—twenty-five percent came from somewhat more extended family; and a refreshing 25 percent collection of highly intelligent and successful non-family members including Asians, Italians, British, and even Blacks—all WASPS—constituted the rest of the imperious board.

A week later, Chava met her mother for lunch at the St. Francis. Rebecca Hershowitz was the family matron of her powerful industrialist clan. Rebecca's mother, the previous matron, had died unexpectedly two years ago just before the marriage of Chava and Rothsberger III. Hers was a family where women had been accepted into important positions in the family business for fifty-plus years. Rebecca's maiden name was Dayan—the richest family in Chicago—and her marriage to Hyman Hershowitz became a merger of dynasties. No one contested her insistence that the middle name of her daughter, Chava, should be Dayan, even though it was not her nuclear family name. Rebecca was already a widow at age forty and, by default, became the richest woman in San Francisco and the unchallenged head of Hershowitz Mining, Ironworks, and Steel, a worldwide conglomerate. It miffed the forty-year-old CEO that Chava's domineering husband was so hide-bound to tradition that he would not even entertain the possibility of his firstborn bearing either the Dayan or the Hershowitz name. There had been a hint that a subsequent boy might take one or the other of those names. In fact, Gideon III knew that it might well give a comfortable nudge to the Chicago Dayans to move their banking business to Rothsberger Family Bankers. That would be a coup that would ensure Rothsberger III's position as the head of the board into perpetuity. He already had planned to have his next child be a boy, and to grant the largess of bestowing the great family name on his boy. He had not let his wife or mother-in-law in on his plans just yet. That might seem to be rushing things—or, worse—to be self-serving.

Rebecca was a tall, statuesque, and proud beauty who could have passed as an older sister of her young daughter, except that Chava was smaller and fair with unruly curly hair and a dainty Danish nose. Rebecca had straight honey-blond hair that she wore in the new longer length having a soft upturn at the level of her graceful shoulders. A diamond studded hairpin kept her thick hair off her face. She wore only the slightest touches of makeup on her exotic olive skin, so subtly applied that it could have been the work of a professional makeup artist. She wore a form fitting eggshell wraparound silk dress and matching pumps with stiletto heels. Unlike her more conservative friends, she did not wear nylon stockings. Her slim, recently shaved legs shined as if they had been polished. Rebecca was a Jewess but—unlike the Rothsbergers who wore their Orthodox Jewishness like a proud mantle,—she was a rather worldly reformed Jew. The Rothsbergers had cringed a bit when the beautiful daughter of a nonOrthodox family was being considered for acceptance as the new bride of the heir apparent of the banking and business fortune. That had evaporated even before the marriage when Chava had willingly adopted full Orthodox practice.

"Have a seat, dear," Rebecca said.

She stood to give her uncomfortable and very pregnant daughter brush-by kisses on each cheek. Chava—absent pregnancy—could have been bikini model in a different world; but, after the marriage, she wore the frumpy greys and blacks of a proper Orthodox matron. After the pregnancy became visible, Chava looked like an inflated black weather balloon.

"How are you doing? You look ready to pop. When is the great day?"

"Any day now, Mom. It can't be too soon. I feel like a big swollen water-filled balloon."

"I want to help, Chava. I know you are all rich as Croesus and can afford all the help that an empress could want, but I want to exercise my motherly prerogative to bustle about and fluff your pillows and change the baby's diapers."

"*The boy's* diapers, don't you mean, Mother dear?" Chava said with a small wry smile.

"Oh, but of course. *He* has decreed that it be so like King Saul or David, and it will be so."

The two women had a small conspiratorial laugh.

"I'm famished," said Chava. "That's part of why I am so fat. I will have a devil of a time getting the weight off after *he* arrives."

"Let's see what this joint serves for us Kosher girls," Rebecca said with a mildly mocking grin.

Chava ordered a small Adler sandwich—assorted deli meats separated by paper-thin Russian rye bread with Kosher mustard and coleslaw—as an appetizer—a salad Nicoise—chunks of fresh tuna piled on field greens, string beans, cherry tomatoes, boiled potato, succulent red bell pepper strips, thinly sliced cucumbers, hardboiled egg, and tart black olives imported from a Kosher olive vineyard in Greece, served with the house vinaigrette—and a potato knish. Her entrée was a half portion of corn beef and cabbage. Rebecca ordered a ham and cheese sandwich and a beer just to get a rise out of her newly Orthodox daughter.

"Are you happy, dear?" Rebecca asked her daughter after they finished their lunches and after an innocuous chat between bites of the beautiful food.

"I am, Mom. Like everybody, I have had to make some concessions. You know as well as I do that the life of an Orthodox Jewish wife and mother is pretty stultifying and altogether too careful. I am used to living with you in the freedom of a reformed household, but I love III. He is good to me and does not carry the male chauvinism too far. It is bearable. I am happy to have hitched my wagon to his star."

"I'm glad of that. I loved your father to distraction, and he loved me as well. He gave me very wide latitude in my life's choices and laughed at my little rebellions. I miss him immensely. However, living with my own star made me strong. You are also strong, my dear, and I have a feeling that you will need to be before you come to the end of your life."

The two women parted with a fond embrace. Rebecca had to get ready for a business trip to Jerusalem, and Chava needed to get her suitcase packed for an immediate trip to the hospital when IV started fighting his way into the world.

The following morning, Gideon III rechecked his arrangements, which now were so ingrained in his mind that he did not have to refer to his notes. Gideon IV would be born in the California Pacific Medical Center's Women's and Children's Center between Presidio Heights and Laurel Heights neighborhoods. It was close to Temple Emanu-El on Lake Street, and only six or so blocks from the Rothsberger mansion. He had timed it: he could have Chava at the hospital in less than ten minutes even in traffic. He had reserved a suite of rooms for Chava and the new baby boy on the top floor of the hospital and had secured the services of David ben Schulberg, M.D. who had emigrated from Israel after medical school, residency, and his obligatory national military service. He had done additional postdoctoral training at the University of California, San Francisco in the specialized area of difficult pregnancies. He was on call at a fee that made cancelling his busy schedule for two days a lucrative rest. Gideon III was not taking any chances. His first son would be afforded every possible chance to come into the world intact, safe, and healthy, and with angels hovering over him.

G.R. III had extended his paternal influence even further. He had made reservations for his son's preschool, kindergarten, and elementary education at the Temple Emanu-El Congregation and preschool and in the adjacent Yeshiva school that would take care of his education until he graduated from high school. Harvard had refused to reserve a place for the boy in the class of 1998 even after a generous offer to build a needed religious studies center on the campus well before that time. So—in something of a huff—G.R. III enrolled his scion in Yale, which was only too happy to accept a multimillion dollar grant to further their State Department studies program beginning the upcoming year. All was in readiness to bring the boy into a world where he would be a member of the dominant class.

It was a good thing, too. Chava came down to breakfast and—as calmly as a cooing dove—announced that her waters had broken and she was in active labor. The chauffeur was in the room in less than a minute; Chava's bags were already in the trunk of the Mercedes; and the couple was whisked out of the mansion, into the limousine, and through the obstetric department doors in eight and a half minutes flat. She was wheelchaired into an examination room and was found to be well dilated and effaced.

"It won't be very long, Chava, Mr. Rothsberger, even though this is Chava's first baby. I am going to give her a little squirt of Pitocin to keep her well on track, then I will do an epidural to keep her comfortable. We'll be taking Chava to the delivery room right away; so, make yourself comfortable, Sir. I'll make sure you are kept apprised of the progress."

Dr. ben Schulberg was the picture of calm and authority, and the nurses and the prospective parents were reassured. G.R. III took a seat in the fathers' waiting room and read that morning's copy of the *Chronicle*.

The epidural went in without a hitch and caused almost no pain. A nurse wiped Chava's sweating brow as she labored. It was a wonderful thing to be free of pain but able to do her job of pushing. It took five hours, and the slight girl was very tired when her baby's head finally crowned. The doctor carefully eased the baby out and placed him on Chava's now slack abdomen, tied and cut the umbilical cord with sterile instruments, and cleaned him up. His

Apgar score was ten. A nurse had been given the sole task of keeping G.R. III informed, and he accepted the preordained fact that his new baby was a boy.

He told the nurse that the baby would be known as Gideon Emmanuel Rothsberger IV, and that was official; she could put it on the birth certificate. When she left the room, he heaved a small satisfied sigh of relief. IV had arrived. He was to start life as a person of importance. Just as the Spanish grandees labeled their sons as *"hidalgos"*—sons of someone!—so would the newest G.R. be recognized.

# CHAPTER THREE

A lot of people resist transition and therefore never allow themselves to enjoy who they are. Embrace the change, no matter what it is; once you do, you can learn about the new world you're in and take advantage of it.

-Nikki Giovanni

Yasmin's breasts began to dry up as Afsoon passed her second year in the isolated hamlet of Qushchu village. She and Astera had taken upon themselves the hazardous task of keeping Afsoon fed and clothed and a secret. Early on, Afsoon's main source of nourishment was the milk from Yasmin's abundant breasts; but—over time—that source waned; and Astera had to sneak food from the table of her husband, Ahriman Shakibaie. Astera had not yet borne a child; so, she had been able to keep her figure and thus her allure for her aging man. As a result, he overlooked her small acts of rebellion and moodiness, because if he punished her too often or too severely, he found her to be as unresponsive as a bag of rice in his bed.

He was busy trying to get his sheep and goats to new pastures during that drought year, and so he was often absent. That gave Astera the chance to take baskets of fruits, vegetables, chicken, and fish to the little hut in the mud flats where the child and Yasmin lived in hiding. Some days, she could get *shish kubide*—kababs made of ground fresh, minced meat mixed with ground bread crumbs when meat was available. On special days, she cooked more lamb *fille kabab* or chicken *juje kababs* sprinkled with spicy *somaq* than was necessary for the communal table and filched the extra for the little girl and her protector. Astera was regularly able to bring Yasmin the makings for *abgusht* or *piti*, as it is known in Azerbiajan, or as *dizi* locally; and Yasmin cooked up the standard food of the poor—cheap soup/stew—in an earthenware pot from which little Afsoon and Yasmin ate with old or broken spoons purloined by Astera from the kitchen of the great tent.

For her second birthday celebration, the toddler and Yasmin sat cross-legged on the dirt floor of the mud hut—there were no chairs or couches—and ate together from their communal pot. They drained off the soupy broth of the *dizi* into wooden bowls—made by Yasmin—and filled with bite-sized pieces of coarse rye and wheat bread. Separately, the two females worked together to grind chickpeas, potatoes, tomatoes, and boiled mutton into a dense mush with a strong metal pestle that looked like a toilet plunger. The batch that day was especially good because it had a few chunks of mutton fat the kind woman saved for her small charge. Afsoon thrived on Yasmin's hearty and healthy food and her love. She grew to be a chubby, gregarious, happy sprite as long as she was isolated with her protector.

For females in Iran, good things are few and far between and do not last. When Afsoon was four years old, she became aware that Yasmin was becoming thinner and had less endurance to play with her. She became listless and less interested in creating rag dolls and small puppet theaters to entertain the little girl.

Finally, Afsoon asked, "Mama, you look sick. What is wrong?"

"Nothing, little dear," Yasmin said. "I am fine, just fine."

"No Mama, you are not. I can see. I can tell. You must not lie to me. I am not safe if you lie to me."

Yasmin had always stressed the need for safety for the two of them in the precarious world in which they lived as semi-fugitives. Afsoon learned early and well that there were great dangers around them and that her beloved Yasmin was her only defense. There were wolves, the occasional bear, and there were bandits. Afsoon did not quite understand the admonition to avoid men, but it was made clear that she must avoid them at any cost. Afsoon was bright and—despite not knowing fully the reason why—she adopted a wary set of behaviors whenever she and Yasmin came near men. Yasmin never let the little girl out of her sight. They went into the village in their black chadors. Although it was not strictly required for a little prepubescent girl, Yasmin had made a small enough chador for Afsoon that she could remain out of sight of the men who frequented the souks and tea houses in Qushchu.

Yasmin was a peasant woman, and a woman of Iran. She was used to harsh realities and knew that little Afsoon could not safely be shielded from the truth.

"Dear one, I did make a little lie for you. I am sorry. I have a bad sickness. I am afraid that I will not be with you much longer. You are right. We must have truth between us. I will fill my last days trying to teach you how to live. Today we will learn how to make some clothes; and tomorrow, with Astera, we can learn how to cook simple things so you can stay fat."

Astera spent more time with Yasmin and Afsoon. Almost every day, she brought a bucket of the water from Lake Orumiyeh that was heavy with healing minerals. She heated the water, and she and Afsoon gently washed Yasmin's pain-wracked body with the soothing liquid. Afsoon was frightened at the touch of the withering sallow skin, but she persisted out of love.

Slowly—under Astera's tutelage—the little girl began to master simple chores and lifesaving skills. Her fingers were nimble but inexperienced, and sometimes Astera hit her when she failed to be able to learn immediately. When Afsoon cried and looked at her with anger or fear, Astera told her that life is hard; and she had to get used to it.

"Stop crying now. You must stop being a little girl and learn to be tough. To be a woman in Iran, you have to be tougher than the men. Shut up this instant."

Afsoon learned that it was futile to cry or to complain to Astera. She learned to keep her fears and her inner pain to herself. Astera took note of the progress the child was making and was heartened at the way she was developing a thicker skin and a better capacity to pay attention and to learn.

Astera also took note of Yasmin's progressively failing health and questioned her friend more insistently.

"Dear Yasmin, I am concerned about you. You do not seem able to do your work. I worry for little Afsoon. What will become of her if you ... cannot ... care for her?"

Yasmin paused for a long silent moment.

"I am ill, very ill, Astera; and I fear every day for my dear little Afsoon. I have a large mass in my breast, and I can feel kernals under my arms. I know that it is the death of women, and I am little more than a walking dead person. There is no treatment, no cure. Soon I will die. Please, dear Astera, you must protect her. You must find a way to get her food and to teach her how to protect herself"

Astera had never considered taking major—let alone full—responsibility for the little girl Azedeh had saved from the freezing mountainside those four years ago. She maintained an expressionless face as she pondered the dilemma. She knew she could count on Azedeh's discretion, but would she help?

"I will do what I can."

"Thank you. It is all I can ask. Consider the beauty, charm, and brightness of this girl, Astera. She is more intelligent than any girl in the village or even the city. She is special. Please find a way."

She turned her head aside and lost her fight to contain her tears.

Yasmin was in pain. She had the worst of breast cancer—the inflammatory form. Over the next few weeks, she turned into a skeleton wracked with pain from bony metastases. The role of Afsoon and Yasmin reversed so that the four-year-old became the nurse and little mother for her beloved mama who now looked like a concentration camp victim. Yasmin had once kept the dirt floor packed down with a little water and swept it every day. She had been able to keep the leaks in the mud hut closed with daily replacement of mud packing. Little Afsoon could not wield the heavy broom well enough and dust from the poorly swept floor now floated up in small puffs when she walked across it. Yasmin could no longer get out of bed. Afsoon spooned a little of the *ash-e mast* [hot yogurt soup with beans, lentils, and vegetables] Astera brought; but Yasmin could only tolerate, two or three tablespoonsful each meal. Some days, she could not eat at all.

Astera could no longer bear to see Yasmin in her condition; so, she came infrequently now. When she did, the food she brought was barely enough for Afsoon, but could be stretched because Yasmin's appetite was so impaired. Before the sickness, Afsoon was a mischievous sprite constantly playing little tricks on her mama and making the hut ring with laughter. She loved her protector exuberantly and showered her with kisses and hugs during the time of plenty. Now winter had come, and the hut was cold. Afsoon shivered in her thin makeshift inside dress and no longer laughed or played. She tried not to, but she cried whenever she looked at Yasmin. Every day the older woman became more haggard. Her skin turned grey, and her eyes were sunken. She seldom spoke, just moaned in pain. Afsoon cried all the time, and Yasmin could no longer comfort her.

The morning was extremely cold. Afsoon took every blanket and piece of clothing that was not required to keep Yasmin warm and wrapped herself in them. She fashioned clumsy foot coverings from the hide of an old dog that had died in the snow, but she still had cold feet. The sad little girl sat for long hours at the side of Yasmin's mattress on the floor and held her hand. Yasmin's breathing was stertorous, but Afsoon barely paid attention because of her own shivering and sobbing. No food had come that day, and Afsoon's pangs of hunger were beginning to trouble her. She lapsed into an uncomfortable sleepiness and dozed for an hour. When she awakened, she worried about being able to find food for Mama. As she awakened, she became aware that there were spiders on the floor and worried that she needed to sweep them out. She turned to look at Mama and saw something very odd. Her eyes were open and staring. Afsoon recoiled as she became aware that Mama's hand was cold. There was a smell in the room—the smell of decay. As the sun began to set, Afsoon recognized the smell in the hut as that which permeated the abattoir a kilometer away from the mud flats where the hut was located; it was the smell of death.

# CHAPTER FOUR

On the first Friday night after the birth of Gideon Emmanuel Rothsberger IV, GR III and Chava invited the crème de la crème of Saint Francis Wood nabe to their home for a *Shalom Zachar*—welcome to the baby boy. Fifty of the richest San Franciscans, dressed formally for the occasion with tuxedos for the men and diamonds for the women, came to offer the heartiest of well-wishes. The occasion was especially significant because the baby boy was the firstborn child who would one day take his place at the head of his family's company and would be one of the movers and shakers of San Francisco.

Chava was home from the hospital and recuperating rapidly. Fifty couples had been invited and seventy-five showed up. The mansion had been cleaned from top to bottom, inside and out, by a small army of professional cleaners. The wood and stone floors gleamed with a mirror shine that surgery could have been safely done there. The carpets had been steam-cleaned and still carried a faint odor of wetness. That odor was overwhelmed by the scent of several thousand flowers situated all over the grand house.

The Rothsberger butler, Joseph ben Aaron, greeted each guest couple formally and with a big smile. The husband of each couple discreetly handed the butler a thin envelope. Non-family envelopes contained checks ranging from $500 to a $1000, and family envelopes averaged $10,000. Gideon Emmanuel Rothsberger II had arrived the night before from Paris. He gave the butler a check for $100,000 accompanied by a terse note: "For the lad's education." Joseph moved away from the main entryway briefly at intervals to transfer envelopes to a footman; so, his pockets would not develop an unseemly bulge.

Each couple—including the gentiles—greeted G.R. III, Chaya, G.R. II, and Chaya's mother, Rebecca Hershowitz, who formed a greeting line, and intoned the traditional greeting: "We welcome the newborn on this first Shabbat that he is with us."

The Orthodox were dressed in simple—but expensive and formal—black and white evening wear. The conservatives and reformed wore black suits and colored power ties, and their wives were resplendent in pastel evening gowns. The gentiles—for the most part—were dressed much like the conservatives and reformed Jews, but a few of the less informed wore grey suits or even sport coats, patterned ties; and their wives had embarrassingly short stylish skirts. Mrs. Hershowitz outshined them all. She wore a form-fitting black Jovani evening gown. The New York City designers had opened for business only that year, and she had been taken by their creative work. Their designs were becoming overnight sensations and were now in demand by Hollywood glitterati. The dress had a scoop neck that revealed more of her opulent chest than most of the Orthodox men had seen of their wives. Attention was drawn to the area below her clavicles by the stunning huge single diamond she wore on a diamond encrusted platinum chain suspended tauntingly in a soft valley. Men kept their eyes rigidly focused upwards, and their wives stifled their comments until they were on the way home.

The beautifully dressed baby was on his best behavior as he was presented to the august gathering of the most highly placed people in San Francisco. There was more money represented in that room that night than most small countries have in their treasuries.

"Refreshments are served in the dining room, ladies and gentlemen," announced the head housekeeper.

G.R. III and Chava escorted their guests into a beautifully decked-out wood paneled room with Philippine mahogany parquet floors and a twenty-two-foot long cedar table rumored to have come from pieces of cedars of Lebanon brought back by victorious Israeli Defense soldiers at the end of the Six-Day War. Jewish tradition suggests that light refreshments be served and that, often, friends and neighbors provide the potluck repast.

Not so in the Rothsberger mansion on that day of days. Family and guests were treated to a buffet that included several kosher wines from the non-kosher winery Château Beaucastel that flash pasteurizes, and its wines are considered among the world's finest. Rabbi Menachum Bergen assured the Orthodox attendees that the controversial pasteurization process used in the winery was overseen by *mashgichim* to ensure the kosher status of the wine, and that the wine did not have to be labeled "Manufactured by Gentiles."

The light refreshments prepared by *baalei teshuvah* chefs from the Los Angeles Mosaica Bistro included: duck leg confit served with white bean cassoulet, house-made lamb bacon, a simple salad of arugula, pickled and roasted beets and horseradish, corn and fava beans carefully layered beneath a succulent, generously portioned piece of Arctic char. Other appetizers included Wagyu short ribs, pickled ginger, frisee, crispy parsnip. The entrée choices were: grilled organic Scottish Salmon with pan roasted artichokes, scallions, maple mustard in a red wine reduction, Black Angus steak au poivre with black olives, mashed potatoes, cipollini onions, endives in a kosher red wine sauce. There were also half roasted chicken, Yukon potato, lemon and caramelized onion. Sides included: Wood roasted cauliflower, pine nuts, tomato, marinated raisins, Japanese eggplant with sweet chili sauce, and roasted fingerling potatoes with garlic and herbs.

Dessert offerings for this set of light refreshments included: passion fruit meringue, passion banana fruit sorbet, coconut sorbet, vanilla ice cream on moist chocolate cake, hazelnut Rocher, synthetic "milk" chocolate praline mousse, toasted hazelnuts, molten chocolate cake, vanilla ice cream, mandarin crème Chiboust brûlée, and fresh fruit in a warm orange liquor sauce.

After the meal, Rabbi Bergen congratulated the new parents and lavished praise on the beauty and vigor of the new boy who had been welcomed into the Jewish world that day. He ended the evening with an invitation.

"You are all invited back to this gracious home tomorrow evening—the eighth day of young Gideon Emmanuel Rothsberger the IV's life—for the celebration of the *Brit Milah*.

The following evening, all of the guests sans a few squeamish gentiles arrived back at the mansion for the celebration. Gifts were not expected this time. The father and mother of the newborn gave their guests short greetings; and when all the guests were assembled, Rabbi Bergen gave a short talk regarding the ceremony they had come to celebrate.

"The *Brit Milah* or Bris, as it is more commonly known, is a ritual circumcision ceremony. The word "*Brit*" means covenant in Hebrew, and this event reaffirms the covenant made between Abraham and God some 3,500 years ago. For the Jewish people, *Brit Milah* is a physical sign of the covenant—an indelible mark on the boy and the man that links him to the Jewish people, the Torah, and its commandments. It is the same for the Orthodox, the conservative, and the reformed. After this ceremony, baby Gideon Emmanuel Rothsberger IV—son of a Jewish mother, and a circumcised male—will be truly and permanently Jewish and will be a member of a proud Jewish family. He will be loved and protected. He will be supported by *k'lal Yisrael*—the entire Jewish community. We will be his family, and he will be ours. His name shall be written into the Book of Life.

"The Hebrew name chosen by his loving parents for their son is Avraham because one of the reasons the Jews were redeemed from Egypt was because they did not give up their Hebrew names. Avraham was the first patriarch of the Jewish people, who dedicated his life to teaching the world about the one God. We know from the Torah and from the writings of the prophets and the Talmud that Avraham was a master of kindness, and we all wish for our new little Avraham that he will live up to such a name. He has been given much; and from him, much will be expected."

Unobtrusively, a small wizened old man—impeccably dressed all in black—stepped up to the rabbi and stood quietly behind him.

Rabbi Bergen glanced towards the man and gestured towards him saying, "This is Abba Cogen. He is the *Mohel* as he is properly known, or the *moy'l*, as he is known in Yiddish, who will perform the *Brit Milah* ceremony. His first name means "father," and he can be regarded as such by all of us. His surname, "Cogen," marks him as a descendant of the tribe of Cohen or Levi, and so he is a priest. Know that Abba is a super-specialist surgeon, who is at once an expert in the laws and customs of *Brit Milah* and the Jewish world; and he is technically qualified to perform the procedure—the circumcision. The difference between a doctor doing a circumcision and a *Mohel* officiating at the *Brit Milah* ceremony is the difference between a surgical procedure and a beautiful and meaningful Jewish life cycle event celebrated by friends, family, and *k'lal Yisrael*—the entire Jewish community."

He nodded to Abba.

The old man picked up the baby and placed him on a small table. In antici-pation of the act, the boy's father had soaked a cotton ball in watered down cognac to soothe him. G.R. IV was sleeping peacefully. Abba produced an exquisitely sharp knife, a metal shield, and a gauze bandage. He carefully removed the alcohol soaked sucker from the baby's mouth. He bared the little boy's penis and washed it with an iodine solution. He then separated the adhesions between the glans and foreskin using a probe. G.R. IV did not move or cry out. The foreskin was then pulled away from the glans penis with a small hemostat while G.R. IV remained asleep. The *Mohel* slid the shield above the glans, allowing the foreskin to enter the groove in the shield. The shield acted as a barrier between the glans and the foreskin being cut. The *Mohel* then very quickly and very carefully cut the foreskin off against the shield with the knife he had been using for over seventy years. The *Mohel* quickly and deftly applied his bandage to the wound so that only one drop of blood fell onto the sterile white linen cloth underneath the baby boy. Only then did G.R. IV make a sudden, sharp, high-pitched squawk and fell back to sleep. The entire process took one minute.

Four weeks later, Chava, Gideon in his baby buggy, and his new nanny, Ruth Kline, walked the six blocks from the Rothsberger mansion to the corner of California St. and Maple—five blocks south of the Presidio and six blocks east of Temple Emanu-El Congregation and preschool where Gideon would one day matriculate and; as his proud father said repeatedly, "will excel." Chava took Gideon in her arms and climbed the three stories to Dr. ben Schulberg's office. The nurse almost snapped to attention when the beautiful young mother and her equally beautiful baby entered the outer office and swept them directly into the doctor's office. A brief examination of mother and child was done in five minutes and both were declared to be in perfect shape. Dr. ben Schulberg gave Chava a short lecture on postnatal care of herself and her baby and arranged for him to see her again in a month. He questioned her carefully about any indications of postpartum blues, and was as relieved as she was when he smiled fulsomely at the state of her psychological health as well as her physical well-being. Everything was as the proud father, G.R. III, had prognosticated. He had even said, "God's in His heaven; all's right with the world." And there was nothing in the Rothsberger world to contradict that sanguine statement of their affairs.

# CHAPTER FIVE

The stench in the tiny hut became unbearable by mid-morning the next day, and Afsoon was faced with a terrible dilemma: leave behind her mama, the happiest place she had ever lived, and face the bitter cold and blowing snow and the wolves that circled the mud flats or stay in the putrid smell and starve to death. She was desperately cold and very hungry. She found an old tattered prayer rug that had fallen into disuse as Yasmin lost her faith and then her health. She cut half of it into strips so she could wrap it around her feet and legs, and kept the other half as a shawl. Her fingers were nearly frozen and too stiff to do any sewing. She could see her breath. There was nothing in the hut to eat. No one was going to come for her. Afsoon began to weep bitterly, but crammed all of the bedding she could under her thin dress and pushed the door open to the hut and ventured out.

In the light of a summer's day, Afsoon knew the way to the collection of tents where Ahriman Shakibaie's clan lived. He was her father; but Afsoon had no comprehension of that, either biologically or sociologically. She had no concept of father as protector, provider, or as a caring human being. Her mind was numbed; all she could focus on was getting to the place where it was warm, where there was food, where Azedeh and Astera were. It was ten miles to the tents as the crow flies; but in the wind and snow and poor visibility, the little girl wandered some, making it even further.

Afsoon labored all through the day. It became more difficult and colder as the sun began to set. Her hands hurt from the cold, and she could no longer feel her feet. She stumbled and fell many times, bruising her knees, which added to her pain. Her stomach no longer pained her; it was leaden. By about the time of the evening meal, she heard the *muezzin* sounding the *adhan*—the call to prayer—somewhere in the distance. The cold air carried his voice—in

Urdu—well enough that she could make out the words of the *Maghrib*—the prayer at sunset, the fourth of five prayers (*salat*) of the day: "Allah is most great. I testify that there is no God but Allah. I testify that Muhammad is the prophet of Allah. Come to prayer. Come to salvation. Come to the best work. Allah is most great. There is no God but Allah."

In her mind, Afsoon could see the venerable old *muezzin* standing at the opening of Shakibaie's tent facing each of the four compass directions in turn—east, west, north, and south—as he solemnly intoned the call once for each direction. The sound was warming, encouraging. It gave her hope that relief was near. She plodded on for half a mile before her feet would no longer support her. She crawled the last half mile to the large dark tent.

The opening to the tent was closed tightly. She had to force her frozen little fingers to fight the knots holding the tent flaps together. They were knotted from the inside, which made her last ditch effort to survive all the more difficult. She did not dare to call out because she knew that neither Shakibaie nor Fereshten, the first wife, would allow her to come in. They would let her die without blinking. Somehow—by dint of sheer willpower—she got enough of an opening in the flaps to allow her to crawl inside. The heat from the braziers and the pot belly stove in the center of the tent was heaven. She began to shiver uncontrollably. She had come to the end of her reserves, and she fell unconscious.

Azedeh was cowering in a back corner of the tent nursing back welts from her most recent whipping from Shakibaie. She had not served the evening nun and berenj—bread and rice—quickly enough and had tripped on a piece of torn carpet and dropped a platter of nun on her lord and master, Shakibaie.

After the whipping, he looked at her impassively and announced, "You will serve me in bed this night. Now clean yourself up and stop the silly crying."

The very thought of him pawing her was galling, but she would have to submit. She was a woman, and women had no choice. She cried all the more. A waft of cold air alerted her to a change in the warmth of the tent. She looked towards the main tent opening for the source of the draft, and it was then that she saw the huddled mass of rags at the opening. She looked about to be sure that she would be unnoticed. Who knew what would set off Shakibaie or Fereshten and bring more abuse on her? She sidled over the rags, curious because they had not been there when she closed the flaps of the tent before *Maghrib*.

She began to riffle through the rags and was surprised to her core to encounter cold and shivering flesh. She removed the outer layers enough to realize that she was looking at the form of a little girl. Azedeh's first thought was to call out for help, to bring her sister wives or the servants to help rescue the pitiful shivering creature on the floor. However, she looked more closely and discovered that it was little Afsoon, the miracle baby whose entrance into life had been from a dead mother and a freezing first night on the Mount of Thorns. Memories flooded back. She calculated the time. This was the child's fifth birthday.

Azedeh left the unconscious girl's side and hurriedly sidled up the Astera and told her what she had found. Astera looked about cautiously. Everyone was engaged in finishing the meal of *khoresht*—thick lamb stew with vegetables and chopped nuts served over rice and talking or sipping scalding spiced *chay* [aromatic black tea] and dipping chunks of *ghand* [sugar] into their cup of tea and sucking on the very sweet confection. One of the boys, Kamin, was playing a bright song on his six-string tar. Shakibaie and Fereshten were raptly attentive to the boy and his song, because he was Fereshten's third son and her favorite; and number one wife had been cultivating her husband's interest in her boy until he was now his favorite as well. Kamin played his own version of an old classical folklore song—a *bard*—which had also become one of Shakibaie's favorites. Twenty-one-year-old Muhammad was politely awaiting his turn to perform for the family. He had memorized a favorite classical Persian poem—from the *Divan-e Hafez,* by Khajeh Shams-ed-Din Mohammed (translated: 'One who can recite the *Qur'an* from memory)— and this was to be his first time to practice on the family. Azedeh and Astera knew that they would not be missed from the evening's entertainment.

The two women and Astera's servant-girl quickly and quietly made their way to the front of the tent to Afsoon's side.

"We must hurry and get her to my tent, or she will die." Ever the pragmatist, she continued, "She has probably already lost her fingers and toes to the cold. Maybe it is better that she should be allowed to die in peace."

Azedeh reminded her, "No. This is the miracle baby who could not be killed by being left on the mountain to freeze. Even the wolves left her alone. Have faith in Allah, the Beneficent. He will provide."

Astera nodded. The three helpers swaddled Afsoon in blankets warmed by one of the fires and slipped outside the tent carrying her. The wide and icy flecks of snow cut at them and made them blink. The fifty-yard trip seemed like miles, and they were all chilled through by the time they made their way into the comfortable warmth of Astera's tent. They laid Afsoon down on the floor thick with large Kermani and rich, soft Esfahani carpets. The latter— made of soft wool and tight knitting around a silk warp and cotton—were especially useful for holding off the cold of January.

"Fetch a tub of warm water, Shokofeh," Astera ordered her servant.

She and Azedeh stripped the little one and gently began to rub her blue fingers and toes.

"Too hot," Astera said when Shokofeh lugged the water tub to where the two superior women were working. "Put some cold in it."

Shokofeh turned and rolled her eyes but uttered no complaint. She did not relish being hit any more than any other woman did. She returned promptly with a pitcher and stirred a portion of the cold water into the tub while constantly stirring.

"Is that better, Mistress?" she asked Astera.

Astera poked a finger into the tub water and pronounced it acceptable. The three women gently lifted Afsoon into the tub. Azedeh held her head above water, and the other two continued to administer soothing massage to her fingers and toes. It was backbreaking, but only Astera voiced any complaint, and even that was fairly good natured.

Afsoon began to rouse.

"Check to see if anyone is coming our way," Astera ordered Shokofeh.

"No one. It's still a blizzard. No one wants to get cold," she reported.

The blue hands and feet turned bright red then lightened to a soft pink as the women continued to massage them.

"Didn't I tell you so, Astera?" Azedeh boasted. "She is the miracle child. Once again, she has come back from the dead."

"You must never say such a thing to anyone but Shokofeh and me, Azedeh. The old women will think she is a jinn, and will report to Shakibaie and Fereshten. They will cut her throat quicker than a fly can evade the swatter to prevent even a hint that a minion of Shaytan could enter the tents of the clan. They will whip us and shun us, or even kill us if they think we had a hand in the works of the devil."

Azedeh nodded her understanding.

"More, hotter water, Shokofeh," Astera ordered.

It came in less than a minute.

Afsoon began to move about and to moan from the pain of the blood rushing back into her frozen fingers and toes. She opened her eyes and gave the three women a wide grin.

She murmured, "*Dostet darnakone*" [Thank you very much.]

Azedeh answered softly, "*Khesh mikonam*." [You're welcome.]

Afsoon slipped back to sleep, now comfortable and unafraid.

Her three saviors prepared a thin mutton bouillon and some *chay* for their little charge to sip when she awakened. Afsoon was indeed made of good stuff as Azedeh had predicted. In less than a day, she was up and about and selecting clothes from the beautiful collection enjoyed by the favorite wife. The blizzard and cold spell lightened in two days; and, on the third day, it was sunny and above freezing. The three adult women prepared soups, stews, rice dishes, and sweet fruit drinks enough to last her almost a week, and admonished Afsoon to stay hidden before they went back to the main tent on the second day to make sure they were not missed.

Afsoon hid herself so well that when one of the women came back to check on her, she would fear that someone had kidnapped the child.

Finally, after a futile search, Afsoon would leap up from her hiding place and call out, "Boo!" or some Farsi or Urdu equivalent, to frighten the worried woman. "Boo," "Okay," and "Tehrangeles" were an integral part of the Western influence—the Great Satan—that had assumed a permanent place in the Iranian lexicon.

"You scamp!" Azedeh would laugh and sweep Afsoon up into her arms.

The warmth of the hug did as much to return the little one to health as the good food and soft, clean, warm clothing and the fire-warmed tent.

Astera usually remonstrated halfheartedly, "Afsoon, you little devil. You will scare me to death or bring the men here when I scream. You must be more careful!"

Afsoon would then hang her head in mock sorrow and repentance, and she and Astera would break down with laughing.

The idyllic situation could not go on indefinitely. Astera and Azedeh planned and plotted on a way to get Afsoon to safety—away from Shakibaie and Fereshten.

"I know a farmer and his wife on the western side of Lake Orumiyeh. Firudin and Mariella Jamshidi owe me. I took in their daughters the last time the Armenian terrorists plundered the west coast of the lake. They are rough people, but they will be kind to our little one. Their daughter, Miriamm, was taken by the Dashnaksutyun and has never been seen since. I shudder to think what happened to the poor child. The Jamshidis will be happy to have a cute little girl in their house once again, don't you think?" Azedeh said pleadingly.

"I certainly hope so for all of our sakes," Astera said with less enthusiasm.

It took some time—time of trepidation—to get a message to and back from the Jamshidis. Mariella voiced a genuine concern for little Afsoon, said she understood how unreasonable and unkind Shakibaie was, and how wonderful it would be to have a five-year-old girl's noise back in her house. She did not seem quite so upbeat about how Firudin would treat her, but at least he had agreed.

Complicated and careful arrangements were made to secrete Afsoon out of Astera's tent and away from Shakibaie and Fereshten's compound. Equally careful effort went into the designing of a means to have the girl transported to the farmhouse. For time immemorial, Shi'ite women have devised ways of circumventing the will of their autocratic husbands and the constrictions of their stifling lives within their religion. They came up with a good plan. At least it seemed to be a good plan, and the best one they could think of.

# CHAPTER SIX

On Saturday evening, December, 21, 1980 after their evening meal, the Rothsbergers sat on their sofa and watched their only child—for the moment, their only child prodigy—move about the floor of the family room on his blanket. No child had ever been more fully scrutinized than Gideon Emmanuel Rothsberger IV, so, when he lifted his head while lying on his abdomen, smiled at them and laughed, it excited attention by both observant parents.

Chava said, "Look, G.R., our boy is a prodigy. He's making milestones well above the average!"

She let her husband know that she had achieved a small bit of one-upman-ship over him by reading up on children's milestones and was able to follow even his smallest actions and to compare them to the children of the bright parents of their inner circle. Over the next several months, Gideon IV stayed consistently in the "Advanced Skills" column—the column listing what only advanced children could do: at a month he could follow objects with his eyes, express himself with "Oohs" and "Aahs," hold his head at a forty-five degree angle, and only cried most of the night. At two months he noticed his hands, gurgled, followed objects across a field of vision, smiled, and laughed easily in response to the loving attention of his parents, grandparents, and nanny, and could do a mini-pushup.

Chava and G.R. III were not the least bit shy about showing off. Their son was progressing at a pace that was significantly more rapid and exciting than all those other cute babies, and they held baby parties to be sure everyone knew that. G.R. IV was a beautiful boy by any objective criterion, but then so were almost of the little boys in their friends' families. Everyone rejoiced at the blessings Yahweh had bestowed upon them and prayed in thanksgiving and in public without any false modesty to let the world know that they—the affluent Jews of Saint Francis Wood nabe—were indeed God's Chosen People.

It is true that babies grow in unique ways. Across the general population, the baby who sits up weeks before his peers might be one of the last to learn how to crawl. Or an eighteen-month-old who still communicates with grunts and gestures giving his doting parents and grandparents a hidden but growing suspicion that he might be mildly retarded suddenly bursts forth with prepositional phrases at twenty-four months. However, G.R. IV's babyhood progress was so remarkable that an enterprising teacher at the Temple Emanu-El preschool sought and was granted the privilege of writing a study about the *Gifted Child*—a direct reference to Chava and G.R. III's son—but who was only identified as "G.R. IV" in the master's thesis that was eventually printed in the *Journal of Childhood Development* with his picture on the front cover. Chava modestly had the cover of the journal framed and hung it in the front hall entryway.

By three months, baby Gideon could roll over from front-to-back and was making progress on his gymnastic back-to-front roll. He easily recognized the face and scent of his parents, grandparents, the rabbi, his nanny, and his doctor and nurse, all of whom lavished comments on his parents for having created such a prodigy. The most remarkable gains made were evidenced in his ability to vocalize: he passed rapidly through stages of squealing, cooing, blowing bubbles, and recognizing voices of all of his close admirers. At three months and a day, he began making clear-cut meaningful sounds. His father was thrilled when his first word was "Dada" and his mother and nanny had to share second place with "Mama" and "Nana." The following week, third place honors went to Grandma Rebecca who became known thereafter for the rest of her life as "Ma." This was a full month to two months early.

His first tooth came in late—at four months (which was actually right on schedule according to Chava's milestone charts), which gave a momentary cause for concern by the parents. He had four teeth when he hit five months. By then, he could distinguish colors, eat solid food, sit upright for a few moments, and began to crawl. He also developed separation anxiety early and could not bear to have Mama, Dada, Nana, or Ma out of his sight for a minute. It was laughable, but Chava worried that she would never get anything done or get any sleep. As it turned out, his progress in that regard was rather more rapid than she wanted. By six months, he was content to be alone or to be in the care of babysitters from the neighborhood—all of whom had been vetted by Pinkertons. Unlike all of the other children in their set, Gideon never really developed a healthy anxiety about strangers. Gideon seemed to be developing independence too early and too rapidly. She fretted that this development by her prodigy might be a harbinger of things to come, and she was right.

Gideon's most rapid progress came in his development of speech. He jabbered away contentedly at five months—a month early, correctly and understandably called to Mama, Dada, Nana, and Ma at five and a half months—nearly two months early; and he regularly communicated in one, two, and sometimes three-word sentences by the time he was nine months old. At a year, he sounded like an adult with limited interests and vocabulary; but over the next six months, he could converse with his family and their friends with an astonishing level of information, endless questions, and even began to repeat simple jokes.

He handled objects with dexterity, scribbled with crayons, and could draw stick figures with a pencil that would have made Picasso proud by the age of two. He was beyond peek-a-boo and patty cake, eating with his hands, and crawling by nine months and could sit, stand, and walk entirely unsupported at thirteen months. He understood "No" but refused to accept its implications at eight months, and vehemently yelled "No!" when he received instructions or admonishments from anyone—four months early. That was also something of a harbinger of the future as well.

He pretended to read board books by age fourteen months, was toilet trained at sixteen months, had an accurate five-hundred-word vocabulary by the time he was seventeen months old, and was able to handle most of the activities of daily living of a four year-old before he was three. Chava was sure she was losing him by the time he was four.

Gideon could read first grade books, count to fifty, add simple numbers, and understood the concept of a=b, a+b=c, and a-b=d intuitively. He had no patience for his little playmates who could not keep up with him. By that time, his biographer of *A Gifted Child* reckoned his vocabulary to be better than more than three-quarters of grade schoolers. He began clamoring to go to preschool, and pouted as he watched the older neighbor children being walked or driven to school every morning. He was far more than ready when the new school year started when he was age three years and two months. He was the top of his class—indeed, of the entire preschool—by the time he was four and had a year to go before kindergarten.

By that time, G.R. III and Chava were less amused by his prodigious accomplishments than they were concerned. How were they going to be able to feed his voracious appetite and capacity for learning? With his remarkably rapid advancement, how would he fit in with his peers, or would he have to venture out to educational levels that would leave them behind and him in a social situation for which he might not be ready?

The problem was solved—like most others that the Rothsberger clan faced—by money, ingenuity, and discipline. Gideon IV soon tired of his childish playmates in preschool and was more than ready for kindergarten. By California law, he could not start kindergarten in public schools until he was five. So, his parents enrolled him in a private kindergarten run by a well-known former U.C. Berkeley professor of early grade school education. It was a rigorous curriculum that included beginning to learn German—she was a German Jew whose parents were holocaust victims—Spanish, because she was convinced that it was the language of the *untermenschen*—whom people like the Rothsbergers would have to employ as time went on—and Mandarin, because they lived in San Francisco with its large and vibrant Chinatown and Chinese business people. There was no question of scrimping on the extra tutors required. The education paid off handsomely. By the time he was to go into the first grade, Gideon could speak English and all of the other add-on languages as fluently as native speakers of age twelve. Not least among his several capacities as a prodigy was the spongelike ability to absorb and recall foreign languages. Gideon was a natural polyglot, and he was only beginning.

First grade, even in the lofty confines of the exclusive Saint Francis Woods Hebrew Academy, was far below Gideon's capacity. Chava and G.R. III Rothsberger seduced Frau Miller to give up her own kindergarten and to convert it into an auxiliary grade school to augment Gideon IV's Hebrew school experience. She had no qualms about him skipping grades because she equated him with young Mozart, and the boy moved through grade school two grades a year and still thirsted for more. By the time he finished sixth grade at the age of four-and-a-half, he could speak all of his languages from kindergarten with fluency and had added French and Japanese with which he was rapidly becoming facile. He still had a ways to go to master writing and reading in popular essays and books in all of those languages, but he was progressing. He could add, subtract, understand number theory and equations, and could do simple algebra in his head. He was larger, stronger, and more agile than his agemates and less than patient with peers and unwilling to tolerate challengers or bullies. That got him into some trouble.

# CHAPTER SEVEN

The escape took place just after *Isha* [evening prayer]. *Isha* is defined in the *Qur'an* and writings of the scholars as that time when one can last see a hair, and the night of the escape was a particularly black one. The inky darkness facilitated the work of Azedeh, Shokofeh, and Astera, as did the intense cold, because both features of the late evening kept any but the most intrepid inside the tents. Afsoon was small enough to fit into the center of the donkey cart surrounded by a pile of Astera's clothes and covered by a few old carpets that were ostensibly being transported down the lakeside trail to the market in Silvaneh, fifty miles away, should the cart driver be questioned. Urmia [Azerbaijani] or Orumiyeh [Kurdish] County of West Azerbaijan Province was sparsely populated with less than 450,000 people in 125,000 families. There were only five cities, and it was not at all unusual for the women in Shakibaie's hamlet to trade with any of the five. It was not usual—but also not rare—to leave at night.

To avoid suspicion should anyone discover the donkey cart with its merchandise, Astera took an enormous risk. She enlisted the aid of Farhad Sharifi, a handsome young shepherd with whom she—the third wife of unforgiving Shakibaie—was having an affair of the heart. Because such a liaison was a capital crime—death by stoning—sidelong glances, let alone sexual trysts, were carried out with near-infinite caution by Astera and her lover. It approached the ultimate sacrifice on the part of Astera and Farhad to risk their lives to help Afsoon escape.

No one spoke a word outside Astera's tent. Afsoon had been thoroughly admonished to keep silence until she and Farhad were well away from the clan tents, and then only when Farhad initiated conversation. The donkey's mouth was muzzled to prevent it from braying and alerting sentries or tent occupants. Farhad flicked the leather reins, and they departed into the darkness and cold. They traveled for more than two hours before Farhad deemed it safe to speak.

"Afsoon, *haletun chetor e* [how are you]?" he asked in Farsi.

"*Khubam-shoma chetoin? Dastet dormakone, bar a dar* [Fine, and you? Thank you big brother]," Afsoon's cheery little voice came from the depths of her cocoon.

"*Khubam.* Can you breathe, little one?"

"Yes *bar a dar.* I am well."

Farhad kept his communications to a minimum but took pity on the frightened little girl alone there in the depths of the cartload and in the pitch dark and cold. He spoke to her or sang one of the popular songs that made its way into the culture from the hated Great Satan, recited a stanza from Omar the Tentmaker, or from a poem from Rumi, the great thirteenth century dervish. His mellifluous voice soothed Afsoon, as much for its implicit kindness as for the beauty of his voice.

The sun was just above the horizon when they entered the farm of Firudin and Mariella Jamshidi. Mariella had been watching for them and hurried out to greet Farhad and Afsoon. She looked over her shoulder to be sure that Firudin was not coming out to disapprove. She had convinced him to do this favor for Astera, but he had not seemed entirely convinced that it was wise or that they would be able to afford to keep her. She would have to earn her keep, he kept insisting whenever they had a conversation about her coming to stay.

"*Sabahiniz xeyir*" [good morning]" she said, speaking Azerbaijani as did most of her neighbors and the traders who passed by the farm.

Firudin's cattle business required that the family use Azerbaijani in preference to the more popular Farsi used throughout the county.

Farhad returned the greeting in the same language, and from beneath the pile of carpets and old clothing, Afsoon repeated the words precisely although she had not heard Azerbaijani before. She had a very good ear for languages.

Mariella took them into their small farmhouse that they shared with sheep and goats. Cattle were corralled just outside the rear door of the people's area of the home. She fed them *sahar yemayi.* Breakfast throughout Iran—and the farmhouse of Mariella Jamshidi was no exception—was simple fare. There were steaming pots of *chay,* and a pot of left-over *lavash*—feta cheese and carrot-flavored jam. It was not of very good quality, and it did not taste very good, but Farhad and Afsoon were starving, and it filled the emptiness in their bellies well enough.

They both thanked Mariella as Haji Firudin came in through the rear entrance. He was proud of having completed the required hajj—so much so that he had made a handsome sign over the front door announcing that this was the home of a haji. He nodded at them and took his seat. He gave Afsoon an appraising look that he usually reserved for buying cattle at auction.

"Did you have a good trip, boy?" he asked Farhad.

"We did."

"Did you enjoy the *səhər yeməyi*?"

"Yes, Sir," the young man said.

"Good. We have much work to do here. Mariella will find suitable clothing for the girl, and we can get her to work in a few minutes after I finish my breakfast. Is there anything you need for your return trip?"

Firudin had evidently not bought into the standard Iranian cultural trait of hospitality.

"No, Sir, I'd best be getting back. Thank you for the chance to get warm and to enjoy the meal."

Farhad then did an unusual thing: he gave Afsoon a quick affectionate hug and bade her farewell. He was none too hopeful that the sweet little girl would have much of a childhood in that austere family; but she was just a female; and it did not pay to waste energy on a concern that Allah had ordained. He stepped out into the cold and pushed the little donkey to get them home before dark.

"Mariella, get clothes for her. We have to get dirty today, and she needs to get used to it," Firudin ordered.

The clothes were two sizes too big and were rough and scratchy on Afsoon's skin; but with a few minor tucks and pulls, Mariella got a reasonably utilitarian fit. Afsoon had learned early in her short life that complaining or otherwise calling attention to herself never turned out well for her. She kept quiet and kept her head down, which seemed to please Firudin. Her new master/father-figure was not abusive as he showed her the new chores she was expected to do and to do well and quickly.

They started with one of the most difficult.

"Bring that bucket and a washcloth, girl. We are going into the corral and learn how to milk goats. Did you ever do that before?"

"No."

"Did you ever see anyone do that?"

"No."

"Good, then I won't have to make you learn how to do something better than what you were taught by some fool. You look like a smart child. I expect you to do a good job."

It was uncommon to rare in Afsoon's experience to be praised. It was unknown to her to have a man give her even a tiny modicum of praise. She thought that maybe this time in her life would not be so difficult. With the incentive of that bit of encouragement, she resolved to do a good job.

Firudin showed her how to hold the goat still. Afsoon was smaller than the goat, and it kept getting away. Firudin made her take a strong, almost a wrestling, hold. That worked better. He showed her how to strip the milk down the nearly cylindrical udders to the teats and to be able to express some milk. In five minutes, Afsoon could get a decent stream going. It was going to take her quite a while every day, but Firudin thought there was hope for her. He left her to it for an hour. She had filled her first bucket.

"Carry it to the house. Don't dawdle," he ordered.

Afsoon struggled to lift it. She put her legs in a squat and hoisted the heavy bucket with two hands. Her arms and legs trembled as she strove to stand upright. The heavy fat milk sloshed around and spilled a few drops at first, then larger amounts as she became tired and began to stagger. Just short of the threshold of the kitchen, her foot in the oversize rubber Wellington boots stuck in the sticky clay mud, knocked her off balance, and she and the bucket fell to the ground, spilling the precious milk.

Firudin was right behind her and slapped the back of her head hard enough to knock her down face first into the icy mud. She was stunned and wanted to protest and to cry, but she fought to suppress her need to respond.

"Get another bucket. Run!" the taciturn farmer barked.

Afsoon learned quickly. She filled another bucket, but this time only three-quarters full. With all her strength and a desperate fight against her awkwardness and the slippery mud, she succeeded in getting the milk into the house.

"Good girl," Mariella said.

Afsoon was puffing. The blow to her head was hateful; so, she made a vow not to make any more mistakes. Firudin seemed satisfied. Afsoon thought she had gotten over a hurdle.

"We go to take care of the steers."

The overdressed child hurried behind him as fast as she could, but had to run in the clumsy boots to keep up. The boots chafed sores on her ankles, but it was not as bad as having no shoes at all as had been her lot before coming to the farm. Firudin had fifteen cows left of the thirty-five he had bought—leased actually—from the giant agribusiness Agrolizinq the previous spring.

The price of milk in the western villages and in Baku was thirty-two kopeks a liter. He was able to get between 20 and 25 liters of milk from a cow every day. In the towns, the price was half what Firudin was getting, and the cost of feed was more than half of what he could take in, leaving nothing to build necessary new buildings or even to repair the old ones. He had to haul water from the Zarrineh River because nearby Qushchu, Lake Orumiyeh was nearly as salty as the Dead Sea. The river emptied into the lake. Rivers such as the Sirvan—which eventually empties into the Tigris in Iraq, and the Simineh—were plentiful and easy to access, but it was hard work to haul the large plastic tanks in his old trucks. He was unable to keep up with the totality of the work required to manage the cattle farm, and he had had to begin selling off his cattle at a loss; so, he was in a lose-lose situation. It made him frustrated, angry, fearful; and he needed someone who he could take out his ill feelings on and not protest. Mariella had begun to protest and find little ways to get back at him when he abused her. Afsoon came at a perfect time for them.

"Get busy and clean this place up," he ordered.

The task was too daunting for him. Just looking at the mess was disheartening. The metal roof pieces were falling off and hanging forlornly from the eaves. There were large gaps between the vertical slats of the sides, which let in the cold and rats. Spiders, and even snakes, crawled on the floors; and larger creatures got in and ate the expensive cattle feed.

Afsoon stood and looked at the huge task and wanted to cry. She had no idea where to start. She had no familiarity with tools; and all of the shovels, rakes, and brooms were too big for her. She turned up her face to Firudin's with a questioning look.

Firudin growled and frowned at her and showed her how to use the large tools. They were heavy, clumsy, and hard to move about. The debris—especially the cow manure that had been caked on the floor for years—was stubborn. Seeing no compassion on her master's face, the five-year-old did the best she could. It was cold in the barn, and that proved to be a small boon. As she worked, she put out enough body heat to keep from shivering. By noon, she was exhausted and famished. She worried she would not get to eat, but she kept working.

Shortly, Mariella came to the barn and fetched her for lunch. The very sound of the word gave her hope. Mariella told her to take off her boots and to wash her filthy hands and face. Afsoon walked into the room and there saw the rest of the family. There were two young teenage girls and three strapping boys standing beside their father. In addition, there was a skinny boy who was a little older than the girls. He was standing off from the other family members. He shyly kept his head bowed and had an odd habit of holding his left arm tightly against his side. He gave Afsoon a little smile, more than the others were willing to grant.

"We will have the *dhuhr* [noon prayer], Firudin said. "Think you could give it a try, Nassir? Even you know that this is the time of day to remember the One God and to seek his help and guidance."

He looked at the standoffish boy with undisguised contempt. Apparently, this was a frequent ritual designed to humiliate him. The *Dhuhr* prayer is the second prayer of the day. It starts when the sun begins to decline from its zenith and ends when the size of an object's shadow is equal to the object's size. Nassir was ordered to give it for the family four days a week, and had developed a serious dread of that time of day.

All three of the prayers except the *isha* consist of four *raka'ts* [units] each. What is recited in those three prayers is identical. The problem for Nassir was that each of those prayers had to be recited silently and word for word without error except for the *Isha*, which required two of the *raka'ts* to be uttered audibly. Nassir grimaced noticeably and did his best to comply. Afsoon could see that the boy was struggling to get the words to flow in his mind. He got progressively more frustrated as he tried.

"Oh, give up, retarded one. At least say the first and most important words out loud, Maybe someday you will be able to do your duty. Now, repeat after me: *Allahu Akbar* [There is One God]!"

Nassir summoned up his courage, "All ... All ... All ... Allahu ... ahu ... ahu...," he stammered. "Akba ... a ... a ... a ... ar," and took a deep, painful breath.

Firudin rolled his eyes.

"Next thing: "*Subhaan-Allaah wa'l-hamdu Lillaah wa laa ilaaha ill-Allaah wa Allaahu akbar wa laa hawla wa la quwwata illa Billaah.* [(Glory be to Allah, praise be to Allah, there is no god except Allah and Allah is Most great, there is no god except Allah; and there is no power and no strength except with Allah]."

"S ... s ... s ... *Sub ... Sub....*"

Firudin gritted his teeth and said, "Enough, fool! What have I done to have been cursed with a fool for a son? He started as a baby of the left hand, and it took almost daily beatings and strapping his offending left arm to his body for more than a year to prevent him from using the foul hand. Then ... when he started to talk, he was found to be a stammerer. Perhaps, he was visited by Shaytan, I don't know."

Nassir trembled and wished the earth would fall in on him, as he did every day of his life. But finally the ordeal was over. Everyone knelt on his or her own prayer rug and inwardly recited the necessary Arabic words. Afsoon had never been taught the words; so, she pretended. She looked briefly over at Nassir, caught his eye, and gave him a small empathetic glance.

Lunch is the main meal of the day among Iranians. On this, the first day of Afsoon's stay with the Jamshidi family, they had pearl barley soup, a thick omelet with herbs, and chicken with broad beans. Like everyone else in the family, Afsoon filled the remaining cavity in her stomach with fragrant white rice that came steaming from the pot. Mariella made this first official meal something of a special treat for Afsoon by taking much of the morning to make baghlava. It was new to the little girl, and she made a wonderful sticky mess of her fingers and delighted in licking her fingers clean. It was by far the best part of the day.

Forty-five minutes from the time the ordeal of the prayer started, Firudin stood and announced that the meal was over, and that it was time to get back to work. Afsoon labored until it was nearly sundown to milk the remaining eight goats and to muck out the barn, only taking a break to learn how to milk a cow. The huge beasts did not cooperate in the least, and by the time the day's work was pronounced done, she was hardly able to stand.

She fell sound asleep during the *isha*, and one of the older boys had to carry her to bed without the evening meal. With the rarest of exceptions—mostly Muslim holidays—every day was the same as the day before it. The only differences as time went on were that she got tougher and could tolerate the long hours, the hard work, and the cold better; and she made a friend in Nassir. The two outcasts saw the need for a bond early on, and it was a sustaining compact for two young people who were being robbed of their childhoods.

# CHAPTER EIGHT

## San Francisco, California, USA, Saint Francis Wood Hebrew Academy, 1985

Aaron Schmuel was the school bully, an odd phenomenon in the rarefied atmosphere of Saint Francis Woods Hebrew Academy. He was intelligent—every child in the school was intelligent—and he came from a very rich family, which was also true of every child in the school. Both of those attributes served as a shield against recriminations for his actions. It was against the code of boyhood—and girlhood, for that matter—for a victim of a bully to complain to parents or school authorities. The loss of face would have been an insurmountable social burden to bear. So, almost every child just gritted his or her teeth and considered Aaron's bullying to be one of the negative vagaries of childhood that they had to endure.

The exception was Gideon Emmanuel Rothsberger IV. In sixth grade, Gideon was four years old, and Aaron was nearly seven. Gideon weighed fifty pounds—the upper limits of normal for his age. He stood fifty inches tall, three inches greater than normal, and he had a slim build. Aaron weighed eighty-four pounds and was fifty inches tall—average height and thirty pounds overweight for his age. He was pudgy and pugnacious.

Aaron came from a reformed Jewish family; so, he did not have to wear distinctive clothing or an Orthodox haircut with fetlocks. Gideon and the majority of the other boys in the academy were Orthodox. He had his first haircut when he was three years old and one day, and had never had his forelocks cut since that first haircut. All of the Orthodox boys wore a *kippah yarmulke*—skull cap. In keeping with the modern Orthodox character of the academy, the abbreviated form that fit on the occiput and was held in place with bobby pins was acceptable, and that was what Gideon was wearing *that* day.

Both he and Aaron were dressed in the school uniform: long-sleeved white shirt, the school tie, the school's blue blazer with the logo of the academy embroidered on the left front pocket, long grey pants with cuffs, black stockings, black belt, and shoes. All cloth was sold in Kosher stores to avoid problems with the Orthodox proscription against *shatnez*—wearing cloth made of wool mixed with linen.

Gideon III had explained to his elementary school son, Gideon IV, when he asked the reasonable question about the rule: "The Torah does not explain the reason for *shatnez*, my boy. It is just a *chok*—a law whose logic is not evident."

Gideon IV was beginning to understand—even at his young age—that many elements of religion were just "*chok*."

Unlike Aaron, Gideon was wearing under his trousers a *Tallit Katan* and *Tzitzit*—a religious apron-like garment with fringes and twisted cotton tassels hanging from each corner to remind the boy of his religious obligations and as a reminder of the Exodus from Egypt. He knew all of that; but he had a quiet rebellion wherein he reserved the right not to like it; and on his grumpier days, to think it was silly. He felt the same way about having to wear a *tefillin* [phylactery], and had a genuine rebellion about that. He took it off as soon as he left home and replaced it only when he opened the front door to the mansion when he came back home.

On *that* day, Aaron stuck out his tongue at Gideon. Gideon ignored him. Then Aaron rushed him and tore off Gideon's *yarmulke* and an attached hank of curly hair. Gideon had real difficulty ignoring that, but by force of will he was able to do so. Aaron called Gideon a sissy and a pretty boy with cute sideburns. It was getting harder for Gideon to ignore or evade the larger boy. This much was a daily ritual and—although he did not like it—Gideon had become accustomed enough to let it pass before *that* day. On that day, Aaron made an incursion that was a serious step over the line beyond that which four-year-old Gideon would tolerate.

When Gideon frustrated Aaron by ignoring him, the bully shot a hand forward to grab hold of one of the tassels under Gideon's pants. Gideon brought up both of his clenched fists from the floor with all of his strength and pulverized Aaron's nose. The larger boy howled in pain and threw his opened hands over the agonizingly painful nose and tried to stop the blood geysering out between his fingers. He could only look at Gideon in astonishment. Gideon was not through. When Aaron stepped back away from the little wolverine facing him, Gideon kicked him square on his testicles—both of them. Aaron fainted.

There was a small crowd of boys and girls who had gathered as Aaron was delivering his daily torment of Gideon. Some were laughing; some were giving disapproving looks; and some were quietly saying "*Bushah, bushah* [Hebrew: shame, shame]," at Aaron. When Gideon struck back, there was a moment of astonished and respectful silence.

As if on cue and the work of a chorus, the gathering crowd of elementary school children began to clap and cheer. Most of the children—both boys and girls—had had their own share of bullying and humiliation from Aaron Schmuel, and they were thrilled to see his comeuppance and afraid of the inevitable consequences.

Headmaster Rabbi Pinchas ʙᴇɴ Yisroel, ha-Rav, an Ashkenazic Jew known for his austere approach to infractions and Leopold Antal Lavigne—the dean of students—a social climber in the California Yeshivish school system, and thus disinclined to show a soft attitude towards malefactors that might cost his school the enrollment of the children of affluent families, were on the scene within seven minutes.

"What is the meaning of this outrage?" demanded the headmaster of one and all.

No one spoke. Aaron Schmuel was retching and unable to speak. Gideon IV looked thoroughly guilty. His coat was torn; his shirt was disheveled, and he was rubbing his knuckles.

"Mr. Rothsberger?"

It was the first time the four-year-old had been referred to by the title of "Mister." He might have thought his father—or perhaps even his grandfather—was standing behind him, but that did not seem likely. He was quiet. It was a pregnant moment.

Four harsh judgmental eyes bored into his. It was outside his experience to be afraid of adults, and his eyes locked with theirs and did not look away.

"Well," insisted the dean of students, "screw your courage to the sticking place, boy. Speak up."

Lavigne was the English teacher who was very fond of Shakespeare and overly fond of quoting him, especially from Macbeth and Hamlet.

"Yes, Headmaster," he said with a slightly quavering voice.

"What do you have to say for yourself?"

Gideon had had time to compose himself during the short pauses in the conversation. He thought to himself that if he were talking to his father—and the most important man in his life was angry—he would demand the truth and nothing more or less. This man was not even the most important in his life.

He had full control of his voice now and said simply, "He bullies me. Today he attacked me. He insulted me, pulled my forelock, tore off my *yarmulke* and some hair. I tried to ignore him, but then he grabbed for my privates. So, I smashed him in the nose and kicked him in his balls. Really hard. That's when he fell down."

The dean shooed away the students.

Headmaster ben Yisroel held out his hand to Gideon and said quietly, "Come with me to my office, young man. We are going to call your parents."

It came across as a death sentence, and Gideon had to screw up all of his courage not to cry. He was determined not to cry. His rigid father had told him over and over again that "big boys don't cry," and "not even little boys cry, not Rothsberger boys." So, Gideon remained dry-eyed and silent. He followed the headmaster to his offices.

"You know what must take place now, don't you, Gideon my boy?" ben Yisroel said without rancor.

"You are going to beat me," the little boy responded dispassionately.

Corporal punishment was not only the rule of the academy, but it was from the Torah. Although his father had never laid a hand on him, nor even threatened to do so, Gideon was sure that he was a believer in the 'spare the rod, spoil the child' admonition in the Torah. He recalled having had his father read that passage in one of their nightly scripture studies.

"I am hardly going to beat you, Gideon, but you must pay for your disobedience to the rules with a few swats."

Gideon held the headmaster's gaze with a rather unnerving intensity.

"Confess that what you have done is a sin, and I will make the paddling only a swat or two at the most."

"No."

"No?"

"No."

"Well, then, lower your pants, boy. Cry if you like, but the punishment will begin."

Ben Yisroel knew he was in the right. It was the right—even the obligation—of the parent or teacher to strike a boy in the course of his studies and had officially been so since the tenth century.

"A man shall not look on the nakedness of another. My rabbi gave a *derasha* [sermon or homily] about that. He was telling us how to be careful with strangers who might do something to hurt a boy. You may beat me with my clothes on all you want."

"I said before, this is not a beating; it is a proper punishment. I am not a brute, a thug, or a Nazi. I am your headmaster. Take down your trousers!"

His voice had raised a couple of decibels.

"No." Gideon's voice was quiet and unafraid.

Ben Yisroel shrugged his shoulders and gave a little sigh.

"Very well then, you have earned a dozen stripes for your brazen disrespect, your chutzpah! Bend over and put your arms on my desk. Prepare yourself."

Gideon did as he was told. The first blow from the thin paddle missed its mark and hit Gideon on the back of his thighs, causing his legs to buckle and him to fall. The pain was terrible, like nothing he had ever known in the four years of his gentle upbringing. It was difficult to stand because the muscles in the back of his legs would not hold him. He did not cry or even make a sound. He pulled himself up by his arms and stood unsteadily on wavering pins.

*"Oh, dear,"* thought ben Yisroel, *"that will leave a mark. This cannot end well, but my authority cannot be challenged, even by a very spoiled, very rich little genius."*

His aim was better after that. He delivered eleven more blows, all to the boy's buttocks. It infuriated him that the boy would not give him the satisfaction of crying. Each blow became more emphatic than the last. The twelfth landed with a sharp crack that could be heard in the outer office. Ben Yisroel looked at the paddle that was split down its center. Gideon Emmanuel Rothsberger IV—scion of the richest and most influential family in California—was now lying on the floor looking at him with reproach. The headmaster knew that he had acted in anger, had lost control, had possibly injured the boy; and he knew that there would be consequences. He knew that the boy who deserved a paddling had been Aaron Schmuel. Now, he would not be able even to be just. There had been enough violence for one day.

Taking an example from little Gideon, ben Yisroel quoted his second-in-command's Shakespearean admonition to himself, *"Screw your courage to the sticking place,"* and dialed the number of the Rothsberger residence.

"Good afternoon, Rothsberger residence," came the crisp businesslike voice of the family butler, Joseph ben Aaron.

"This is the headmaster of Saint Francis Woods Hebrew Academy. I must speak to Mr. Rothsberger."

"May I ask which Mr. Rothsberger do you require—G.R. II or G.R. III?"

Ben Yisroel considered the underling on the phone to be impertinent, but it would not do to sound abrupt or brusque; so, he calmed himself.

"I wish to speak to the father of Gideon Emmanuel Rothsberger IV," he said.

"Is young master Gideon ill? Has he been in an accident? Is the boy all right, Sir?"

"He is. Now I must speak to his father."

"He is not at home at present."

It was infuriating.

"May I speak to Mrs. Rothsberger?" ben Yisroel asked through gritted teeth.

"I will see if she is in residence and if she is taking calls. May I tell her whether or not it is an emergency, Sir?"

The butler's voice was annoyingly correct, calm, and to Ben Yisroel, condescending.

"It is important, but it is not quite an emergency."

There was five minutes of silence on the other end of the line before Chava Rothsberger came on.

"Yes, Headmaster, what can I do for you? Joseph said it was about my boy, Gideon."

"Indeed, Mrs. Rothsberger. While I would have preferred to communicate with your husband, I will convey my message to you and ask that you have Mr. Rothsberger call me at his earliest convenience."

Ben Yisroel gave the short version of what had taken place, not leaving out the fact that he had paddled Gideon. He left out the facts that the boy was now on the floor of his office unable to get up, that he had only been defending himself against a bully, and that nothing had been done to bring justice to the bully who was now out of his grasp because his mother had come to the school to take him home.

Mrs. Rothsberger's voice was stony.

"I will inform my husband. You can rest assured that he will investigate the circumstances and will most definitely get back with you."

She put down the receiver, called the chauffeur, and drove to the school to pick up her son. Unfortunately for all concerned, the child was still resting on the floor of the headmaster's office when Chava arrived. Chava was a little out of breath from having hurried into the school due to her advanced state of pregnancy with twins. She marched past the headmaster and directly into the man's office against the protests of the strait-laced secretary. Ben Yisroel had stepped out to wash his face in cold water. Chava walked over to her son, picked him up from the floor, and marched back out again.

The secretary put her hand to her mouth and asked, "Is the boy all right?"

Chava pointedly ignored her and strode purposefully out to the car. Chauffeur Abram Silberberg leapt from the driver's seat and opened the rear doors of the Mercedes to allow Chava to place Gideon gently on the backseat.

"Home," she said.

# CHAPTER NINE

> "Evil in the name of evil is bad enough; God save us from evil in the name of good."
>
> -Herodotus, *The Second Essay*

## Urmia, Capital of West Azerbaijan Province, Iran, April, 1990

Afsoon grew rapidly during her ninth year. She was almost as tall as her two "sisters," Dina and Elaheh. During occasions when Firudin was gone for two or three days to take cattle or sheep to the market in Urmia or to get supplies in Silvaneh—which was not so far away—and Mariella was busy keeping the farm running, Nassir and Afsoon played together. Afsoon had never known play before coming to the Jamshidis. Neither of the children had ever had a friend; and their bond grew stronger and deeper with every passing month and with every insult, beating, and privation the two of them endured.

With Afsoon, Nassir lost his stammer. Otherwise, he cowered before his autocratic religious father every time he had to speak out loud. *Isha* was a nightly torture for fear that he would be forced to be the one who uttered the two *raka'ts* that had to be spoken aloud. Elder brothers Mozaffarian and Gorgani were merciless to the young stammerer and indifferent to little Afsoon. Thankfully for both children, they often accompanied their father to market or were in the hills tending sheep and cattle.

Nassir was eleven, but was not as tall as Afsoon—and was frail. Afsoon was brave, and he cringed when approached by an adult and hid whenever he could to evade contact with his father. He was intelligent—but not as intelligent as Afsoon, and she had to learn not to become impatient with his inability to learn as quickly as she did; but most important, he was empathetic and even kind to her. He taught her the concept of "birthday," and every year in January, he arranged a little party for her. Together, they had decided that she was born in January based on the irrational concept that her chronology should have started in January four years before she joined the Jamshidi family. Since she had no idea when she had actually been born, it was fun to accept the pleasant fiction. Nassir was the brother she never had, and she loved him unreservedly.

For her tenth birthday, they hiked up to the top of the knoll behind the farm and sat in a small copse of mixed native trees—stands of oak, ash, elm, and cypress—which were regarded as a valuable asset of the Jamshidi family. The trees were thick and provided a place where the two children could not be observed from the outside. Nassir presented her with a wrapped present— the first time in her life that she had even seen a gift-wrapped package. He would not let her open it until they had eaten a small meal—a salad—he had prepared himself and after he had given her a little cupcake he had saved from dinner three nights before. It was stale and not very good, but it had a tiny candle stuck in its middle. Nassir lit the candle and clapped his hands as Afsoon ate her half with as much gusto as if she were enjoying a large piece of fresh baghlava. The two children savored their morsels of sweet cake and each other for several minutes. Finally, Nassir let Afsoon open her present.

"*Tavalodet mobarak, khahar kuchulu* [happy birthday to you, little sister.]," he said shyly.

She carefully untied the string and set it neatly aside on a clean rock. Next, she took her time to undo the cloth that covered the treasure. She stared with wonderment and joy at the gift. Nassir had spent his free time for the past month fashioning a doll out of rags. He was clever with his hands, and the doll was nearly a foot in length and had a well-designed Azerbaijan festival dress complete with hat and shoes. Afsoon was quiet. She folded the cloth wrapping and set it aside with the string. Then she clutched the beautiful little doll to her chest and began to croon to it as if it were a real baby. Nassir glowed with pleasure at his great success. After a few minutes of savoring the thrill of having her first present—in truth, her first personal possession—she threw her arms around Nassir and squeezed him until he begged for mercy.

Without reservation, Afsoon said to Nassir, "*Dooset daram* [I love you.]!"

It was an idyllic day, perhaps the only day of pure happiness either child had known in their entire lives.

Afsoon had an obscure hiding place in the back storage room of the farmhouse where she kept her secret things. She hoarded food because she was never entirely sure there would be enough to sustain her. She could not forget the lean times with Yazmin and especially in Shakibaie and Fereshten's tents. Once—when she was afraid of Firudin—she stole one of his skinning knives and hid it with her food stash. The doll—her treasure—was kept wrapped in the same cloth Nassir had placed it in, and hidden where no one else could find it. The rag doll was a girl, of course. Once in a while—when no one was around—she brought her out and sang to her; it was her baby; and she lavished all of the pent-up love and affection of her soul upon it. If she received a cuffing or felt the bite of a switch for some small infraction, she took her baby to bed with her. Her name was *Fereshte* [angel].

On those nights, Afsoon often told her baby, "*Shab be khey Fereshte* [good night, angel]," "*Dooset daram*"; and when the day had been particularly painful, she told angel, "*Man ehsas e nakhoshi mikonam* [I feel sick.];" or that she was afraid of the *shab* [dark]. It was a rare night that she was not afraid of the *shab*.

Nassir provided another wonderful gift beginning as early as when Afsoon turned five. He brought her books from school. Reading and writing were forbidden to girls, but some math—very simple accounting—was permitted to allow girls to help in family businesses. Nassir had to secrete a book to use for teaching his little sister. During off-work times, the two of them found places to sit and enjoy the intellectual exercise. Early on, Afsoon was enchanted by the poetry and even the mundane nonfiction works. Nassir was amazed at the brilliance Afsoon displayed. Like her ability to soak up new words, new phrases, and new languages, she was able to learn to read and to retain what she had read with truly remarkable facility. Over the nearly five years that they worked on her reading, she began to be better at it than Nassir. He had no jealousy, only pride at his sister's prowess and his own contribution to her learning. She waited with great anticipation each day when Nassir returned from school to find out what book they would next be able to read together. She often kept books—hidden in her back storage room hiding place—for a few days to go over and over the material. She treated books as friends, and the knowledge they imparted to her as a treasure.

By the time she was ten, Afsoon had absorbed from Nassir's books the poetry of Ferdosi, Omar Khayyam, Hafez, Rumi, and Sa'di. She learned geography, the grand history of Persia, the marvelous accomplishments of Grand Ayatollah Sayyid Ruhollah Mostafavi Musavi Khomeini, blessed be his name—the savior of Iran from the wicked Shah—who came into power the year before she was born. She already knew of the murders and tortures inflicted on the Kurds during the Pahlavi Dynasty from 1925 to 1979. Every

Kurdish person—including children—could recite chapter and verse of the litany of horrors described by the Ayatollahs. She learned the essentials of Islam—which she rejected as both boring and fantasy, although she never breathed a word of that opinion even to Nassir. She was fascinated by the concept of a novel—a book of fiction that made history real. Her favorite was Simin Daneshvar's *Shavushun* [*A Persian Requiem*]. From that great novel, she was able to transport herself back in time to watch life in Iran between World War I and II. She learned social commentary from the novels of Jahal al-e Ahmad—*The School Principle* and *The Pen*—which were originally written in Farsi, but now had been translated to several dozen languages, including that of the Great Satan, the United States of America.

It was there that she first encountered English; and she strove to learn as much as she could, spurred on by contrariness to the vitriol voiced by everyone she met about that strange place. She had no idea how the words were pronounced; but by dint of the prodigious effort of comparing the Farsi version with the English version, she began an acquaintanceship with the first truly foreign language she had encountered. Nassir often told her that she was intelligent, even brilliant. At first he had added "for a girl"; but as time passed and she exceeded his level of reading and learning, he dropped the insulting phrase.

At first, Nassir understood mathematics far better than did his little sister. She had difficulty recognizing the numbers and with trying to comprehend why there were so many. She doggedly worked at learning to manipulate numbers and problems that came from little stories. When she was eight, a sort of light turned on; and, not only did she begin to understand; but she began to be able to internalize both the numbers and the intellectual concepts behind them. Nassir told her that the Arabs had excelled in math when the Europeans were still swinging from trees. It was one of the great accomplishments of the Islamic world. By the time she turned nine, she could work with algebraic equations, concepts of geometry, axiomatic systems, statistics, trigonometry, and pre-calculus, which was as far as any school in Western Azerbaijain Province could go. She had no teacher other than Nassir, and she had outstripped his abilities a year ago. She did not know it, but she was a mathematical prodigy. She just needed better teachers to set her free to soar in the difficult disciplines.

To learn English, Afsoon had had to learn a new script. Since 1932, most Kurds used the Roman script to write Kurmanji. The other form, Sorani, is normally written in an adapted form of the Arabic script. From a linguistic or at least a grammatical point of view, however, Kurmanji and Sorani differ as much from each other as English and German. Afsoon had already mastered both forms as well as Azerbaijani and Turkish, all of which used different scripts. Kurds use the name "Kurdish" to refer to their ethnic and national identity and use "Kurmanji" to refer to their language. Afsoon spoke all of the languages well, having learned six languages and scripts during her childhood. English came fairly easily, even with its peculiar lettering. Because of the demand that Arabic be used for religious purposes, especially for communicating about the instructions of the *Qur'an*, Afsoon was working at learning that language as well. She had an unconscious but stubborn resistance to learning the language of the religion. She was unsure exactly why.

No one else had any idea of exactly when her birthday was. Mariella decided it was in April because that was the month she and her two daughters had to go to Urmia. She had not told ten-year-old Dina the purpose of the trip. Thirteen-year-old Elaheh already knew, and was silent and glum for two days prior to the trip. Afsoon was thrilled to have a major break in the monotony of farm work and stultifying Islamic ritual.

The day came. All was excitement and anticipation by the two ten-year-olds. It was not lost on Afsoon that Elaheh did not join in the enthusiasm. Afsoon presumed that she was just being her moody teenager self. The three girls and their mother donned black chadors open in the front. All four of them took care to be sure that their long hair was modestly tied in the back. Mariella drove the farm truck over the rutted dirt roads to Nushin, where they first encountered paved highways. The ride to Urmia took six hours, and they had to stop in restaurants twice. Afsoon had never seen a restaurant before and found them exciting. She could hardly wait to get to the capital city of West Azerbaijan Province, Urmia, to see what it had to offer.

Mariella obviously knew her way around the city. Afsoon and her sisters marveled at the huge mosques, skyscrapers, green parks with fountains and playgrounds, *madrasehs* [Islamic schools], and the University of Urmia with many of its 10,000 students seemingly thronging the surrounding streets. They did not stop to get out and get a good look at the marvelous city sights. Mariella had a resolute purpose—it seemed—and that purpose was as opaque to Afsoon as what America must be like. Mariella drove directly to a slum, which was strange, because there were so many beautiful places. The neighborhood where she finally stopped was worse than the worst sections of Qushchu, which was only a large village without even paved roads.

"Get out, girls." Mariella ordered after parking the old truck in a filthy trash-ridden alley in a row of tenements adjacent to the *Shahar Chay* [City River].

It was a mystery to Dina and Afsoon, and they opened their mouths to ask a question but were shushed by their mother who was obviously nervous and in a hurry. Elaheh hung back.

"Please, Mother. I don't want to go. Let me stay in the truck."

"No, Elaheh, it is not safe here," Mariella insisted.

All of the girls were apprehensive now. Elaheh appeared pale and walked in silence with her head down. They went three or four blocks through narrow dark passageways and between dilapidated buildings until they came out into the sunlight of a trash-strewn empty lot. The place was obviously the site of a former large building that had long since vanished, likely a victim of an attack by the Shah's army during one of it incursions into Kurdestan. On the far side of the empty lot near a lifeless building, Afsoon saw three mothers with three young girls her same age. Mariella and her three daughters walked up to them and nodded a greeting, but no one spoke.

From the shadows of an alley that emptied into the open concrete field, a figure approached. It was a man dressed in clerical clothing—a dirty white shirt with no tie—because ties were considered to be a Western affectation—a black turban, and a black *aba*, a light dress-like garment made of camel hair, under his black cloak that was open in front. All of the women bowed immediately upon seeing not just a cleric, but a *sayyid*—a clergyman descended from Muhammad, Peace be upon him.

Behind him from the shadows came two women in severe black burqas with nothing showing except their eyes through a slit in a face covering. Unlike the modest but face revealing chadors worn by the girls and their mothers, these women could have been imported from the Afghan outback. They carried a padded portable folding table with obstetrical stirrups extending from its sides. They opened it full, adjusted the stirrups, and left for about five minutes. They returned carrying a black leather satchel and a canvas bag full of clean rags. The two specters then stood obediently—heads bowed—on either side of the table.

The cleric faced the women and their ten-year-old daughters. He held them with his stern eyes for a few moments.

"I am Imam Ali Abedi. We will now learn the way of the Prophet, may Allah's peace be upon the *Rasul u Allah* [messenger of God] from whom I descend. Do not speak. This is the most important day of your lives, and you are to give full respect to me and to the sacred ceremony that will take place here today.

"Allah has spoken through His *Rasul* in the *Qur'an* that women must guard their modesty, and they must not entice men or seduce them to sin. In Sura

24:31, Allah told Muhammad, 'Say to the believing women that they should lower their gaze and guard their modesty; that they should not display their beauty and ornaments except what must ordinarily appear thereof.'

"The men of the law, according to the *Fiqh* schools through the ages since the One God made His decree, have established that clothing must cover the entire body; only the hands and face may remain visible. The material must not be so thin that one can see through it. The clothing must hang loose so that the shape of the body is not apparent. The female clothing must not resemble the man's clothing. The design of the clothing must not resemble the clothing of the nonbelieving women, especially those loose women found in the Western world. The design must not consist of bold designs or show figures of man or beast. That is a violation of the commandment of Allah that 'Thou shalt not make unto thee any graven images.' Those patterns attract attention, and clothing should not be worn for the attracting attention or for the sole purpose of gaining reputation or increasing one's status in society.

"No Muslim woman can be friends with a man. Why? Because there is a chance of sex. Muslim women cannot laugh or smile at a man or flirt with a man as the nonbelievers in the lands of the Great Satan do. Why? Because one or both of them could begin to think about sex. Muslim women and Muslim men must not share the Western intimacy of shaking hands. Why? Because such touches lead to sex, and men cannot control themselves. That is why men and women stay separate. That is why women must dress modestly; a woman must not allow anyone outside her family circle to see her face, her hands, or her ankles and feet. It is forbidden. Such displays cannot be permitted for male friends, for distant family members beyond those expressly described by the Prophet and the Companions, may Allah bless their names forever, or by physicians as is the practice in the Western world.

"Even women and girls may be tempted. A touch may cause excitement that leads to the great sin. There are body parts in females that are overwhelmingly tempting to poor men who were born without adequate control. When touched, those parts can cause an unnatural excitement; and that cometh of evil. Those parts must be removed in order that a female believer may remain pure and safe. It is for the good of the girl that *khatneh* [circumcision] be done. You are aware that in our Kurdish areas believers know that it controls women's sexual desires and makes them clean. Food prepared by uncircumcised women is considered unacceptable, and children of an uncircumcised woman may not call her 'Mother.'

"Abu Hurayra, a companion of the Prophet, may his name be praised, quotes him as saying, 'Five things are *fitrah* [the natural way or instinctual way]. They are: *khetneh*, shaving the body with a razor, trimming the moustache, paring one's nails and plucking the hair from one's armpits.' Today we shall attend to the ancient and sacred ceremony.

"I am of the Shaafi school of law, and I am proud to report that almost all of our girls have been made clean by removal of their male parts."

He paused for a moment then pointed at Mariella and Dina. He waggled his finger at them to come forward. They obeyed in silence, heads down. The two women in burqas and Mariella lifted Dina up onto the table. She began to cry when they lifted the skirt of her chador and placed her feet in the stirrups. She sobbed when the women bound her wrists and ankles to the table with leather straps and cinched up the buckles.

Afsoon and the other girls looked on in fascinated terror. Elaheh suffered agonies of memory and looked away. It was too much for her to bear.

With quick practiced movements, Imam Abedi opened the leather satchel and extracted two clamps and a knife. The knife was none too clean, Afsoon observed. He told the women to hold her still lest she come to harm, then he began methodically to cut Dina, who screamed a high–pitched, otherworldly sound. The girls and women fell against each other for a sense of protection that every one of them knew would not come.

It took twenty minutes to complete the Type III *khetneh*, known in the Muslim world as infibulation.

Dina screamed over and over, "*Komakam kon! komakam kon!* [Help me, help me!]," a plea that fell on the deaf ears of the adults and the ears of children who had no power.

When the agony of the cutting with the dirty and dull knife was done, ten-year-old Dina had suffered removal of the normal structure of her greater and lesser labia and her untouched clitoris. Using a large needle and heavy silk thread, Imam Abedi fused the gaping wound with blood still gushing out onto the tabletop, leaving a small hole for the passage of urine and menstrual blood. The tiny opening in the fused wound must be recut on the night before a girl is married to permit intercourse, which is extremely painful, and cut open with a wide gash to allow childbirth. Even beyond the Jewish and Christian biblical observation that a woman must bear children in pain and suffering, the acts of procreation and the delivery of a baby by a woman who has suffered female genital mutilation are torture beyond the comprehension of people outside the Muslim world.

One of the other ten-year-old girls was next. Afsoon released her bowels and bladder into the skirt of her chador before that patient was finished with her surgery. The girl's blood made a wide puddle on the ground and covered her shoes. When it was done, the little girl's agonal struggles had resulted in six fractured ribs, and both of her upper arms were broken—one of them had a bone fragment protruding from the skin—from the women's and the mother's efforts to hold her down.

Afsoon fainted before the women laid their hands on her. In the distance, Afsoon heard an unholy keening scream coming from somewhere in the world as the cruel knife sliced into her little woman's parts that are the most tender and sacred to women the world over. She was unconscious before she realized that the sound was coming from her. When it was over, Afsoon, Dina, and the other two girls joined the other 140 million living women and girls of the Muslim world who have undergone female genital mutilation and who suffer the pains of hell whenever they menstruate, are required to make love, and when they have children.

The imam and his two spectral women took the money the three mothers handed them and disappeared back into the darkness from which they had come, leaving the mothers and the mutilated and bleeding girls to fend for themselves. Each girl was given a pile of rags to staunch the bleeding. Each mother wrapped the rags in place with a long strip of muslin. Somehow, they all walked back to their homes or vehicles. Afsoon was in unbearable agony, but Dina was worse. Blood seeped out of the edges of the makeshift bandage; and by the time the three of them were back to the truck, it was a sodden mass. Mariella placed the two girls supine on a straw-filled mattress in the back of the farm truck and began to replace Dina's bandage. Afsoon was limp and helpless. Elaheh sat in stony silence in the passenger side of the truck cab.

Dina's wounds were re-covered; so, hoping for the best, Mariella started the truck and sped as quickly as she dared through the streets of Urmia to get home where she would have help to save her daughter. Afsoon heard the plaintive moaning from her adoptive sister; and when it would not stop, she tried to help. Blood continued to soak the bandage and the cover on the mattress despite all of Afsoon's efforts to press on the tender wound with the remaining rag bandages.

Dina at last could bear no more and begged Afsoon to leave her alone.

"It is better to die than to have any more pain. I am a little girl, and little girls should not have such suffering. Let me have peace."

Afsoon wept until there were no more tears. She became aware that Dina was no longer crying and moaning. There was only the sound of the truck jouncing over the rutted dirt road. She was afraid to look, but at last summoned up enough courage to see how her little sister was doing. Dina lay motionless staring into the sun. She would not move when Afsoon shook her and called to her. She felt guilty that she was too weak to do more and not even strong enough to yell to Mariella to stop. She finally had to admit that Dina's color was so white that it had to be free of blood. She had seen dead staring animals on the farm. It was the second time Afsoon had seen a dead person. In her own weakness, she could do nothing except slip into a troubled slumber of exhaustion.

# CHAPTER TEN

Chava took Gideon up to his room and closed the door.

"Let me see your back and behind, Son," she said.

Gideon reluctantly removed his clothing and stood facing away from his mother.

She took in a short gasp and asked, "How was this done?"

"Rabbi ben Yisroel hit me with a paddle."

"Is that like a board?"

"Yes, Mama, a thin one."

"How many times?"

"I'm not sure. Several."

"All right, Gideon. You take a rest now. When you wake up, I want you to tell me why he did that to you."

"Yes, Mama."

Chava left Gideon's room and went into the library, where she sat for three hours reading a novel, forcing herself to remain calm and not to think about what had happened to her little boy. She wanted to be fully composed when she met with her husband.

G.R. III had received a message from his secretary giving a report of a telephone conversation from Headmaster Rabbi ben Yisroel at Gideon's school that was somewhat vague—something about a fight, and corporal punishment. He left the bank early to surprise Chava with a quick dinner out at one of her favorite restaurants. When he arrived home, Joseph ben Aaron took his coat and hat and handed him a glass of his favorite kosher wine, Domaine Du Castel, Grand Vin, '82. The banker walked up to the second floor towards the master bedroom. Chava met him as he passed the doorway of the library.

"G.R., we need to talk."

"I came home early so we could have a little date—go to the Israeli Bistro for an early supper, some wine, and some good talk. Great minds work the same way, I see."

"No, I mean we need to have a real talk about our boy. He has had a bit of trouble, in case you don't already know."

Chava was generally quite sensitive to anything that involved their first-born, especially now that she was heavily pregnant with twins. However, he had never known her to be irrational; and now she wore her determined look.

"I did get a message at the bank. Rabbi ben Yisroel called, and Mrs. Weis left a short written account. What do you know?"

"The information I have been given was pretty scanty, Gideon, but what I have seen tells a great deal more."

She told him that Gideon had been in a fight and that the circumstances were not altogether clear. She described the paddling and their son's significant bruising in some detail with a quavering lower lip. She began to cry when she finished. Chava almost never cried, and never used feminine tears as a bargaining tool or to manipulate him. G.R.'s interest was greatly heightened.

"I'll have to get to the bottom of this," he said.

"Wait until tomorrow morning until you have heard Gideon's side and have seen his back. Then, you can have your talk with the headmaster, all right?"

"I guess I have no real choice. It will be hard to get hold of the man until morning anyway. I guess the Israeli Bistro is off now."

"I don't have an appetite. Let's have the cook bring us some leftovers; would that be okay with you?"

Joseph took a phone call and interrupted G.R. and Chava.

"From a Mr. Schmuel. He says it is important."

"Mr. Schmuel," G.R. said, his voice businesslike.

"I am Levi Schmuel, the father of Aaron Schmuel, a classmate of your son's at the academy, Mr. Rothsberger. Our two boys had a fight in school today, apparently a rather serious one. Aaron has a broken nose and a set of extremely swollen and tender testicles. We took him to our pediatrician who is concerned about the testicles—says they could be permanently damaged. We have an appointment with an ENT about his nose."

"I see," G.R. said.

He liked the matter-of-fact manner of Mr. Schmuel's communication and his lack of evident anger.

"My wife suggests that we wait to get the facts from the school tomorrow before we make any decisions, especially rash ones, Mr. Schmuel. Maybe this was nothing more than a harmless bit of school boy misunderstanding. I would say that we really don't know at this point."

"I agree. I suggest that we go see ben Yisroel together tomorrow. I don't want to make this into trouble; but my boy is injured; and your boy did it. Aaron tells me that your Gideon is considerably smaller than he is; and I, for one, would like to get to the bottom of it, then let the chips fall where they will."

"I like your plan. Would it be all right with you to meet at the headmaster's office at ten tomorrow?"

"Fine. I will see you then. Thank you for talking with me."

"Good night, Mr. Schmuel."

In the morning, the parents carried a tray of breakfast up to Gideon's room. He was alert; and although he had some aches from his bruises, most of his discomfort was tenderness. If he did not touch or put pressure on the sore areas, he was all right.

"How are you doing, Son?" asked G.R. III.

"Okay. I want to go to school. We are starting to work on our math project for the science fair. I am the chairman. I can't just sit around here."

He gave a little moan as he turned to gesture at his bed.

"That's my boy. Now let's take a look at your behind, shall we?"

"Do I have to?"

"Yes, Son. I want to know what all of this is about."

Gideon obediently bared himself for his second parent. G.R. III's face screwed up in disapproval, but he waited before he spoke. Chava covered her mouth with her hands. The bruises had coalesced into deep purple welts. It looked as if the skin might break down from the pressure of the blood beneath it.

"Tell me every detail, Gideon. Start as far back as necessary and don't leave out a thing. You know that I despise lying, and what I do about this depends on what you tell me."

Gideon started at a point two years ago when the bullying started.

Chava interrupted, "Why didn't you come to us, Son?"

Gideon sighed, "Oh, Mama, boys can't do that. Everybody would think I was a sissy boy."

G.R. III said, "Let him tell his story his own way, Chava. He is being unemotional, and that is the kind of information I have to have."

Chava nodded her assent.

The rendition of history was clear, succinct, and left nothing out until he started to tell about the fight. He covered that in a couple of sentences.

"So, I hit him and I kicked him, and I knocked him down."

"Slow down a bit, Gideon. Go back to the first of the fight itself. Did you hit Aaron first, or did he hit you?"

"He yanked my forelocks, then he poked me in the chest after he said a bunch of rotten things about me."

"I remember about what Aaron said. When he poked you in the chest, did you think he was going to punch you?"

"Dad, do you think I am a dummy? I can tell when someone is going to hit me. Jeez!"

Chava said, "That particular word is one we do not use here. Let the Christians be irreverent about their deity; we won't be."

"Sorry, Mama."

"Now, Son, let's hear about the fight itself," G.R. III said.

"When I made Aaron frustrated by ignoring him, he moved real fast to grab hold of one of my tassels under my pants. I thought he was trying to grab my privates, and that would really hurt; so, I threw an uppercut with both fists with all my strength and smashed Aaron's nose. He made a big howl and threw his hands over his nose and tried to stop the blood, but it kept coming out between his fingers. Then I kicked him in the balls, and he fainted."

G.R. III turned aside to suppress a smile.

Chava looked as if her gently reared son had just cursed a rabbi and said, "Where on earth did you pick up that kind of language, boy!?"

"At school, Mama. I thought I would sound like a doctor instead of a kid in a fight if I said 'testicles.'"

G.R. III laughed out loud, which earned him a scornful look from his wife.

"All right, Gideon. I have my day's work cut out for me. Let's see you walk and sit; if you can do both, you can go to school. You'll have to get a move on."

The son went to school; the mother pouted and worried; and the father set to work. The first thing he did was to call the bank's intelligence division. Every major bank kept a set of records on its rich clients, politicians, gangsters, bank employees, and potential clients or business associates who might have compromising areas in their backgrounds or lives. He learned that Levi Schmuel was both a client and one of the people with a checkered enough past to have a red flag placed by his name.

G.R. III had a courier bring everything the intelligence division had on Schmuel, and it proved to be both copious and compromising. G.R. skimmed through the general material on the Israeli mafia and focused on Levi Schmuel and his family. The bank intelligence team had generated information and evidence proving that Schmuel was a criminal. He had been arrested twenty-one times, but only indicted three times and convicted once. He spent two years in

Folsom prison for racketeering and money laundering—1962-1964. He was suspected of participating in illegal gambling, protection and extortion rackets, fencing stolen goods, and diamond smuggling. He had made a substantial reputation in and out of the Israeli and American Jewish mobs as a mob accountant, money launderer, and computer hacker. His past known associates—but nothing on the radar for several years—included Zeev Rosenkranz, head of one of the major organized crime syndicates headquartered in Tel Aviv, Israeli gangsters Rami Amira Segev, Ronan Alyian, Moussan Haya, and Eitan Mizrachi, who had criminal interests involving the United States—particularly New York City—Russia, South Africa, the Netherlands, and throughout the United Kingdom.

It was quarter to ten when he finished skimming the contents of the intelligence division's packet. He drove himself to the Saint Francis Woods Hebrew Academy and parked in faculty parking where his contributions to the school had earned him his own reserved parking place. He met Levi Schmuel in the anteroom of Rabbi ben Yisroel's office, easily recognizing Aaron's father from the intelligence dossier's photographs.

"Good morning, Mr. Rothsberger," Schmuel said with an unrevealing face.

"Good morning, Mr. Schmuel, I am pleased to meet you."

There was a dramatic contrast between the two men. G.R. III was the Jewish community's movie celebrity—tall, dark, handsome, curly haired, with a finely chiseled nose, and patrician. He was dressed in a $1,800 conservative black suit and a stiffly starched white shirt with French cuffs and gold Rothsberger Family Bank cufflinks. He wore coal black Gucci tasseled shoes that Joseph, the butler, had shined to a light-catching gleam that morning. His face was smoothly shaven and lined with superficial smile-line wrinkles. His skin had just the slightest olive complexion. There was no hint of grey, and his face and body appeared as young as he—in fact—was.

Levi Schmuel would have been typecast as a movie thug except for his piercing intelligent brown eyes. His $2,400 Saville Row suit was tailor made, but somehow did not quite fit perfectly. He was a foot shorter than G.R. III and solidly built with heavy shoulders, thick arms and thighs. His suit was grey; his shirt was light blue; and Schmuel had not been quite able to get the upper button done up. His tie was the center of attention—a Hawaiian beach scene—and it was tied too short. He wore expensive—but out of place—penny loafers the color of which clashed with the rest of his ensemble. Although he had shaved, the shadow of his beard was evident.

The men shook hands. G.R. III made a small mental note to remember the powerful thick hands of Schmuel. His hand smarted a little after the physical encounter.

"The headmaster will see you now," announced Ruth Weinberger, Rabbi ben Yisroel's elderly secretary, who had been in her place thirty-five years longer than the present headmaster.

Levi Schmuel stood and gestured politely for G.R. III to precede him. The headmaster stood up from his chair and walked around to the front and gestured for the men to sit down on one of the three comfortable stuffed chairs. He took the third one.

"Perhaps, I should speak first. I realize that both of you are very busy, and this may seem a trivial matter. However, I will fill you in on all that I have learned about the fight between your two boys and its antecedents. I will do so in all candor, as I think you would expect nothing less."

The two men nodded their agreement and remained quiet as the rabbi told of each of the boys' accomplishments in the school. Both were intelligent, even brilliant. G.R. IV was the brighter of the two, but he had in the negative column of his ledger entry the fact that he was much younger and smaller. The headmaster spared no feelings of Levi Schmuel and gave a remarkably detailed rendition of the evidence for labeling Aaron as a bully. He cited more than a dozen boys and girls who were victims of Mr. Schmuel's son. The majority of the children had confessed that Aaron had been running his own personal protection and extortion racket.

Levi glowered but held his peace as the headmaster spoke his full piece.

Likewise, G.R. III remained quiet and—in his case, expressionless—while Rabbi ben Yisroel recounted exactly how the fight that brought everyone into his office that day had taken place. Ever meticulous, he cited fourteen students' accounts of the scene.

He looked at the two men. They gestured for him to finish.

"Uh, hmmh," he coughed when he reached the subject of his possible culpability—the paddling of G.R. IV. "Now, I shall recount what took place in my office when I dealt with young Rothsberger."

He again gave an objective rendition, not sparing himself. The only defense he offered was that he had the obligation both from the Torah and from school policy to inflict corporal punishment when it was necessary.

He added the salving comment that, "four-year-old Gideon behaved with courage, and the gentle manners I have been striving to instill in my charges. The boy did not cry or whimper. He was a *mensch*—a person of honor and rectitude."

With that, he ceased his narrative and looked at the two fathers seated facing him.

"Any questions, gentlemen?"

Schmuel—ever the gentleman—gestured to G.R. III to go first.

"Headmaster, I have three questions. Please give me an answer to each in its turn. The first is what—if anything—was done to punish Aaron?"

That produced a moment of hesitation and a quickening of the headmaster's pulse. He stammered a couple of times, but finally told G.R. III that he had not yet done anything. Aaron had gone home almost immediately after the altercation.

"My second question is, why not? But it would seem that you have answered that. I still retain more than simple curiosity about what you plan to do; but I will leave that to be decided by you and Mr. Schmuel, whom I consider to be a man of stern values.

"My third question is: how is it that a big strong man, a cleric, should consider such a savage beating of my little four-year-old boy whom you knew at the time to be innocent of any wrongdoing? To that question, I shall require a very detailed and forthright explanation. Your behavior was entirely unacceptable."

Rabbi Pinchas ben Yisroel, ha-Rav, had never in his life been spoken to in that manner. He blanched visibly; and, despite himself, looked down and studied his shoes.

He said softly, "I shall give you a full account, Mr. Rothsberger."

"Good, I expect it by morning. I am now finished. Mr. Schmuel?"

Levi Schmuel was physically intimidating even when sitting, but he stood up and drilled holes into the headmaster with his unfeeling beach stone eyes.

"You will administer exactly the same punishment to Aaron, Headmaster. You will do that today without fail. I will guarantee that my son will never again act the bully in your school. I will expect a biweekly report on his behavior for the remainder of the year. I am somewhat old-fashioned. Corporal punishment is to be meted out in the home—spare the rod and spoil the child—the Torah puts it. However, I am modern enough to tell you here and now that no child will ever again suffer what Gideon Rothsberger did at the hands of the greatest bully in the academy. Am I clear, Sir?"

"Perfectly. Is there anything else?"

The two fathers glanced at each other; and as if they had practiced their lines before coming to the school, said in unison, "We will get back to you."

As the two men walked out of the administration building, Levi lightly touched G.R. III's arm and said, "We have to talk."

# CHAPTER ELEVEN

"What do you have in mind?" the starchy banker asked the Jewish Mafioso.

"Let's sit in my car, if you don't mind."

G.R. III nodded, and they climbed into the backseat of Schmuel's limousine behind the chauffeur who never even chanced a glance at the two men. He was—by occupation—deaf and suffered from profound amnesia.

"First, I admit without reservation that my boy was wrong and was the aggressor. I will deal with him in a way that he will not soon forget; you can take that to the bank."

He smiled.

"Second, allow me to compliment you on your son. He is young but a strapping lad with fire in his belly. I admire that in a man and more so in a boy. He was brave, did not let himself be bullied; and he fought back like an Israeli soldier. That leads me to an observation that I would like you to consider. There have been 2,000-plus years of Jews bowing their heads to the Christians, the Cossacks, the Nazis, and now the Muslims. They have been good little mensches—people full of honor, rectitude, and submissiveness—docile as sheep on the way to the slaughter. They have been willingly characterized as possessing great tolerance, quizzical, head bowed intellectualism, and gentle manners. Like members of the Molokan Sect, they have assumed their roles as pacifists and God-worshippers. In a perfect world—a lamb lying down with a lion world—that might be a plausible way to go. However, I personally would rather be the lion than the lamb in that situation. Many people I know think differently. But some of us are of the opinion that a Jew cannot be a member of a persecuted people for 2,000 years without yearning to be like their enemies—holding the power. You are at least as familiar with

Jewish history as I am, but please allow me to drive home my point. Your boy will never be a *nebbish*. Someone once said that a *nebbish* is 'someone you feel sorry for.' I respect your son. He is one of those who will fight with all of the weapons at his disposal, and he will be one of the powerful.

"Benjamin Netanyahu—my favorite Israeli politician—said, 'You know, Jews are complicated people.' That's true. Some Jews have refused to be sweet gentle little mensches. Consider Samson in the Torah. I think that every time that big Israeli brute, Samson, brandished the jawbone of the ass, it meant murder and mayhem to the persecutors. He murdered more than a few of them. It seems to me that—then and now—a murder of a few more Philistines wouldn't cause Yahweh any loss of sleep. And there was Golem who was the medieval Prague progenitor of Frankenstein. That Jewish monster was built by a rabbi to fight anti-Semitism. It was the defender of the Jews. If you are a reader, you know that story is for all Jews for all time.

"And you know that a group of Jewish businessmen in Liverpool after WW II raised money to buy guns for the Irgun and the Lehi to drive the anti-Semitic British out of Palestine. The Lehi were known to the British as the Stern Gang; well, so be it. Israel and hundreds of thousands of Jews survived the follow-up of the Holocaust because of them. They weren't all bad. Our own fathers grew up in the thirties and forties when Jews were docile punching bags. American soldiers came back from the war and reported on the Holocaust, the mass murders in the ovens, and the Nazi's disregard for Jews as human beings—they were the *untermenschen*. The newspapers and magazines and later on TV brought it into every home. At the same time as they were being presented the image of murdered, degraded, and starved Jews being bulldozed into mass graves, there was another image. The Zionists and the Kosher Nostra made their own image closer to home: big, bad, tough, fearless Jews *with guns*. They put out the message to everyone that even thought of being an anti-Semite or of pulling off a pogrom. It was, don't be fooled by a guy in a yarmulke. He's gonna kill you before you can get round to killing him.

"I know you have read up on me. I don't deny my past—which is my *past*, by the way. But my family goes way back, far enough that I count as my heroes guys like the soldiers of the IDF and the spies in the Mossad, the sixteen Israeli mafia families, and yeah, the Kosher Nostra. My family knew guys like Bugsy Siegel, Meyer Lansky, Jacob Levinsky, 'Dopey' Benny Fein, and Joe 'The Greaser' Rosenzweig; they made the goyim think twice about discrimination and persecution of us Jews. You wouldn't want one of the Molokans to marry your daughter, and you probably wouldn't want her to marry into Meyer Lanksy's or Bugsy Siegel's family either. But, you know, when someone like an Iranian or a Syrian needs to have an attitude adjustment, you'd make a call to Moise Levinsky or Dangerous Adam Gonen before you'd get on the horn with the likes of Woody Allen or some prissy art history prof at Yeshiva University.

"The Russian Jews who emigrated to Israel from Russia included some scientists, some chess grandmasters, some prima ballerinas, and others who formed the country's new industry of organized crime, drug dealing, and prostitution—I admit that. The tough guys—the shtarkers and the real menschess—were corroded by 75 years of Soviet socialism and corruption. But they weren't Molokans or lambs.

"Okay, I've gone on enough. You get my drift. We have been patsies long enough, and our boys need to be friends. They need to learn to work together. They need to be tough and smart enough to stand up to the goyim everywhere. It will be their battle to deal with the ragheads who murder our people just because they are Jews. I know a guy. He was an instructor in the Israeli Defense forces and for the Mossad—we had some dealings with each other. He can teach our boys Krav Maga, the IDF self-defense system. We can link up your bankers and other international businessmen and bankers—our people—the Mossad, and the World Zionist Organization, the *Sayanim*. We can link up with the *edah* [the entire Jewish people]."

The *Sayanim* are Jews who live in and hold the citizenship of lands *outside* Israel; they are recruited clandestinely by Israel's intelligence agency, Mossad, to further its operations. The *Sayanim* respond when asked to provide safe houses, transportation, access to communications networks and other facilities, official documents, money, secure banking, forgeries, etc.

G.R. III smiled as Levi took a breath. Levi had something of a sheepish grin at his long-winded and emotional defense of any and everything Jewish. G.R. III had mixed feelings about the man. He regarded Schmuel with a combination of distaste and pragmatic acceptance, and decided at the end of Schmuel's impassioned speech that he would, indeed, be able to work with the man; but he would have to keep him at arms-length.

G.R. III took a short turn in the conversation, "Mr. Schmuel...."

Levi interrupted, "Could we be Levi and Gideon?"

"Levi it is. Most of my friends avoid confusion by calling me G.R. III, because all of the family males are named Gideon."

Both men laughed.

Levi said, "I won't tell you what most of my family and friends call me most of the time."

Spontaneously, the two fathers shook hands.

"Levi. I have to get to the bank very shortly. However, I want to talk more to you about your association with the *Sayanim;* so, I can get involved discreetly. If it is not presumptuous of me, may I suggest that you make arrangements for our boys to study Krav Maga, and I will take care of matters at the school. I think our different kinds of expertise would be best used with that approach."

"I knew we were going to be able to work together. I will let you know how things go on my end when we meet again. I would like to meet with you on a banking matter on Monday. Can you fit me in for about an hour in the morning? I believe you will find it worth your while."

"I will make room, Levi. Until then...."

They shook hands and went their separate ways, both thinking about how they would handle the other man who might as well have come from the opposite end of the earth.

# CHAPTER TWELVE

Afsoon was carried from the back of the truck and placed in her bed in the house without ever awakening. Early the next morning, she came around to find Nassir holding her hand.

"Good morning, little sister," he said softly.

"Good morning, big brother."

"You have to get up now. We are going to bury Dina. We only have a few hours left."

Muslim burials must be within twenty-four hours of death if at all feasible.

Afsoon began to cry. Nassir could not resist and started to cry with her.

"Was it so awful?" he asked timidly.

"Worse."

There was a heartfelt emphasis as she enunciated the word emphatically. Nassir did not want to know more. He left her and brought back Mariella and Elaheh, who poured Lake Orumiyeh water over Afsoon's blood-matted bandages. The sting was horrific, but Afsoon had determined on the truck ride home from Urmia the day before that she would never let anyone see her cry or hear her give in to screaming again. She knotted up her face to lock against any sound sneaking out. After fifteen minutes of soaking the bandage rags, they fell away from the open wound. The washing had removed the clotted blood and scabs and left the raw tissue bare and dry.

"Lie like that for an hour, then get dressed and come down. We have to go up the hill then," Elaheh said.

Mariella said nothing to Afsoon—no soothing or affectionate comforts, no expression of dismay, and no mention of Dina. Afsoon thought of Firudin and Mariella, the imam and his spectral assistants, of her elder brothers,

Mozaffarian and Gorgani, and back all the way to Ahriman Shakibaie and his first wife, Fereshten.

She silently said to herself, "*Az hamashun motenaferam* [I hate them all]."

She had love for Nassir and hate for most of the others she had encountered in her ten years of life. All other people were inconsequential. As she prepared to face the dreadful parting with her adoptive sister, she knew she had lost whatever religion she might have had. She did not believe in prayer, in ceremonies, in God, in the faith, in clerics, in the traditions. It was clear to her that no God who condoned murder by government or terrorists—which she had read about in newspapers brought home by Nassir—or who caused women to suffer so much at the hands of all men and of women of Islam was worth a passing thought, let alone worship. She vowed that somehow—someday—she would escape. It was a hope that would sustain her for the next four years of pain, trouble, and strife.

Mariella and Elaheh were in the back laundry area. Tradition demanded that the preparations of a dead body for burial be done outside; but it was freezing; and the ablutions could not be carried out there. Dina's nude body lay supine on a laundry sorting table facing Mecca in preparation for the washing ceremony. Mariella called to Afsoon to come in. She obeyed, but was afraid and cowered as she looked on the little girl's body; she seemed so small and white. The doors to the room were closed and locked, and shutters were closed on all of the windows to protect the deceased from the prying eyes of men and from the sun and sky as the three females set to work.

First, the odious task of scraping off the caked-on blood around her missing genitals was done. Copious amounts of soap and water and scrubbing clothes were necessary before she was clean. Dina's nails were cleaned and trimmed, and her hair shampooed. The sight of the mutilation was horrifying to Afsoon and Elaheh, but Mariella worked like an automaton, as if she did not see what had been done—what she had allowed to be done—on her daughter in the name of Allah and the religion.

They cleaned the table thoroughly until everything appeared to be pristine. Then they performed three complete washings with three different solutions—the *Mordeh Shoor*—were performed. The solutions were as prescribed by believers throughout the ages: *Sedr*, an ancient cleansing substance—with *kafoor* (camphor) for scenting the body, then plain freshwater from the river, were used. Dina's hands were washed first, then her genitals, then her head, then the right and the left side of her small body. The nine washings were ritualistic; all nine washings consisted only of lightly rubbing with the solutions. Finally, at the end, all of Dina's bodily openings—ears, nostrils and genital areas—were blocked with cotton balls. Before her mouth was blocked, Mariella placed a few drops of *ab e torbat* [spiritually blessed water the family believed had come from Kerbalah where Hussein lies buried]. Mariella recited the specific prayers then repeatedly asked Allah to forgive little Dina for whatever sins she might have committed. Afsoon though it absurd that her little sister could have committed sins.

Dina's body was tightly wrapped in a *Kafan* [white burial cloth] and tied with white cotton ropes. It was a sin to sew the *Kafan* anywhere. Around her head was placed an embroidered band holding the handkerchief used to wipe Dina's tears from her attendance at *Moharram* gatherings for Imam Hussein. Thus, it was indicated to the spirits that they have shed tears for Imam Hussein. As with other females, a prayer bead from Kerbala brought home by Firudin from a long ago journey was placed around her neck to show the spirits she had been a good Shi'ite and has mourned for Imam Hussein. More prayers were recited.

Imam Zamaani Fard drove to the house that morning and brought three of his sons to assist in the burial ceremonies. Two of them hoisted the open empty plain wood casket onto their hands; and one of them, along with Furidin and his sons, Mozaffarian and Gorgani, carried the coffin up the hill to the copse of trees followed by the females. Every few feet, the funeral procession paused to call out *"Allahu Akbar."* Firudin had at first insisted that only males be in attendance at the procession and burial, but relented when he saw the fury in his wife's eyes, her having suffered the entire ordeal of her daughter's death and the washings.

The grave had already been dug by Dina's brothers. She was to be placed in the same unmarked grave as her elder sister and brother who died of scarlet fever six years previously. Such multiple burials in the same hole were frowned upon, but the poor working people of North Western Iran could not afford to follow such requirements to the letter. The coffin was placed next to the hole; the wrapped corpse was gently placed into it; and the members of the family looked down to see the rotting wood from the previous caskets. Together, all members of the family—Afsoon was excluded—asked for Allah's forgiveness of their newly departed daughter and sister and recited the *Namaz e meyet* [prayer of death]. Dina's face was then exposed. The part of the *kafan* covering her face was folded under and placed over the brick that was there to support the head. Dina was turned onto her right side to face *Ghebleh* [Mecca]. Firudin placed a copy of the *Qur'an* on Dina's abdomen to protect and bless her. Each member of the family sprinkled rose water on the wrapped body, and then each picked up a few handfuls of dirt and sprinkled it into the open coffin.

Imam Fard gave a short sermon: "All of Allah's people and even *kaffirs* [nonbelievers] will be resurrected. At that time, the divine book in which all human deeds, good and bad, are recorded will be opened in heaven. The list of the deeds of Dina Jamshidi will be read aloud for all to hear. If the book is placed in the right hand of Dina, she will go to heaven, if in the left hand, she will be doomed to hell. None but Allah can know what their fate will be. Dina—like all of us—will cross the Sarat Bridge. Crossing the bridge will decide her final fate. Blessed ones—as we hope Dina is—will cross and end in heaven. The unbelievers, the people of the left hand and of the land of the Great Satan are doomed; the bridge becomes so narrow that it is like the edge of a knife; and they drop into hell."

The family recited the prayer of death again and again asked for Allah's forgiveness for Dina. The procession made its sorrowful way back down the hill to the house for a simple meal. Dina's name would never be spoken again. After the meal, the sons of Firudin and Imam Fard returned to the gravesite and filled it in with dirt. By the end of summer, all traces of it would be gone.

§§§§§

1992 was a year of troubles in Kurdish Western Azerbaijani Province. During the first week of the new year, there was a bombing in the great market in Urmia. Twenty-eight people were killed, including an important imam and his wife, and one hundred thirty-one were seriously injured. The bazaar was wrecked—Persian carpets, fine miniature paintings, ceramic marquetry pieces, and elegant glasswork were shattered and strewn about a thirty-meter square area. Mid-month, Kurdish nationalists took to the streets in several cities such as Mahabad, Sanandaj, and Urmia and staged mass protests against the government and in support of transnationalization of the Kurdish movement. These protests were violently suppressed by the government forces.

A week later that same month when Afsoon turned twelve, the first of two things of importance happened to her. She had finally healed and had become accustomed to the discomfort and tightness of scarring in her genitals. She had some difficulty keeping herself clean because her excretions did not pass out of her in the natural way, but she learned to live with it. Then, during the second week of that frigid month, she was alarmed to see seepage of blood coming from the scarified upper opening. She was terrified that she was being punished for sin, that she was infected, or that her blood vessels had opened up again after two years, and she might have to have something done to her extremely tender private parts. After three days, she gathered up her courage and went to Elaheh to tell her of this dreadful new problem.

"It is only the woman thing, Afsoon. We must get you to the bleeding tent. I will teach you, and you will be fine."

Elaheh taught her that a menstruating woman is unclean.

"It is a punishment for all women because it was Eve—the first woman—who led Adam—a man and a superior being—astray and caused the two of them to be cast out of paradise and for all people thereafter to be prevented from knowing paradise until after death. You have to go to the red tent before the men see you."

Afsoon was—like all Muslim women—shunned during her menses and forced to live in seclusion till she stopped bleeding. None of the other members of the household would eat or sit with her, not even Nassir. She was forbidden from practicing the activities of the religion, and she was prohibited from working. As it turns out, menstruation that first time and thereafter posed no problem for Afsoon. She loved the rest and did not miss the religious elements that pervaded her life otherwise. It was difficult for her that she was only allowed to eat dry foods, salt and rice. She had her own utensils that could never be used by anyone else lest Afsoon's monthly impurity be passed on to the other person.

Two days after her bleeding stopped and she was allowed back into the company of the pure, a man from Ahriman Shakibaie and Fereshten's hamlet drove a Land Rover up to the house. He had a hurried consultation with Firudin and Mariella then sped off to give his message to other outlying farmers. The gist of the message was that Grand Ayatollah Ali ibn Abi Rahimi, the Supreme Leader of Iran, had sent the Republican Guard to quell what the majority powers considered to be a Kurdish insurrection. From the early days of the Iranian revolution, relations between the central government and Kurdish organizations were fraught with problems, and the Grand Ayatollah was determined to put an end to all resistance.

Ali ibn Abi Rahimi had only recently been declared to be a Grand Ayatollah, and it would be two more years before he was elevated to the title of *marja'-e taqlid* [source of emulation] for the Iranian people. His status as the Supreme Leader was unchallenged by the conservatives, and the conservatives held all of the power in the relatively new Islamic state.

On September 17, 1992, three Kurdish opposition leaders and their interpreter were assassinated by intelligence operatives controlled by Rahimi. The murders took place in the Mykonos restaurant in Berlin. Berlin's highest criminal court issued an international arrest warrant for the Iranian intelligence minister for ordering the assassination and implied that Ali ibn Abi Rahimi was the mastermind behind the attack. Rahimi, his senior military officers, and the conservative clerical political leaders of Iran took great umbrage at the temerity of Germany to suggest that the great religious leader could be involved in murder. He arrested his head of intelligence and executed him.

In November, the Iranian Republican Guard Army moved into Western Azerbaijan Province to avenge the bombing of the grand market of Urmia, and to end the audacity of the KDP-I—*Hizbi Demokrati Kurdistani Iran* [Democratic Party of Iranian Kurdistan]—the oldest and largest Iranian-Kurd political party inside and outside of Iran.

That action ushered in the second important event that affected Afsoon.

The Supreme Leader was no stranger to war, having been a senior officer during the Iran-Iraq War of the 1980s, and he was not the least bit timid at enforcing his will on those who differed with him or dared to stand up to him and his regime. The Baha'i suffered loss of all their civil and political rights in the face of his juggernaut, and now it was the turn of the Kurds. Two days after the first warning, the messenger returned to report the devastation that had occurred in the five cities of the province. Most of the buildings had been razed to the ground; most of the Kurdish men who fought back were dead—their bodies taken away and dumped into a desolate area known as Kafarestan—Land of the Unbelievers—and Lanatabad—Land of the Damned. Women were raped, children were murdered, fingers were amputated in a green machine transported from Evin Prison for the purpose of shock and awe. Law and order on the Rahimi plan was restored. At the time of his report, it was seven o'clock in the morning.

"What about the Shakibaie clan?" Firudin asked.

"Nearly wiped out. Ahmad and Fereshten escaped to the old family village in the north west at the foot of Mount Kuh-e Sahand in Kandovan. They are safe there."

"What of Astera and Azedeh?" asked Mariella.

"Azedeh is safe there as well. I take it that you have not heard. Astera and a lover named Farhad Sharifi were caught in the very act by Fereshten. Astera was stoned and Farhad was banished."

"How awful," Mariella said.

"Yes, women are evil in their hearts. It is well that the Prophet, may peace be upon him, understood that and decreed the burqa and the chador. Were it not so, all decency would perish, and we would become as degenerate as the *kaffirs* of the west."

Mariella did not venture to express any sympathy for Astera or her lover. It was *inshallah*.

Everyone on the farm galvanized into action. Firudin and the boys rounded up all of the weapons they had stashed for just such an eventually as this. Mariella and Elaheh gathered up stocks of food for a siege. They had scarcely begun when a thrumming sound like thunder was heard in the distance. Firudin ordered Nassir and Afsoon to take every animal they could up the hill to the trees; so, they would not be seen. Halfway up the hill, they could see the terrifying tanks, troop trucks, and artillery caissons in the far distance advancing on their little farm. The two youngsters hurried as fast as they could to get the animals hidden.

"My baby," Afsoon cried. "I am going to get *Fereshte*. I have to."

She began to run down the hill.

"No!" yelled Nassir. "You can't make it. The Republican Guard will get you. No one is going to survive!"

Afsoon paid no attention. She was strong and fleet of foot and made it to the house in a few minutes. Nassir trailed in behind her, frustrated at the willfulness of his little sister. Together they raided her hiding place in the back storage room of the house. In the front of the house, all was chaos and action. The family—now reinforced with half a dozen other outlying families—was creating barricades, distributing weapons and ammunition, cooking, gathering jugs of water, and piling soap and bandages in a makeshift infirmary. Afsoon and Nassir ignored them. Nassir had assured his little sister that what the rest of the family was doing was a lost cause and that they had to save themselves. First, she had insisted that they save Angel and the mathematics books. They were treasures that had to be kept out of the hands of the terrorists.

The thunder was louder now and had a bone chilling menace to it. The two children knew that it was the sound of Shaytan and Death on the march. They work feverishly to carry Angel and the books to the trash heap behind the sheep and goat corral and buried the books in the refuse so they could not be seen.

"They will burn everything else, but they will ignore the trash, Afsoon," Nassir said with more certainty than he felt.

"Run, Nassir. I have Angel. We have to get to the trees before they get here. It will only be a few minutes!"

They ran straight up the hill as fast as possible, lungs screaming, hearts pounding out of their chests. The first rattle of machine guns started before they disappeared into the trees. By the time they could breathe again, artillery fire got underway. Afsoon clutched Angel to her chest, and she and Nassir crawled on their bellies to where they could see the action without being seen. It was over in five minutes. The military juggernaut of the *pasdaran* [Revolutionary Guards], constitutionally mandated to protect the country's Islamic system, rolled over the farm as if the house, barn, and barricades were made of match wood. There were survivors. Firudin, Mariella, Mozaffarian, Gorgani, and three men from other farms, stood with heads bowed in front of the commissioned and noncommissioned officers of the Republican Guard detachment.

Mariella was wounded and had to be supported by Firudin. Gorgani had a severe burn on his back and was supported by his brother. Behind them, what was left of four generations of Jamshidi family work, blood, sweat, and tears was now a raging inferno sending a grey plume of smoke skyward. The family's flagpole had been knocked over by a tank, and the two offending flags—the colors of the KDP-I, and the Iran portal of the flag of the autonomous region of Iraqi Kurdestan—were torn off the lanyard and spread out on the ground in front of the vanquished farmers.

The colonel, dressed in his smart, starched, and spotless desert Airborne Detachment uniform studied a set of photographs for a moment. His epaulets were new with three ten-point gold stars on an ink-black background. The medals displayed on his broad chest included the Medal of Honor, the Conspicuous Gallantry Lion, and a dozen campaign ribbons—for the victorious Iran/American war in Balochistan, for the invasion of Bulgaria, for the Iran/Asia conflict, and the Iran/Israel campaign medal. The effect on the cowed prisoners was chilling.

He deliberately stood on the flags with their handsome green, white, and red colors and the emblem of a full bright sun. He then urinated on them to demonstrate his disdain by desecrating them and to show his and his government's absolute power over the Kurds.

"You," he said, pointing at Mozaffarian and Gorgani, "come here. Kneel."

They were beaten and obeyed robotically.

The colonel looked down at the young men with angry disdain.

"These two men are part of the terrorist anti-Iran group who murdered innocent citizens in Urmia in May of this year. They have been tried and found guilty. The punishment is outlined in the *Holy Qur'an*."

He nodded to a sergeant standing behind him. The man stepped forward, crisply carrying a large curved scimitar that gleamed in the cold sunlight. He stepped behind Mozaffarin, placed the point of the sword lightly against his upper back, and looked to his colonel for a signal. The signal came in the form of a slight cutting motion from the gloved hand of the colonel.

The sergeant gave a hard jab of the sword into Mozaffarin's back, which caused the young man's head to arch backwards in sudden response. As he did so, the great sword arced through the air and decapitated the eldest son and heir of the Jamshidi family with one stroke. His head rolled in the dirt and was shortly surrounded by almost his entire blood volume.

Despite her resolve to be stoical, Mariella screamed. The colonel nodded to his left, and a soldier shot her dead. Firudin was leaning on her, and both of them toppled to the ground. Gorgani was horrified and tried to back away on his hands and knees. The swordsman swept the great blade down on him, but Gorgani's movement caused a miscalculation. Instead of a clean-cut decapitation, the blade scored a huge swath across his back. It was a terrible wound, but not fatal. The sergeant swung the sword again; but, this time, Gorgani's head was bowed and canted to his right, and the sword slashed across the back of his skull. There was a dreadful wound that opened his scalp, cut through the muscles, and crushed his occipital bone. Gorgani moaned in desperate fear and from pain beyond anything he could have ever imagined.

The colonel frowned at the sergeant, which created a serious incentive in the executioner. He kicked Gorgani to the ground, bent down and adjusted the young man's head into an acceptable position, then gave a mighty swing of the bloodied sword, which separated the head from the neck and cut a gouge in the earth six inches deep. The dispassionate colonel signaled his approval.

"Finish the rest of the traitors to the Revolution," he ordered.

Two guardsmen stepped forward and machine-gunned the rest of the men. Firudin's body leaped and bucked from the excessive bullets that tore him apart.

On the hill, the two children had a perfect view of the macabre scene, and they watched in horrified fascination. They were silent and hugged the earth. Afsoon gripped Angel as if her life depended on protecting her baby. They remained riveted to their hiding and viewing spots until the Revolutionary Guard column pivoted and moved out, headed for the next Kurdish farm. The Jamshidi farm was now a two-foot high pile of smoking ashes. Guardsmen discovered the family's animals and slaughtered them with a flame thrower.

Nassir and Afsoon waited over an hour before daring to venture out. It was not yet ten o'clock. They had survived because they had chosen a perfect hiding place that the soldiers ignored. When they again returned to what was once the tidy bustling Jamshidi farmstead, they found that the only thing remaining that indicated that life had once gone on there was the trash pile that was left intact. The mathematics books were unscathed. Nassir hiked two miles to the north field and returned with the old—but functional—tractor that had sat in a swale undetected by the marauding Iranian army.

Without looking back, they loaded up Angel, the books, and Afsoon's skinning knife—which, along with the tractor and the clothes on their backs, were the only possessions left in the world of Nassir and Afsoon. They turned the tractor towards Kandovan village. 1992, like 1990, had been a very bad year for Afsoon.

Before they had gone a mile to the north, they were met by Elaheh. Nassir stopped the tractor, and he and Afsoon leaped off and ran to embrace their sister. Nassir reached her first and swept her up in his arms.

"Allah be praised for His mercy. We've found you. You were lost, but you are found. We thought you were dead, but here you are, alive!"

Afsoon hugged her from behind, and together she and Nassir compressed Elaheh into a human sandwich.

"Let me breathe," Elaheh said. "Are they all gone?"

"Yes, the Supreme Leader's killers are gone."

"And the family?"

"All murdered just like all of the Kurds in the rest of Western Azerbaijan Province. We cannot stay here."

"Where can we go, Brother?" Elaheh asked, in shock now because of the overwhelmingly bad news.

Nassir was now the man—the patriarch—of the family by default. He took charge.

"We go to Kandovan Village in the secret hills."

Afsoon and Elaheh nodded.

Afsoon asked Elaheh, "How did you get away?"

"Mama told me to go and hide in the ditch above the milk shed as soon as we heard the murderers coming. I begged her not to make me go, but she slapped me and ordered me to leave. She said, 'Someone has to live, my little one; all the rest of us are dead people walking. Now go, and know that you are loved.' So, I ran to the canal and pulled a lot of dead branches and weeds over me. I could hear the guns and screams. I saw the fire and the smoke. I was terrified, but I stayed down. I begged Allah, may all submit to Him, for protection; and here I am. How did you get away from them?"

Nassir and Afsoon filled Elaheh in on their adventures.

"See what we have, Elaheh," said Afsoon.

She showed her the tractor laden with food. Elaheh smiled her approval at that. When Afsoon showed her the load of mathematics books and her rag doll, she was less impressed.

She said, "So, that's all we have."

"Yes, but we will be welcome in Kandovan. And Ahriman Shakibaie and Fereshten will be there. They will help us, too," Nassir said enthusiastically.

"No they won't," said Afsoon, and she knew better than her adoptive siblings.

Elaheh and Nassir would not allow anything to dampen their elevated spirits as they fired up the engine of the antiquarian tractor and pointed it in the direction of Kandovan and their new lives.

**"Toto, I have a feeling we're not in Kansas anymore."**
**-L. Frank Baum, *The Wizard of Oz*-**

# THE IRANIAN REVOLUTION

**"Could thou and I with Fate conspire To grasp this sorry Scheme of Things entire, Would not we shatter it to bits—and then Remold it nearer to the Heart's Desire!"**

-An eleventh-century Iranian scientist
Quoted in *Modern Iran: Roots and Results of Revolution*, by Nikki R. Keddie

The separation of religion and state has been a foreign concept throughout Islam since the time of the Prophet Muhammad; so, it should not be surprising that there was a yearning for an Islamic state during the years that the royal dictator, Mohammad Reza ShahanShah Pahlavi, attempted to drag the Persians kicking and screaming into the modern, progressive, American/European-based, world with secular governmental administrative, military, and judicial practices, a semblance of democracy, and the despised Savak [secret police]—all of which were anathema to the ultraconservative Shi'i hierarchy. The Shah came to power via a CIA/MI6 backed coup, and that was a further large thorn in the side of the impassioned Shi'i hardliners.

After the coup, the Shah instituted a "White Revolution" in 1963, which was considered an all-out challenge to the *ulama* [powerful and privileged Shi'i religious scholars]. "A major concern of the trained ulama against the Pahlavi regime was its continual whittling away at ulama power and influence, accompanied by the growing power of Western infidels and their ways.... A drastic 1977 cut in government subsidies to the ulama for various purposes ... also increased ulama discontent." [Nikki R. Keddie, *Modern Iran: Roots and Results of Revolution*, pp. 222-223]. In early 1963, sixty-one-year-old Sayyid Ruhollah Mostafavi Musavi Khomeini issued a strongly worded declaration denouncing the Shah and his plans. For that, Khomeini, a Grand Ayatollah, was imprisoned in Tehran and later exiled to Turkey, then Iraq, then France. In all, he spent the next fourteen years fomenting revolution. In exile, he consolidated his position as the leader of the opposition, and the paramount Iranian politician and religious leader. In 1978, ulama and bazaari leadership organized massive memorial demonstrations for those killed by the Pahlavi regime in previous incidents that took place during the traditional forty-day religious intervals (about 2,800 persons). For the first time, the chant, "Death to the Shah!" began to be heard. In 1979, Khomeini and his forces overthrew the corrupt Shah, and Khomeini became the Supreme Leader of Iran and an absolute religious despot in the newly created Islamic Republic of Iran.

He was a charismatic personality, a tireless leader, and an absolutist proponent of Shi'i Islam. He gained control of his country and became an international celebrity—in 1979, when he came to power, he was named Man of the Year by *Time Magazine*. The new constitution of the Islamic Republic of Islam created the office of Supreme Leader—which was shortly improved to be a lifetime appointment—endowed with extraordinary powers. The coverall was that he was to "determine the interests of Islam," and under that rubric was to set general guidelines for the Islamic Republic. In the office and person of the Supreme Leader came to rest the ultimate power to supervise policy implementation, mediate [here, read "have the veto"] over the executive, legislative, and judiciary branches, grant amnesty, dismiss presidents of the republic, vet candidates for the presidency, and be the commander-in-chief of the military. He was, therefore, solely responsible for the declaration of war, to establish peace, mobilize the armed forces, appoint and dismiss military commanders, and appoint and convene a national security council. He was given the authority to appoint a wide variety of senior officials of the civil government in all its branches, which gave him control over the media, the clergy, and to vet candidates for public office. These powers exceeded even the dreams for power of the Shahs and were altogether comparable to those of the divine-right kings of Europe, the historical oriental despots, Mao Zedong, Adolf Hitler, and Joseph Stalin.

In the decade of Khomeini's rule, there was ever-growing power of his followers and elimination—often by naked violence—of his opponents. This occurred despite any and all resistance by opposition groups and came about—in the end—due to enforcement of ideological and behavioral controls on the general population. He gained and maintained control by draconian measures: he created a new Republican Guard who stamped out opposition such as the Baha'i and the Kurds in waves of lethal persecution. "He ordered the swift and brutal execution of anyone who seemed to oppose his vision of an Islamic Republic.... Old army officers and aging former politicians were arrested and summarily executed, as were young revolutionaries, juvenile activists, Kurdish rebels, women protesting the imposition of a medieval code of conduct on them, religious minorities, poets, journalists...." [Hamid Dabashi, *Iran, A People Interrupted,* p. 163]

He supported student hostage-takers at the American embassy and gave approval to the 444-day Iran Hostage Crisis, which catapulted him into general favor throughout the Muslim world. He issued a murderous fatwa against British Indian novelist Salman Rushdie who was considered to have slandered the Prophet. His iron fist visited calamity throughout Iran: human rights violations of Iranians included a mass campaign of forced closing of opposition newspapers and attacks on opposition protesters by club-wielding vigilantes, torture, rape, and execution against political opponents as well as their families, close friends, and anyone who was accused of insufficient Islamic behavior including Jews. Khomeini instituted a level of abuse against females unknown since the Prophet Muhammad gained his pinnacle of power. His reign resulted in the deaths of thousands of men, women, and children, who were tried in secret kangaroo courts run by hard-line clerics. In 1988, he ordered the execution of 30,000 political prisoners. He was responsible for the decision to throw wave after wave of children to die as cannon fodder in the Iran/Iraq War in which more than 700,000 Iranians died by some estimates.

Under Khomeini's rule, Sharia [Islamic law] was established throughout Iran with the concept of rule being to stamp out democracy as the *Qur'an* requires, and to substitute it with *velayat-e faqih* [rule by the jurist]. Khomeini and his faithful followers were—and are today—quick to proclaim that any Muslim should not hesitate to demand *velayat-e faqih* over democracy because Islamic jurist rule represents the voice of God himself. The new rule required the citizens of Iran to comply with Islamic dress code and that it be enforced for both men and women by Islamic Revolutionary Guards and other Islamic groups.

Women were required to cover their hair, and men were not allowed to wear shorts. Alcoholic drinks, most Western movies, and the practice of men and women swimming or sunbathing together were banned. The Iranian educational curriculum was Islamized at all levels with the Islamic Cultural Revolution. The "Committee for Islamicization of Universities" carried this out with a thoroughness that rivaled the Chinese Cultural Revolution under Mao Zedong. The broadcasting of any music other than martial or religious on Iranian radio and television was banned by Khomeini in July 1979. The ban lasted for the rest of his life.

Under Khomeini's "inspiration," a "Cultural Revolution" was instigated by which so-called leftists were purged from the universities and political life. As a result, the nation suffered a major blow to its cultural life and achievement by eliminating those with real—nonreligious—educations and strongly encouraging a massive exodus of students, professors, and other professionals. A specific example underscores the new Islamic attitude: the magnificent Roman ruins of Persepolis were neglected and turned into a public urinal. Coca Cola in Iran was nationalized and became Zam Zam Cola. The Revolution ushered in an era of transportation of terrorism against Israel and the West through Iran's surrogates, Hezbollah and Hamas. Health care delivery, especially to women, deteriorated, resulting in a general increase in mortality and especially in maternal and infant death. Grand Ayatollah and Supreme Leader for Life Khomeini died in June 1989.

Khomeini was replaced by Grand Ayatollah Seyyed Ali Hosseini Khamenei, who was elected Supreme Leader by the Assembly of Experts on 4 June 1989. The same level of brutality and bigotry continued to prevail. His rule differed from that of Khomeini by becoming an established clerical oligarchy as opposed to Khomeini's unabashed totalitarian autocracy. He is in power at the time of this commentary. For most of the life of the Islamic Republic of Iran, the nation has been in a financial crisis to one degree or another. Domestic spending has been hampered by the large expenditures toward perceived military needs, possibly including development of atomic weapons. Foreign investors have tended to treat Iran as a pariah. The intelligentsia and creators of progress, business, and innovation have fled the country to escape persecution.

Sanctions by Western nations have been of a moderate degree and moderate negative result, but more stringent sanctions to halt nuclear weapon production altogether could be put into place. Oil revenues have plummeted; the value of the rial has declined. Prices for staples like rice, sugar, and butter have risen significantly (tripled)—there is general inflation. Iran's isolation has increased. Unemployment has reached 30 percent during some periods. Obtaining a visa has become more difficult, and travel curtailed. The government—state-religious foundations—controls 60 percent of the economy, which stifles growth. In the past six years, liberal Western governments have loosened their sanctions and their purse strings and the economic crisis appears to be lessening.

-Sources: *Walden University Online—LookLex Encyclopedia; Open Course Ware*, University of Notre Dame. *Faith, Practice, and Law in Sunni and Shi'i Islam. ugu.edu—University of Georgia online*; *Wikipedia.* Michael Axworthy, *A History of Iran: Empire of the Mind;* Ervand Abrahamian, *A History of Modern Iran*; Nikki R. Keddie, *Modern Iran: Roots and Results of Revolution;* Hamid Dabashi, *Iran: A People Interrupted;* Amnesty International, *Iran: Violation of Human Rights, 1991; Pour Mohammadi and the 1988 Prison Massacres, Human Rights Watch Report*, December, 2005. *Iran, Lonely Planet*, Andrew Burke and Mark Elliott, 2008, Wilfried Buchta, *Who Rules Iran?* 2000.

# CHAPTER THIRTEEN

"No, this is not the beginning of a new chapter in my life;
this is the beginning of a new book! That first book is already
closed, ended, and tossed into the seas; this new book is newly
opened, has just begun! Look, it is the first page! And it is a
beautiful one!"

-C. JoyBell C. [her Twitter name],
*Saint Paul Trois Châteaux,* 1948

## Kandovan Village, Kurdestan County, West Azerbaijan Province, Iran, November 12, 1992

Saif-al-din [sword of the faith] and his wife, Parveen, were taking their turn at watch. It was an unseasonably warm evening and more pleasant to sit in the shade of the overhang of the cave in which they lived than to be inside. Six other watchers peered out across the semiarid flatlands towards the direction of Albania where the Armenian bandit/terrorist group Dashnaksutyun originate and have their base for savage raids on innocent travelers and villagers. What was once a reasonably safe and profitable commercial journey from Kandovan Village to the main city of Dashkasan was now far too dangerous a trip for any but the army to undertake. The last raid by the Dashnaksutyun occurred only a month and a half ago, and four villagers were killed and three women were kidnapped and had not been seen since. The village was on high alert.

The desert sun was almost ready to pass behind the far mountainous horizon.

"It is nearly time for *Asr*," Saif observed. "We should get the carpets and say our prayers out here."

He was speaking Aramaic, a holdover from early refugees who had dug the first caves in the soft mountain rock and had lived there—protecting their language, culture, and homes—for more than 2,500 years. The Aramaic alphabet is adapted from that of the Phoenicians and became distinctive from it by the eighth century BCE. Modern Aramaic is spoken today as a first language by many scattered, predominantly small, and largely isolated communities of differing Christian, Jewish, Muslim, and Mandean ethnic groups of West Asia.

He and Parveen also spoke the lingua franca of trade—Azerbaijani—and the national languages—Farsi, Urdu, and Kurdish—out of necessity. They understood that theirs was a culture in peril of extinction, and their language was spoken by only a few remaining people—perhaps no more than 400,000 worldwide—and young people were moving out of isolation and away from the language that is little used outside their cloistered cultures.

"Look, Saif, someone is coming across the open area towards our hills."

Parveen pointed at the slowly moving tractor clattering over the hard scrabble ground on its treaded bare metal wheels. Saif moved to the high power spotting scope mounted on a tripod and focused in on the vehicle.

"A boy and two girls," he said. "Not a threat."

"Wherever they came from, they must be very tired," Parveen said. "I'll get some food and drink."

The news of the government's raid on the Kurds had not reached them in Kandovan yet. It took the better part of an hour for the slow moving dilapidated old tractor to arrive at the base of the hills. From a distance, it was not possible to make out the cave openings, and one had to have some idea of their location in order to get to them. Nassir was very familiar with the caves and with many of the cave dwellers. He looked up and saw Saif and Parveen watching him and the two young girls. He waved.

Saif and Parven gestured for them to go around to the back of the large rock jutting out from their cave home. Nassir stopped the tractor, and he and the girls ascended the steps carved out of stone to a rope ladder hanging down from a steel spike seventy-five feet higher up. Saif stood by the spike waiting to give them a hand up when they climbed to the top.

"Greetings and welcome," he said, then remembered that the visitors likely would not be Aramaic speakers. He repeated the message in Urdu, and they responded in kind.

Saif led them to where five prayer rugs were lying in wait. They all knelt and offered the formal silent *Asr* prayers. Afsoon merely went through the motions.

"You must be famished after your long trip," Parveen said. "Come and share our food."

In a few minutes, the three young people told their whole story. The gracious couple had known Firudin, Mariella, Mozaffarin, and Gorgani fairly well after several years of mutually profitable trading. They were saddened by the terrible rendition, and began to fear for their own safety. What if Rahimi's men came after them?

After a sparse *halal* [religiously sanctioned] supper of coarse corn bread, lamb sausage, oranges, and *doogh* [goat yogurt and water], Saif dispatched Nassir to warn the neighboring cave dwellers about the government's bloody raid; and Afsoon and Elaheh helped clean up the plates, cups, forks and spoons. As in other Iranian homes, knives were not used. Everyone took a few moments to stretch out their knees and thighs after squatting at the very low table.

"We have room, you three will stay here in our protection," Parveen said.

Afsoon was tired, sleepy, and now full. The idea of moving on was most undesirable, and the invitation was very welcome. The three females moved all of the worldly goods possessed by the new guests from the tractor to the back rooms of the cave in half an hour. Afsoon considered the cave to be the best place she had ever lived. The floors and walls were carpeted with rugs handmade in Kandovan and from the north. The family was affluent from their rich trading linkages. They had Dag Kasaman, Gazakhcha, Shikhli, Borchali, Qaymaqli, and Agqoyunlu carpets around the cave. The most prized carpets were the Azerbaijanis that depicted fights between two opposite forces, evil and good. There was electricity from a generator that Afsoon had only seen in her brief visits to the cities of Western Azerbaijan Province, and had never lived in a house with that wonder of the modern age. There was a flush toilet, also a new experience for the twelve-year-old girl, and an electric stove that excited her.

Nassir called into the depths of a cave about three miles from the home of Saif and Parveen to warn the inhabitants as he had done in his race around the cave system. A gruff voice came from the interior.

"What?" the voice demanded.

Nassir recognized the voice as belonging to Ahriman Shakibaie, the master of the tent village near Qushchu.

"I am the son of Firudin and Mariella. They and my brothers were murdered by the Grand Ayatollah's soldiers, and our farm was burned to the ground. My sisters and I have come to live in the caves. Saif-al-din sent me to warn you that the army might come here."

Ahriman walked out of the cave to stand face-to-face with Nassir.

"I already know, my boy, they raided my hamlet at the same time. It was also burned, and people were killed. We have made our preparations. Thank you for your effort. I hope you have found a good place to live. As you can see, our home is much too small to have room for others."

Their cave was nearly twice as large as Saif and Parveen's, but Nassir let it go without comment. He knew Ahriman's reputation as a hard and stingy man.

"Peace be with you, Brother," he said with slight bow, then turned and left.

Afsoon, Elaheh, and Nassir lived in peace and plenty in the cave system for two and a half years before more trouble came. Afsoon had access to books on astronomy, including the passion of Saif for astronomical physics. She reveled in the mathematics in his books, and he was excited to have so apt a pupil in the disciplines that were his passion. He imparted every scintilla of knowledge he had about math and science to the eager girl, whose mind was a sponge soaking up information. Parveen had her speaking Aramaic in a year, and the girl sounded like a native speaker when she had been there not quite two and a half years.

The evening before trouble came, the family invited three other families to a party. Afsoon, Elaheh, and Parveen worked from dawn to prepare. Saif and Parveen were celebrating their twenty-fifth wedding anniversary. No party could be held without *saz* music. Everyone in the caves admired *saz* music—which refers to a family of plucked string instruments popular for centuries around the region and into Turkey. The cooking of *khingal*, the regional party dish, was a major ceremony there; it required the efforts of three women: under Parveen's direction, Elaheh made the dough, flattened it into leaves, and sliced it. Afsoon melted *qurut* [dried goats' milk]. The *qurut* had to be soaked in water one day before, and then smashed inside the water. After melting it completely, she added onion to it. Parveen prepared fried onions, cutting the large sweet onions into long, thin pieces and frying the strips in sheep butter. When those tasks were completed, the three women of the house sliced chicken into bite-sized pieces and boiled them in water and a little chicken stock.

Then, they boiled water in a large shallow copper pan—by tradition, all dishes used for cooking *khingal* have to be old copper dishes. The prepared *khingal* was stirred and sifted with a copper skimmer by Afsoon. Then, Parveen added the *qurut*, fried onions, and pieces of chicken and placed the mix on the *khingal*. Every region in Kurdestan and nearby Azerbaijan had its own way of making *khingal*, and cooks took great pride in presenting their best in a ceremony of music, dancing, and eating that never grew old for the dwellers of the caves. The guests were suitably impressed and lavishly complimented Parveen and her girls. Saif was proud of them.

Afsoon was happy and content with her life with Saif and Parveen, safe with Nassir and Elaheh, able to expand her mind, and to enjoy peace, freedom from deprivation and fear, and the last time when she could be a child. She no longer hoarded food. That night, she held *Fereshte* to her now budding chest and cooed a lullaby to her angel doll. She looked forward to the coming day because the family was going to make a trip to the mountains; so, Afsoon, Elaheh, and Nassir could see the place that Saif and Parveen considered the most beautiful in the world.

# CHAPTER FOURTEEN

**San Francisco, California, U.S.A., Saint Francis Wood Hebrew Academy, 1985**

At ten o'clock in the morning, G.R. III called Rabbi ben Yisroel at the Saint Francis Woods Hebrew Academy.

"Headmaster's office."

"This is Gideon Rothsberger. I would like to speak the Rabbi ben Yisroel, please."

"I will see if he is taking calls."

"Tell him that he is taking my call."

She was affronted by his brusque tone, but given that it was Mr. Rothsberger, she let it go.

She knocked on the headmaster's door.

"Enter."

"Mr. Rothsberger is on the phone. He is quite insistent ... even rude, Sir."

"I'll handle it. Put him through."

"Good morning, Mr. Rothsberger. What can I do for you today?"

"It is what I can do for you, Rabbi. I have found you a new place to work."

The headmaster was stunned both at the brusqueness and the presumptiveness of his caller. He composed himself before replying.

"I beg your pardon?"

"You are to report to the Oholei Torah Yeschiva in Crown Heights, Brooklyn in four days. You will carry with you a laudatory recommendation from the board of regents here at Saint Francis Woods Hebrew. The letter will extol your kindness and compassion for the students, and the level of your scholastic achievements. You will present yourself to the headmaster for a few preliminaries largely to establish your bona fides as a serious Orthodox rabbi. That seems to be of paramount interest in the headmaster's office. After that interview, you are scheduled to do a three-month sabbatical to study the Torah with Rabbi Moises at the Chovevei Torah synagogue. It will be an opportunity for reflection and deep contemplation with one of the world's most renowned scholars. When you return from the sabbatical, you will have the privilege of being the dean of students."

"It is not a school for a man of my wide ranging interests and capabilities, Mr. Rothsberger. I know the Ohelei Torah. It is an Hasidic institution that hardly offers instruction in English, mathematics, science, civics, or the arts. I have met with students who tell me that they were taught only in Yiddish until the eighth grade then they switched to Hebrew. They learned religion all right, but hardly anything secular. Many never see an English word in written form. I do not think that prepares our youth to live in the world. I take umbrage at having not been consulted before these arrangements were made."

"It is done, Rabbi ben Yisroel. Frau Miller—whom I think you know—has graciously accepted the position of headmistress here and has begun a major overhaul of the curriculum. Let me be blunt, Rabbi, you do not want Levi Schmuel and me to write the other, more detailed letter, I presume."

Rabbi ben Yisroel ground his teeth, but he knew he could make no viable defense if he expected ever again to be able to teach—the only thing he was trained and suited for.

He said, "Your money and your power win. It has always been so. Who am I to resist?

He was gone before the end of the school day.

As soon as G.R. III was done with ben Yisroel's office, he called Gunnhilde Miller.

"Frau Miller, congratulations on your appointment as the headmistress of the Saint Francis Woods Hebrew Academy. You will have adequate funds to bring about the changes we discussed. You can begin today, if it meets with your convenience. I trust that my son will no longer need to travel to your home to be tutored."

"Thank you, Mr. Rothsberger. You will be pleased with my work. Your son will have the best and the brightest to bring to fruition his latent potential."

"Thank you, and good-bye. You have my full confidence and support."

G.R. III and Levi Schmuel met at noon for lunch at Rothsberger & Company Bankers executive dining room. The room was large and lined with expensive dark wood from floor to ceiling. The two men dined alone.

In both their worlds, men waited until the dessert wine was consumed before starting business.

"There is a new headmistress at the academy," G.R. III opened.

"Good. And our sons are now matriculated students in a Krav Maga school near the academy. Lt. Col. Shai Avitan—until two years ago a martial arts instructor in the IDF—has agreed to our generous terms. He now owns a modern, well-appointed school that is fully equipped. He outlined a long-term program to make our boys into men, and then able to take their places in the ranks of the most effective fighters in the world. He will need between twelve and fifteen years to mold them depending on their capabilities and desires. You and I will have to see to it that our boys have that fire in their bellies.

"My goal for our scions is what the Haskalah—'the educated one,' narrative poet Y.L. Gordon—requested of us, 'Be a Jew in your home and a man in the street.'"

G.R. III nodded his approval.

"Now, you mentioned during our talk in the car that you had a banking matter to bring to me."

"I do. It is a long-range one and must be handled only by you and me, Gideon. If we are to do business, you and I must be able to keep secrets more rigorously than the Catholic priest and his confessional. Is that agreed?"

"Yes ... if we come to terms on the business. I must protect the bank as you must protect your interests."

"I agree fully with that, but I add one more level of protection. We must protect each other and our families. We are not adversaries; we are partners. In time, I trust that we will also be friends despite the differences in our apparent lifestyles."

"What is your proposition, Levi?"

"I can never give you details of where the money I will entrust to the bank comes from, but I will now and forever guarantee that all of it is legitimate and no one will ever be able to associate that money—my money or the bank's— with the Kosher Nostra or any other criminal enterprise. I give you my word."

"And I accept it, my friend."

Gideon was not nearly as certain that there could be mutual trust or that the Jewish organized criminals would not squeeze their way in, but he did not let his doubts show in his face.

"This is what I propose," Levi said and began to lay out a plan to invest huge sums of money in the bank, which would make Levi Schmuel and his business partners the largest account holders in the bank's history.

The two men talked for two hours about safeguards, secrecy, investments, business networks, and came to a full agreement that Gideon would control all of that money and business enterprise through the bank; and in so doing, would become richer by two or three million dollars per year. They easily came to a mutual agreement that they would become serious and secret supporters of the Mossad and the World Zionist Organization, the *Sayanim*. Through his contacts—most of whom Gideon preferred not to know about—Levi would coordinate the arrangements with the Israelis.

# CHAPTER FIFTEEN

**Berkeley, California, June, 1992**

By the time Gideon Rothsberger IV graduated as the valedictorian of Saint Francis Woods Hebrew Academy, and a National Merit Scholar, he was eleven years old. With Gunnhilde Miller's careful shepherding, the boy was fluent in German, Italian, French, Hebrew, Yiddish, Arabic, Mandarin, and English; taken alone, this prodigious linguistic feat would have qualified Gideon as a genius in the minds of most ordinary people. It was helpful that the results of the Stanford Binet Intelligence Quotient test he took at age ten revealed him to be a certified genius with an I.Q. of 185—an intelligence level achieved by only one or two people out of two million. G.R. IV had been subjected to a number of natural intelligence studies during his formative school years and had proven to be a genius in several of the multiple intelligences loosely accepted by psychologists: linguistic, logical-mathematical, spatial, interpersonal, naturalistic, and existential. He scored high but short of genius in bodily-kinesthetic and intrapersonal categories. He failed in the musical category even despite his brilliance in mathematics. He was tone-deaf; he could not even whistle a tune.

He proved his prodigious mental gifts in Jewish studies, Jewish-Muslim relationships honors classes, in European, Middle-Eastern, and American history, in English, and in the literature of the languages in which he became fluent. His teachers and friends were awed by the sheer volume Gideon could absorb and recall. If ever anyone did, G.R. IV had a photographic memory. He could recite long excerpts from Shakespearean tragedies, passages from *Grey's Anatomy,* and the lyrics of whole operatic scenes without glancing at a written sheet of paper.

Mathematics was Gideon's most singular natural aptitude. Over and above his naturally acquired gifts, he learned to work hard under Frau Miller's stern eye and Professor Samson Bernstein's equally task-oriented hand. The U.C. Berkeley professor agreed to tutor Gideon one hour five days a week after he read *The Gifted Child* in Gilda Rogdonavich's master's thesis printed in the *Journal of Childhood Development,* and after being shown the boy's phenomenal mathematics test scores. The professor worked with Gideon from the time the boy was nine until he graduated at the top of his high school senior class two years later.

Professor Bernstein had Gideon tested in an experimental educational laboratory. Before he had a single class in calculus, Gideon sat for an examination in both differential and integral calculus and—during the tests—he intuitively reasoned out the process of doing the math and achieved correct answers in record time. The mathematics department at the University of California at Berkeley studied his sometimes novel approaches to the arcane disciplines to which they had dedicated their lives and came away with a twinge of envy. It was not until the 1600s that the two European geniuses, Isaac Newton and Gottfried Leibniz, separately came up with the concepts of calculus after years of effort. This boy had come up with basically the same intuitive understanding during a three-hour long test at a Jewish school in San Francisco.

Setting aside for the moment his obvious bias towards having the boy prodigy go to Berkeley, Professor Bernstein made a study of the finest universities in the world for the teaching of mathematics. He decided that Berkeley was as good as any other, but it was obvious that Gideon Rothsberger IV would need very special teachers and a virtually unique environment in which to learn. With the help of Rothsberger and Schmuel money, and a dogged approach to accomplishing his goals, G.R. IV was given a place at the University of California Berkeley designed for his unique needs and aptitudes. Instead of Gideon having to choose among the many fine universities in the world, arrangements were made for the best-of-the-best teachers to come to him when he matriculated in September of 1992 at the tender age of eleven.

U.C. Berkeley's reputation is the equal—if not the superior—of any of the top ten universities in the world. The University of California itself was chartered in 1868, and U.C. Berkeley on San Francisco Bay, with a 1,232-acre campus as its flagship school. 42,192 students applied to be in G.R. IV's class. When he entered the university, there were 32,218 students—19,814 undergraduates and 10,404 graduate students. 62 percent were males, 56 percent whites, 21 percent Chinese, 1.2 percent Japanese, 0.8 percent Latinos, 0.5

percent African-Americans, and 0.2 percent Jewish. Of the undergraduates, 93 percent ranged in age from 17 to 25 for all four years; 6 percent ranged in age from 26 to 40; 0.9 percent ranged in age from 13 to 17; 0.02 percent were less than 13; one student was over forty; and one student—Gideon Rothsberger IV—was younger than 13. The student-to-faculty ratio was 21.1 to 1—the best in the nation—with 61 percent of classes having under 30 students. Gideon's math classes had three students for his entire undergraduate career—two years long. There had been seventeen Nobel laureates during the illustrious history of the university, and seven of them were still on the current faculty. At one time or another, five of the seven taught classes that Gideon attended, and two of them tutored him personally for varying periods of time.

Gideon did not look the part of a boy genius. He was handsome but had a minor offset of his nose and slightly cauliflowered ears that made him look a bit tough, but devilishly attractive to the opposite sex—not quite a Davidic demigod, but enough ruggedness to give a more mature look to the boy. That was just one of the benefits he reaped from Lt. Col. Shai Avitan's Krav Maga school in upscale Presidio Heights. The broken nose with its imperfect repair and the thickened ears, with an assortment of bruises, scars, and one broken arm along the way had caused Chava recurrent angst, his father a few laughs; and Gideon to admire his own developing toughness. He was one of the Jews who would one day be a man in the streets.

Once Gideon settled into the routine of university life and the newness of his considerable youth had worn off with his classmates, he was able to set to work and establish several serious goals for himself. Gideon had apparently been born old and serious. He was a self-starter and a relentless worker. His classmates joined fraternities, had keg parties, played Frisbee games, and drove their cars erratically to let off steam. Gideon found martial arts to be his fun. He found a Brazilian Jiu Jitsu school where he could compete and try his skills in real time with bigger, stronger, and uncaring opponents. Lt. Col. Avitan had found the place for him, and to no one's surprise, the Jiu Jitsu master was a student of Helio Gracie from Rio de Janeiro, a seasoned street fighter, a dedicated Jew, and one of the Mossad's *Sayanim*. Because he was able to master his core curriculum with ease, he had plenty of time for his soaring education in math and to improve his fighting skills to the point that he was able to defeat most of the blue belts in the club and even a few of the purple belts in his four-nights-a-week grappling schedule. During the summer following his completion of his combined freshman and sophomore years at

U.C. Berkeley, Gideon resumed his Krav Maga training under Lt. Col. Avitan and competed in two age and weight appropriate tournaments that he won.

The first year of university education was quite like what every other undergraduate went through to complete the core classes in biology, chemistry, English, language studies, history of ancient civilizations, political science, and art appreciation. He skipped basket weaving with the jocks. The differences in Gideon's educational track were that every one of his classes was an honors course; each was tailored to his particular aptitudes; and each pushed his professors to the limit of his or her own level of expertise. Another difference was that Gideon's class time was truncated to half of the usual time scheduled each semester, and he completed the core years in one instead of the usual two years.

He had team teachers in mathematics brought in from around the world owing to the prestige of U.C. Berkeley's math department and the challenging phenomenon presented by Gideon. It became a friendly contest to see which professor could trip him up, stretch him beyond his limits, or teach him something he could not figure out by himself. Many of them succeeded in their endeavors, but all of them taught him mathematics at its frontiers.

During his first two semesters, Gideon raced through the standard mathematical disciplines to ensure the solidity of his base—advanced algebra, geometry, trigonometry, statistics, and introductory calculus. After his excellent preparation at Saint Francis Woods Hebrew Academy, much of what was covered constituted a review; but the university-level courses widened and deepened his grasp of the complex subjects and gave him a better foundation upon which to improve his intuitive abilities in math.

The third semester, Gideon was introduced into the history of calculus and its philosophical underpinnings.

Dr. Stephen Ammon Rhodes taught the class attended by three students, of whom Gideon was the youngest.

"Sometime in the mid first millennium B.C.E., a Greek philosopher named Zeno conjured a paradox which now bears his name. He spent time observing flights of arrows moving through space towards a target. From his work came a very useful concept—one of the most productive paradoxes ever posed. He pointed out that the arrow's motion has two properties, namely, that it occupies a given place at any instant; and, in addition, it is obviously moving. He posited the idea that one could consider the position of the arrow at any other instant and the time elapsed to advance to that position ad infinitum. His notion was indeed a fundamental paradox related to both infinite and infinitesimal space and time. He could not provide answers to resolve his paradox. That had to come with the genius of the invention of calculus—a fundamental historical human intellectual triumph.

"Although calculus is a difficult and taxing discipline, it is based on common sense; and understanding the concepts does not require much in the way of technical mathematical background. Any intelligent person—regardless of age or educational experience—can come to understand the concepts and the value of calculus. At its core, there are only two very basic concepts of calculus, both of which come from an understanding of the elements of motion posed by the Paradox of Zeno: differential calculus concerns itself with the understanding of the rates at which quantities of all types change—a measure of how a function ($f$) changes as its input ($x$) changes. To look at it from the perspective of Zeno, a derivative of the position of a moving arrow with respect to changes in time is the arrow's instantaneous velocity.

"Integration, on the other hand was elucidated by Bernhard Riemann, and calculus became able to acquire a firmer footing with the development of limits. This other part of calculus is used to measure the exact area under a curve. Riemann postulated a limiting graphic procedure that approximates the area of a curvilinear region by breaking the region into thin vertical slabs, which is the inverse of differentiation. His concept postulated an integration of an infinite sum of rectangles of infinitesimal width. Together, differentiation and integration are the two principle operations of calculus, and the rest of the mathematical procedures come from those two brilliant concepts.

"These basic tools of calculus—developed from algebra and geometry—form the foundation of every branch of the physical sciences: physics, biology, computer science, statistics, engineering, economics, business, architecture, aviation, and medicine, to name only a few. By finding the average of a function, one can determine the path of an airplane, a car, a truck, a bus, or anything that moves along any path. Furthermore—with calculus—you can calculate the average cruising altitude, velocity, and acceleration for any of those moving objects. Consider the seemingly minor examples of the speedometer of your car, calculating the maximum volume of a box, the maximum area of a corral of any shape and dimensions, the rate of filling a swimming pool by knowing the rate of flow of your hose, and other such *related rates*—one depending on the other—the faster the water is poured in, or two cars approach an intersection, the faster the water level will rise and the sooner a collision would occur if changes are not made. It becomes critical to know how rapidly the distances between those two vehicles are changing.

"Tomorrow we will take up how to determine marginal cost, marginal revenue, and marginal profit in economics for young Mr. Rothsberger, our banker, and for you budding scientists. I expect you to study pages eight through thirteen on these concepts for our next session. Bear in mind the value of knowing with precision about *marginal cost*—the approximate increase in cost of producing one more item and that marginal revenue and marginal profit work very similarly. Good day."

Every day held the same excitement for Gideon. He loved the theoretical functions of calculus and knew that the practical applications were of inestimable value towards his eventual career in banking. He could easily foresee the future needs for his education in math and economics so that he could one day take over the bank and the global enterprises of the Rothsbergers.

By the end of his first year, he had inculcated into his mind for automatic recall the method of exhaustion for determining integrals developed by the ancient Greek astronomer Eudoxus, the method of calculating areas for parabolas and the area of a circle that came from the Greek Archimedes and Chinese Liu Hui, and the volume of a sphere from two other Chinese mathematicians, Zu Chongzhi and his son, Zu Geng. He learned the application of thinking of integrals by how if a retailer wants to sell a given number of items, the demand function tells him or her what the selling price should be: the lower the price, the higher the demand, or that a demand function can operate the other way around by finding out with precision how many items people will buy at that price, with the price being determined as a function of the number demanded.

Gideon learned the value of understanding—for business purposes—optimization problems—how many apartments should a business rent in order to maximize profit when considered against the costs of building, maintenance, and collections issues? The businessman and the banker cannot simply assume that renting all the apartments will generate the most profit, which is counterintuitive to superficial common sense. The same mathematics applies to the everyday questions asked by drug companies and other manufacturers—how many items per day should they produce in order to minimize production costs? Gideon made up his mind to follow the pragmatic path of his no-nonsense forebears; he was going to go into banking; and he was going to be the most successful banker of all time because of his brains and his education. It was final. He had not yet quite turned twelve.

# CHAPTER SIXTEEN

"One is never afraid of the unknown; one is afraid of the known coming to an end."

-Jiddu Krishnamurti, *Permalink*

## Kandovan Village, Kurdestan County, West Azerbaijan Province, Iran, November 12, 1992

Saif awakened the sleeping family prior to dawn for the *Fajr*. A few minutes later, the family members were all dressed in time to hear the muezzin call the faithful to prayer. All of them went through the time-worn familiarity of the ceremony. Only Afsoon blanked out her mind as the others silently recited the words of the prayer by rote.

Suddenly, lookouts from around the valley signaled the emergency call to arms. The sounds of their ram horn megaphones carried from five miles away: Danger!! Danger!! Danger!!

All other routines were abandoned, and the al Din family and all the rest of the cave dwellers went to their arms lockers and took their muster places fully ready. For twenty minutes, there was little sound coming from the outside, and no one inside the cave fortress complex spoke a word.

Afsoon concentrated, and her excellent young ears were the first to hear the clanking of the buckles of horse tack.

She whispered breathlessly to Saif, "Horses coming."

He nodded to her in the near darkness and passed the message on. Five minutes later, there was no doubt about the threat. The roar of dozens of pickup trucks and vans and scores of galloping horses filled the air. Screaming men began climbing the ladders and stairs leading into the cave complex. The sound of gunfire, wounded men and women, and the chilling advance of men on foot approaching the al Din cave was unmistakable.

Saif recognized the language.

"The Armenians are here! The killer Dashnaksutyuns have broken through! Girls, run and hide. Take the little ones with you. Boys, get ready. There will be killing here today. Fight for your home, for your family, for God. *Allahuh Akbar*!"

Nassir grabbed hold of Afsoon and Elahehs' hands, and the three of them sneaked back into the labyrinthine hallways and rooms of the cave system until they came to a hidden bunker. They found knives and several guns and a supply of emergency food.

"Wait behind the carpets," Nassir ordered, referring to the rugs hanging from bars over openings in the cave walls. "You will be safe here for a while. I am going to get some horses. We have to ride away, or we will die ... or worse."

Afsoon felt as if she was paralyzed by fear, but primal self-interest propelled her to action. She pushed Elaheh into the largest of the auxiliary cave openings.

"Where are you going?" Elaheh cried. "I'm scared."

"I have to get a few things."

She shoved a shotgun and two pistols with their ammunition into the room where Elaheh was cringing in fear. Then, she ran through the dark hallways to the room she shared with Elaheh and one of the daughters of a neighbor family. Not daring to turn on a light, she rummaged around until she found *Fereshte*.

"Come with me my angel," she whispered to her rag doll in a soothing tone then ran back through the blackness of the familiar hallways.

The sound of gunfire, of swords clanking steel-on-steel and of screaming now filled the air. The two young girls—well aware of the fate of women and girls captured by the Dashnaksutyun terrorist bandits—shivered in the darkness of their last refuge. Booted footsteps approached the room. Afsoon and Elaheh held their mutual breaths as men threw piles of clothing, cleaning supplies, and horse tack around the room. It was evident that they were after food, usable household items, and men's clothing; and the two hiding girls presumed that the bandits were also after money or other treasures. Neither dared consider the idea that the brutes were searching for them.

There was brief talking in Armenian, then Afsoon heard sounds indicating that two men were leaving, probably to take their booty to their trucks. She could still hear the heated breathing of one man—at least she thought it was one man. She pulled out the skinning knife she had taken from the Jamshidi farmhouse while she still lived there and fingered its reassuring heft and sharpness. She held it in front of her. To be captured by the Dashnaksutyuns would be like being taken to Urmia for an FGM, and she would die first. Elaheh softly muttered prayers. Afsoon prepared her mind for what was to come.

The two girls could hear the lone remaining man opening each rug-curtained cubicle in the cave and heedlessly tossing the contents of the small auxiliary rooms out into the main room after a cursory inspection. He had a flashlight and waved it around to see if there was treasure or if he might find someone hiding behind the carpet curtains.

As they knew he would, the man threw aside the carpet shielding them from his gaze. He stepped in and began to swing the dim light from his flashlight in a counterclockwise sweep of the room. Afsoon stood immediately to his left as he moved the light. The light came to rest on Elaheh, who screamed.

"Ah, little beauty, you and I will have such fun. This will be your first I bet," he sneered, his voice breathy in anticipation.

Afsoon could see his face clearly from the reflections of his flashlight on the cave walls. She waited in extreme tension until he turned far enough to give her a good target. Then, she swung the thin skinning knife with all her might. The blade entered the man's eye with such force that it impaled his left eye and his brain to the hilt. He gurgled out a loud curse and started to pull away. Afsoon wrenched the knife sideways, slicing the porridge soft brain and its supplying blood vessels in the arc of her movement. The man dropped to the floor without another sound. Afsoon jerked the knife out of her victim's eye. It required both hands and most of her strength. He lay motionless, and she could not hear any breathing.

She picked up the flashlight from the floor where the intruder had dropped it. She held the knife in her right hand and the flashlight in her left. The left eye was a ruined mess, but the right one was open, so Afsoon assumed that he was still alive. She swiped his throat with the sharp blade, opening a fissure from ear to ear that bared the bone. The eye remained opened; so, she plunged the blade to the hilt into his chest where she presumed his heart was located. Since there was no bleeding from either the slashing or the stabbing, she concluded that the man was dead.

She backed away in horror at the spectacle of the grotesquely wounded man, of a dead man, and from the impact on her of what she had just done. Elaheh removed her hands from in front of her eyes and stood up to see better what had taken place. Unlike Afsoon, she gave a little murmur of joy and an "*al-Hamdulillah*" [Praise be to God] and threw her arms around her brave little sister.

Afsoon remained pragmatic.

"We must hide this *jinn's* [devil's] body," she said. "Help me roll him up in a carpet."

He was out of sight, and the blood on the floor was covered up by laying another carpet over it before Nassir came back.

Elaheh told her brother what had happened in a machine-gun staccato. He looked at Afsoon in amazement and pride. There was no time for praises, however.

"I have three horses. Let's get to the back. We have to run or the Dashnaksutyuns will kill us. Saif and Parveen and the two boys are dead. They didn't have a chance," he told the horrified girls.

Afsoon retrieved *Fereshte* from the floor where she had been dropped in the short violent fight, and ran with her only family out into the hallway.

When they arrived to the small corral where Nassir had tied the horses, it was starting to become light outside, at least light enough that they would soon be seen. They had a surprise waiting for them. Ahriman Shakibaie and Fereshten were placing saddles on their two horses. Neither recognized Afsoon or Elaheh, but they had met Nassir several times. Shakibaie's first inclination was to drive them away, but he thought better of that when he saw that the boy was well armed.

"Can you ride, boy?" he challenged.

"I can. And I can shoot, too."

"Can the slaves ride? We can't be held back by anyone. The Armenians will kill us all. The girls will go back to Armenia to fates worse than death at the hands of those butchers. We'd better leave them to take their chances hiding here."

"They can ride. They are my family, and they are coming whether or not we go with you."

Shakibaie shrugged, and they all mounted up. They followed a little known route up the mountains behind the cave rocks, pausing periodically to see if the Dashnaksutyuns were following. It was now light enough for them to see the terrorists or to be seen by them, and they wasted little time in observation. After a hard half-hour's ride up the side of the mountain that left the horses lathered in a thick foamy sweat, Shakibaie announced that it should be safe to circle back and work their way below the lake and to Qushchu by keeping to the fringe of trees stretching from the mountain to the lake. That went well for the first thirty minutes because they were able to descend the mountain through a thick stand of trees with the ground cushioned by a thick layer of sound-insulating fallen leaves. Afsoon clutched little *Fereshte* to her chest for comfort as they rode through the heavy dead fall that cluttered the forest floor.

Shakibaie had been wrong about the extent of the coverage by the trees. They dwindled out until the direction they had to go became a savannah and then there were no trees at all. It would be an open space ride for well over a mile before they came to the margin of Lake Orumiyeh.

Nassir said, "We have to run for it. Once we get to the other side of the lake, there are villages; and the Dashnaksutyuns won't follow us."

Shakibaie disagreed, "They might not see us if we keep quiet and move at a walk across the mud flats," he said.

Nassir started to argue, but Shakibaie and Fereshten shushed him. Who was he—a mere boy—to argue with the headman of the clan? So, the five riders slowly emerged from the trees, looking constantly for signs of the Dashnaksutyuns. There was no sign of the terrorist/bandits until they were halfway to the lake margin. Then a dozen bandits rose up from behind a low hill and began racing towards them, firing shots in the air and whooping curses at the five innocents.

Nassir and Afsoon saw them first and kicked their horses into a full racing gallop towards the lake. The other three quickly agreed with that decision and came along close behind. The race grew more intense as the distance between the prey and their predators began to narrow. When they were within one hundred yards, it was obvious that the cave dwellers were not going to make it.

Shakibaie reined his lathered horse to a stop and leaped from the saddle. Nassir saw at once what he had in mind and jumped off his horse as well. Both men kneeled and took aim with their rifles. They fired three shots, and two terrorists fell from their horses. The remaining Dashnaksutyuns slowed down but kept coming, more careful now. Afsoon slid off her horse and balanced against its rump. She took a very calm and careful aim and shot the leader of the group dead center between his eyes. He was dead in the saddle, but his feet were locked in his stirrups and he kept coming, sagging to the side like a floppy rag doll. The superstitious Dashnaksutyuns looked from one to another and turned around to find cover behind a clump of low lying rocks. Shakibaie, Nassir, and Afsoon remounted; and the five prey species rode off as fast as their horses could carry them. They rounded the lower end of the lake before they thought they were no longer being pursued.

Shakibaie looked at Afsoon in something like an expression of wonder, perhaps mixed with a little praise. The incongruous picture of the sure-shot girl clutching a rag doll to her chest was disconcerting. Fereshten, Elaheh, and Nassir frankly took her in with expressions of mixed wonderment, thankfulness, and wariness. What was one to think about a woman who did things like that?

As they drew within five miles of Qushchu, Shakibaie's sons—Hassanzadeh and Hossein—coming from the clan's tent hamlet for supplies of firewood, saw them in the distance and rode at a gallop to greet them.

"Welcome back, Father and first wife. We were not expecting you even this year," Hassanzadeh said.

"We had no choice," said Shakibaie. "The Dashnaksutyuns raided the caves, and we barely escaped. We had to kill some of them. Even this little slave—Afsoon—killed one. She will be part of our family now. I want you to find her a place to sleep. Maybe she can stay in the tent with Azedeh and the new wife."

"No problem. I'll take care of it," Hassanzadeh said.

The tired riders rode into the tent encampment before *Fihr*. After prayers, Afsoon and Elaheh were settled into the tent where Azedeh and Fatemah—the new wife, who had taken Astera's place—lived. Fatemah was young—not more than two years older than Afsoon—and not as old as Elaheh. Her status—related to her youth and fresh beauty—was that her bed was the best in the tent—the one previously used by Astera. Afsoon knew that Astera's bed had been shared with her lover, Farhad Sharifi, and for that she was stoned to death. There were a few ghosts still lurking in the shadows of that tent. Twelve-year-old Afsoon and fifteen-year-old Elaheh had no illusions about their places among the hierarchy of women in Qushchu, nor did they have any romantic misapprehensions about their place as women in comparison with the status of men in general, even slaves. Nassir's status as an outsider—an interloper—was not much better than that of Afsoon. He was placed in a tent with the four black slave boys who had been brought to the region by Arab slavers from Mali. At least, he outranked them.

A week later, a peddler came through the village and reported what he had seen and learned in Kandovan Village when he stopped there. The caves had been ransacked and wantonly destroyed. The invaluable carpets had been torched. Precious crockery, religious items, and clothing was shredded or added to the fires. Anything of value to the Armenians had been loaded into the armada of trucks that were driven in to bring the raiders and taken back to where they came from. Survivors—and there were no more than a handful—told the peddler of the orgy of brutality, rape, and murder that had taken place in the aftermath of the orgy of stealing. Not a single adult male was left alive. Every female—from babies to grandmothers—was violated. The women over a certain age, the homely, and any who fought back were hacked to death with swords. Children of both sexes below the age of twelve were crammed into vans and driven off to lives of slavery, a pattern that had persisted in the region for more than three thousand years. None of those children would ever be heard from again, and no one could bear to talk about what they would suffer. It would be ten years before the caves would fill up with new owners; and, in all likelihood, they would not be speakers of Aramaic.

Afsoon shrugged at her fate, kept a low profile, and accepted the change that had become the story of her life. She had been happy to a degree with the Jamshidis even though it was a harsh existence. The al Dins were genuinely kind and accepting. Now she was back under the thumb of Ahriman Shakibaie and Fereshten—his unfeeling first wife—who were somewhat less demeaning of her than before but well short of cordial. The women in the tent were not quite family; but, at least, there was some sense of belonging. Afsoon was—once again—the lowest person in the social structure and therefore required to work the hardest and do the chores no one else wanted to do; but she was not abused; and she could find time to do some reading from books that she persuaded boys going to the school in Qushchu to sneak out for her. She devoured the poetry, committed the mathematics books to memory, and began slowly to learn about the outside world from newspapers, magazines, and an encyclopedia that came to her volume by volume. She knew it was out of date, but her thirst for knowledge was such that she could not stick up her nose at a source that was less than truly educated people could obtain. Muslims rightfully took pride in the history of Islamic math and science; and the books at the school and Qushchu library were quite good, unlike those on social issues. From them, she learned the wonder of numbers through advanced algebra, which was as far as the best book in the province could take her.

Winter came early, but was milder than the two previous years. She and Nassir decided to celebrate her thirteenth birthday in January as they had done while they lived on the Jamshidi farm. It was a little confusing to Elaheh, who thought that April was Afsoon's birth month. The three of them made a little cake, sang a happy birthday song; and Elaheh gave her some baby clothes for *Fereshte*. Thirteen was an auspicious age, Afsoon thought. Her body was making some pretty remarkable changes. Elaheh teased her about the rapid growth of her breasts, but it was gentle teasing. She was flat chested and sure that she would never be able to attract a husband. Afsoon had noticed that Hassanzadeh was paying her a fair amount of attention. He had stared at her chest frequently until Afsoon found a more bulky older chador; and he seemed to lose interest, which made Afsoon less tense.

# CHAPTER SEVENTEEN

**And a woman spoke, saying, Tell us of Pain. And he said: Your pain is the breaking of the shell that encloses your understanding. Even as the stone of the fruit must break, that its heart may stand in the sun, so must you know pain.**
**-Kahlil Gabran, *The Prophet*, p. 52, 1973**

## Qushchu Village, Kurdestan County, West Azerbaijan Province, Iran, January 22, 1993

There was nothing important, auspicious, or at all ominous about that day. It was cold, but not severely so. Afsoon's chores were the same as they had been a month ago when she was only twelve. Given her intelligence, the drab routine of her life chafed her; but Afsoon had no recourse; so, she took a stoical view. Life was like that for the masses, not like it was for the rich or for the characters in her books. She worked at being happy, and learned a number of pleasant little songs from the other women to lighten the boredom and sameness of her days.

It was her singing that brought on the trouble. She had a nice clear voice and enunciated the poetry of the lyrics well enough that people who heard her sing thought of it as musical poetry, and poetry is a passion throughout Iran. One who especially appreciated the beauty of Afsoon's singing was Hassanzadeh Shakibaie. He was eighteen years old and longed to have a woman. He romanticized about beauty, about soulful songs, about Afsoon. She was young but had developed the body of a twenty-five-year-old, lissome, nubile, and ripe. He recognized the signs that she wanted him as well. Sometimes when it was hot, she worked outside in a shirt and old pants—no chador. Sometimes when he looked at her chest or her ankles, he knew she was making an effort to make her anatomy attractive for him. Sometimes—when he stared—she stared back and blushed before turning away. When he flirted, she played the coquette. It was obvious to him.

On that day, she was outside in her winter chador hanging clothes and singing an ancient love song. The day was clear and bright. Hassanzadeh knew she was singing to him. He walked up behind her and stood watching as her graceful arms moved from clothes basket to clothesline in a fluid, enticing dancelike movement. Then, she made an overt flirtatious sexual movement. She had to know he was standing behind her. Afsoon hiked up the skirt of her shapeless chador to step on a wood chopping block to gain enough height to reach the line with a blanket. She had to strain and made sexual sounds as she did—just for him. Hassanzadeh's blood began to race. His face flushed, and his entire body was suffused with desire. The girl of his dreams was presenting herself to him for love.

He moved up behind her and wrapped her in his strong arms. He stood nearly two feet taller than her, and the contact between his powerful large body against her delicate softness was electrifying. She cried out in mock, flirtatious alarm.

"Hassanzadeh! What are you doing? Let go of me. Take your hands off me!"

Her arousal was intoxicating to the young man.

"I know you want me, Afsoon. You are beautiful and ready, and I am a real man ready to give you great pleasure."

"No. Stop!" she screamed.

The passion of her scream drove his level of passion to the bursting point. Some of the other boys had told him that when a girl says "no, no," she means, "yes, yes." She was struggling but no match for him. He could tell how much she wanted him as her body writhed against him.

"Stop. Stop now. I will tell your father and mother. You will be caned. Let me go!"

There was now a note of real fear in her voice. Hassanzadeh knew it was the virgin in her trying to break free, to have fulfillment with him. He was so ready.

Afsoon was no match for Hassanzadeh's height, weight, and strength. She squirmed to reach the skinning knife she carried under the sleeve cuff of her chador, but he had her arms pinned. He threw her roughly to the ground. She shrieked. He clamped a calloused hand over her mouth. She bit the palm of his hand. He pulled it away. She screamed. He slapped her across her face then backhanded her. It was time for the girl to stop pretending, he reasoned. This was their time, and nothing was going to prevent him from having her.

Afsoon was dazed and unable to think. She could not protect herself against the power of the man. She refused to cry. Instead, she tried to kick and bite him, to squirm away, anything. But it was futile. Everything she did only further inflamed him.

It was over in a minute. The penetration of the tiny virginal scarred opening was as if she had been wounded by a glowing red poker from the cooking fire. She cried for help. Nobody heard. She fainted.

Hassanzadeh regained his mind when his moment of crisis was over. He looked at the half-naked severely bleeding girl beneath him and recoiled in horror. What had this conniving vixen done to him? The *Jendeh* [bitch]! He leaped away from her in revulsion.

"*Kunde*," he shouted, "*kunde, kunde, kunde*!!![whore, whore, whore]" he screamed at the top of his lungs.

He knelt over her and began to pound her with his clenched fists. He bruised her face, her breasts, her ribs, her belly. He stood up and kicked at her legs. When she made a feeble defensive gesture with her left arm, he grabbed her wrist and viciously hyperextended it until it snapped. He was unaware of his surroundings, and he was unaware that one of the slave girls and Azedeh were now watching in fascinated horror.

When the red blur of his vision cleared enough from him to see, he became aware of the two young women staring at him.

"See what this *kunde* has made me do? See?" he yelled at them.

Then, he hitched up his pants and ran away in the direction of the unmarried men's tent.

As soon as Azedeh and Shireen—the slave girl—were sure they were safe, they rushed to Afsoon's side. She was barely conscious. Blood poured from both nostrils, from a large cut on her lower lip, and covered her ravaged young womanhood.

"What can we do, Azedeh?" Shireen asked. "Fereshten will be furious. Hassanzadeh is her favorite son. She will beat us."

"I know, but there are two of us. We can both testify, and we will be equal to one man. But first, we must get her inside and stop the bleeding. Hurry."

It was difficult to get Afsoon into a position to carry her, and they stumbled over the uneven hard ground. Twice they dropped her. She just moaned quietly. Afsoon did not cry out or shed tears. Fereshten, Fatemah, and Nassir rushed out of their tents to see what the commotion was about. Nassir hid his eyes from the terrible hellish scene. He began to cry.

When it became known to her, Fereshten muttered imprecations against the wicked girl who had befouled her pure son. Fatemah gasped and turned her face away from the brutally injured young girl but was the first to rush to help. Fereshten stood by like an angry statue. Nassir rushed to his adoptive sister's side and helped the women carry her to Azedeh's tent. The bleeding stopped with a little pressure, except the lower bleeding site continued a slow dribble. Violaceous bruises were beginning to form. Her wrist was canted at an abnormal angle and caused terrible pain. Afsoon was now awake but did not cry or even moan. She had sworn that she would never allow anyone to be able to make her cry again after she had undergone the hellacious FGM procedure. Her anger was kindled to a level that it drove away her tears.

Nassir and the women made a splint for the broken wrist and covered her nakedness. Shortly, Afsoon drifted off to sleep clutching *Fereshte*. In less than half an hour, the tent flaps parted abruptly; and Ahriman, Fereshten, and Hassanzadeh Shakibaie rushed into the enclosure.

"Where is the *kunde?*" demanded the furious Ahriman.

He held a short knotted eight-strand camel-hide whip in his right hand. He pointed it at Fatemah.

She bowed her head and stared at the ground then pointed at the corner where Afsoon lay asleep.

"That's the *jendeh*," Hassanzadeh stated in an authoritative voice that mimicked that of his father.

Fereshten spoke in her coldest voice, "Bring her outside, boy," she said to Nassir.

"No, it is wrong. She is the victim of a vicious *zina bil Jabar* [Urdu: rape]!"

He planted himself between Shakibaie and Afsoon. Ahriman and Hassanzadeh shoved him aside, and Hassanzadeh knocked him to the ground and pinned him there.

Nassir shouted, "You cannot do anything to her. She is a victim. She has been raped. For shame! For shame!"

Hassanzadeh punched him in the mouth, stunning the smaller young man.

Hassanzadeh shouted to his father, "Father, you must behead the *kunde*. Take her outside. Shireen, fetch my sword!"

Fereshten spoke again in her frigid voice, "No my beautiful son, that is too good for her. She must be shamed before the courts and sent to prison for her crime. Your father will whip her, then we will call the Sharia police. They will see to justice for us."

Hassanzadeh could see the logic and the justice in that, and he nodded his head in agreement. Ahriman walked over to Afsoon and tore off her covers and slashed off her fresh chador. He gripped her hair with iron fingers and dragged her outside into the cold with no more effort than if she had been a two-year-old. He and Fereshten draped the unresisting girl over a stump of a log. Then he applied the lash. Each application of the whip yielded eight bloody cuts and counted for eight lashes until he had made cuts from her ankles to her neck—thirteen strokes in all to come a little over the required one hundred lashes prescribed in the *Qur'an*.

Afsoon twisted and twitched with each punishing whiplash, but she did not cry out. That infuriated Ahriman so much that he kicked her repeatedly. Still, she was silent—looking at him with a demonic hatred.

Finally, the bloodlust subsided; and the Shakibaies left the tent to summon the police. Azedeh, Fatemah, Shireen, and Nassir gently carried Afsoon back into the tent and washed her wounds again with Lake Orumiyeh water. They barely had time to get the limp girl back into a decent chador before the police van arrived in the tent village. Knowing that *Fereshte* would be lost to Afsoon forever, Nassir hid the doll in a carpet trunk, hoping to be able to get it to her sometime, if she survived. He began to mourn Afsoon as soon as she was thrown into the police van. She was just shy of the end of her first month as a thirteen-year-old.

# CHAPTER EIGHTEEN

**Berkeley, California, January, 1993**

M ost undergraduates choose a major after their second year in their university training. Gideon Rothsberger IV was hardly a typical undergraduate. He did not have a major in the usual sense; rather, he specialized. He focused his energies on becoming a world-class banker as was expected by his father and grandfather (III and IV). Toward that end, he specialized in banking and business management, the mathematics of economics, accounting, and finance. Because of his intense interest in the mysteries and intricacies of higher mathematics, he pursued a course in math designed by his major professor, Samson Bernstein, and his math tutor, Dr. Stephen Ammon Rhodes, just for him. Gideon had every intention of going his own way, but he allowed his most trusted adult advisors to help guide him—his mother and father, Frau Gunnhilde Miller at the Saint Francis Woods Hebrew Academy, Levi Schmuel—irrespective of his Kosher Nostra leanings—his Krav Maga instructor, Lt. Col. Shai Avitan, his major professor, and his math tutor at Berkeley. Most undergraduates take four, even five, years to complete their work for a bachelor's degree; Gideon completed his freshman and sophomore years in one year and his junior and senior years in the second year at Berkeley.

He graduated *maxima cum laude* [with very great honor], which was the highest possible honor, rarely given by any university and never before awarded at U.C. Berkeley. He was one day past his thirteenth birthday and was the sixth youngest person ever to receive a degree at any school in the University of California system. The *San Francisco Chronicle, Oakland Tribune, Los Angeles Times*, and even *The New York Times* and *Life Magazine* ran feature articles on the "boy prodigy." *The Daily Californian*, U.C. Berkeley's newspaper, put out a special edition on Gideon and other past prodigies who had graduated from Berkeley. He appeared on the *Johnny Carson, Maury Povich,* and *Oprah Winfrey Shows* on television.

The articles and appearances caught the attention of important people well beyond the usually intended readers and viewers in the popular media. One of those was alerted to the young man's potential by Gideon's Krav Maga instructor, Lt. Col. Shai Avitan, and that man communicated with his opposite in the United States.

The call came through Rear Admiral Neal Daastrup's scrambled home telephone at two o'clock in the morning. He was grumpy whenever anyone disturbed his sleep, a condition he wanted to be sacrosanct; but all too often, he got disturbed anyway.

The encoded caller ID showed the caller to be Major General Zwi Rosenstein, Daastrup's counterpart in the Mossad.

"Zwi, you old criminal, this had better be good. Do you know what time it is here?"

"I do. It is about the only time I can get to you without having to deal with everybody who runs interference for you."

"Okay, I'll assume it is at least reasonably important. It's your nickel, shoot."

"Do you read the papers and watch a talk show or two?"

"Sure—in my copious free time."

"Did you happen to notice some attention being paid to a nice Jewish boy by the pompous name of Gideon Emmanuel Rothsberger IV?"

"Can't say that I did. So what's up with him that captures the interest of the Mossad?

"The boy is just thirteen and a certified genius in a lot of areas, especially in very advanced mathematics. He just graduated with, and I quote, 'very great honor' from U.C. Berkeley. I am not calling just to have you know how smart us Jews are. I have something in mind for this boy. His father is one of the richest bankers in the world, and his family is becoming best friends with another very bright Jew by the name of Levi Schmuel. I'll be right up front about him. He is something of a mover and a shaker in what we call the Kosher Nostra. He may be semiretired, but he is still in contact—in fact, in business—with my brother, Max, who is second in command in the Zeev Rosenkranz Israeli mafia gang operating out of Tel Aviv. And yes, there is a family relationship there as well. Anyway, both Gideon Rothsberger III and Schmuel are active contributors to the *Sayanim*, need I say more?"

"No."

"I see long-term benefits by establishing mutual contact with the father and the boy and Schmuel that we can capitalize on to deal with the nasties in Iran one day. I think the boy's career would be wasted if he were to become nothing more than a banker. We could maybe steer his postgraduate career towards nuclear physics and nuclear engineering, and see if we can't get a bit of high stakes spying underway down the line. What do you think, Neal?"

"Boy, you do plan ahead. Do you have any idea if the kid is made of the right psychological material to engage in our mutual interest?"

"I am pretty sure that he has had significant indoctrination into the 'We hate Iran and its Nukes' club from his family and acquaintances, and we have something of an ace in the hole in that regard. The boy is being trained by a former IDF lieutenant colonel who worked with the Aman, and who still maintains some very close ties with army intelligence and the Institute. Our man was an instructor in Krav Maga for IDF special forces, and has been teaching the lad the niceties of that sport. Our guy says that—for a youngster—he shows real promise; and in his conversations with the boy, it seems that he has a strong pro-Israeli and anti-Iran bent. I think he is ripe for grooming by such as you and me."

"Sounds good if I live long enough to see a plan come to fruition. What do you have in mind?"

Rosenstein elaborated his plan, and the two spies agreed to meet G.R. IV before he went off to graduate school.

Zwi arranged a meeting with G.R. III and Levi Schmuel in San Francisco during the first week in June. They were both amenable to having their sons and "*dohd*" [Hebrew: uncle] be approached by the Institute and even the Aman, if it seemed likely to be of value. G.R. III had meant it when he said that he would support Israel and the *Sayanim*, but he wanted it to be understood that he would never approve dangerous fieldwork for his scion.

Zwi Rosenstein and Neal Daastrup met G.R. IV at the Presidio Heights Krav Maga School during the third week of June. Both men were conservatively dressed in expensive suits and could have been banking friends of G.R. III.

Lt. Col. Avitan waited until the two men could watch his protégé defeat two larger opponents in full contact sparring matches before he introduced them. He kept his introduction vague.

"Gideon, I want to meet a couple of my best friends who are interested in all that you are accomplishing. This is Zwi, he's from Tel Aviv, and this is Neal Daastrup. He works for the government in Washington, D.C. Gentlemen, may I present Gideon Rothsberger IV."

They shook hands all around. After some congratulations about Gideon's accomplishments, Zwi led into the more important subjects for which the two senior officers had traveled considerable distance.

"We expect great things from you, Gideon. Your father and Mr. Schmuel feel the same way. Let me ask something about your plans now that you've graduated."

"I'm kind of torn after studying all of the programs. Almost everybody has been recruiting me, and they all have offered full-ride scholarships. I have less than two weeks to commit. I want a master's in math and an MBA. The best school for math is the University of Michigan in Ann Arbor, and it has a good MBA program, too. There is a thriving Orthodox Jewish community there; so, I would feel right at home, maybe more than I have at Berkeley. I could specialize in any one or even more than one of the business studies and have a good useful masters at the end of a couple of years."

"Have the schools you are interested in agreed to let you finish in two years, provided you can cut it?"

"They all said I could have whatever I wanted. I kind of think they want to show me off, if that isn't bragging to say so."

"Admiral Daastrup and I—I'm a general—have a suggestion for you to consider. The world of computers is taking off and will involve almost every activity that people are interested in over the next few years. Maybe you could get the masters in math and start getting a nuclear engineering master's instead of in a business discipline."

Gideon started to interrupt.

"Wait a second, Gideon, let me finish before you make any kind of decision. The world of nuclear physics and nuclear engineering is going to take off and will make brilliant people and innovative companies a pile of money. Computers are completely woven into physics, engineering, and business; and you could master them all and be the best prepared and most sought-after man in the world. I am not just shining you on, Gideon. Adm. Daastrup and I don't do that kind of thing. In our line of work, truth is what prevails, and we are the most practical of men. Two years from now, I see you walking off the stage with a pair of masters' degrees—one an MBA with a specialty in computers, and the other in nuclear physics. You can go on to get a Ph.D. in nuclear engineering and combine all of your education and talent into a great and growing field."

"I'm not sure...."

"There's something else. You must realize that the two of us represent two different allied countries, and in this we have a shared goal. You can't have missed the fact that Iran is working feverishly to produce a nuclear bomb and will probably succeed in four or five years, maybe as long as ten; but they will finally succeed unless Israel and the United States step in."

"I don't understand what it is I could do."

"We want you to swear to keep a secret, if we talk any more about this to you, Gideon," Adm. Daastrup entered the conversation for the first time.

"Wow, that's pretty heavy stuff. I'm just a kid, even if I just graduated from college."

Zwi looked pointedly at the thirteen-year-old boy, "You are about ready to have your Bar Mitzvah, aren't you Gideon?"

"Next week."

"Tell me what it means to become a Bar Mitzvah."

"Well, besides reciting from the Torah, I guess it means like it says, 'For today, I am a man.'"

"Do you think age thirteen is too young to be a man, Gideon?"

"I guess not. Jewish boys have assumed their place among men for millennia, even getting married. It is kind of scary, but I actually think I'm ready."

"We think you can wait for a couple of years before you get married, but we do want you to shake our hands and guarantee that you will keep our secrets, just like we will keep yours. We can work together to save the United States and the *edah* [the entire Jewish people]. What do you say?"

By way of his answer, Gideon Rothsberger IV extended his hand to an admiral and a general and swore a pact with them. It was heady stuff for a boy who had not so long ago played army with his friends, attacked Muslim strongholds in the backyard, and dreamed about being a superagent for the Mossad. From stories told to him by his father, G.R. IV developed a deep hero worship for Eli Cohen—Gideon even remembered the full name of Israel's greatest spy ever: Eliahu ben Shaoul Cohen—who spied in Syria and was then murdered by the Syrians in 1965. When he and his friends played heroes, Gideon always chose to be Eli Cohen. He recalled a documentary that told the story of "The Year of the Spy"—1985—when multiple spy cases were discovered in the United States. He had been just as interested in the *Back to the Future* movie which was replayed dozens of times during Gideon's preteen years. He longed to have a DeLorean ever since. The stupid movie, *The Goonies*, had been one of his favorites, and *Scooby Doo, Where Are You? Attack of the Killer Tomatoes*, and *Darkwing Duck* on the TV had occupied his afternoons. He guessed that thirteen as the age to become a man was well chosen by the ancients. He felt a serious and protective responsibility as the big brother to his eight-year-old twin siblings Tahmineh and Leila who loudly resented his bossiness and loved him unabashedly. He guessed that counted in the steps of manhood.

The two senior government officers took a few moments to tell him about their respective agencies—the DIA and the Mossad. They told him that he could possibly play a powerful role in the silent war against the Persians by being well enough educated to interfere with their nuclear plans. In closing, they let him know that they would be meeting with him periodically and that they would always have his back. His schooling would sail along even better than he could do by himself, which they admitted, would be well above what the average genius could do. The day would come when he would be an important but unsung *gibur* [hero] of the *edah*.

In the parking lot, Adm. Daastrup asked Gen. Rosenstein, "Think that boy really understands what we're telling him? I don't mean is he smart enough, but is he mature enough? He is still a child, after all."

"This is a long-term proposition, Neal. We are likely to have a few Murphy's Law moments; but yes, from the long-term perspective, I think backing him and teaching him will be well worth the effort and the risk."

They shook hands and went their separate ways, both still wondering about what they had gotten themselves and that boy into.

On the first Sabbath after Gideon's thirteenth birthday, the Rothsberger clan met together for the first time in over a decade for the purpose of celebrating his Bar Mitzvah. The importance of the Orthodox ceremony to the Rothsbergers was underlined by the fact that no such complete family gathering had taken place when G.R. IV graduated from Saint Francis Woods Hebrew Academy or from U.C. Berkeley with the highest of honors. They were unlikely to do so again until G.R. IV took his place as president of Rothsberger & Company Bankers. Chava had controlled the project of preparing the mansion for the event and had studied every source she could to be sure that her son's Bar Mitzvah came off correct in every detail.

Gideon worried more about doing his part in front of the impressive gathering of Orthodoxy—reciting from the Torah, etc.—than he had when he faced major examinations at the university.

Rabbi Bergen stood in front of the great room and held up his hand for quiet.

"Greetings and welcome to all. This is a joyous occasion for us to meet with one another and before Yahweh to receive a new man into our community, into our family. I am convinced that Gideon Emmanuel Rothsberger IV is ready to assume his duties among the *k'lal Yisrael*. He is thirteen and able to become a son of the law. Under the law, he shall hereafter be fully responsible for his actions. He shall bear responsibility on his own to participate in and to obey our 613 *mitzvot* [laws of the Torah] and all the *Halakha* [the collective body of religious laws, including biblical, Talmudic, and rabbinic statutes], tradition, and ethics and to have the right to participate in all responsibilities of Jewish community life. He now—on his own—has moral responsibility and can no longer shift that burden to his parents. He may now be called upon in the synagogue to read from the Torah, to participate in or even lead a *Minyan* [a quorum of ten Jewish men—Orthodox—required for the performance of specific religious obligations, the most common obligation being public prayer.]. As a man, Gideon may possess personal property, may testify as an accepted witness in a *Beth Din* [rabbinical court], and may legally marry.

"Gideon, rise and come to the front and give the *Aliyah* [blessings from the Torah]."

Gideon was very nervous. He stood before the assemblage of Orthodox notables and collected himself. Most boys needed help to read from the Torah, both because of their shyness and because of inadequate preparation. Some were even unable to read and had to settle for giving a prayer. G.R. IV reached into his encyclopedic memory and recited the necessary verses verbatim.

Rabbi Bergen smiled at him and gave a little admiring shake of his head.

"Now, Gideon, please read from the weekly portion of the Law as the first of our seven men tonight."

Gideon read in the original Hebrew and was perfect in pronunciation and delivery. Next he obeyed the command to read the *Haftarah* [selections from the Prophets]. Seeing that Gideon had sailed through that set of tasks, Rabbi Bergen finally asked him to give a *d'var Torah* [a discussion of a Torah issue]. Not one to shrink from challenge, Gideon gave a penetrating and lucid discussion of how the faithful should regard Yahweh for having required Abraham to sacrifice his son, Isaac. Was it caprice? Was it a mere test since a ram was provided from the thicket? Was it fair? Could God be faulted?

Many a man strained to keep from rising to present an argument; but it was Gideon's night; and they stayed in their seats admiring the boy.

"We will now lay the *tefillin* [Hebrew. Also known as *phylacteries*—Greek]. Gideon, these are sacred, and it is one of your obligations under the Law to treat them so."

The rabbi placed the set of small black leather boxes containing scrolls of parchment inscribed with verses from the Torah, on Gideon's arm and forehead.

"Hereafter, you will wear your *tefillin* during weekday morning prayers as you take your place among the men as a sign and remembrance that our God delivered us from bondage in Egypt."

He gave a small nod to Gideon's father, who stepped forward carrying a carefully wrapped bundle. He opened the package and unfurled a beautiful *tallit* [prayer shawl] and draped it around Gideon's shoulders. The boy stood tall with his *tefillin* and *tallit* in place and faced the *k'lal Yisrael*.

Rabbi Bergen and G.R. III then said together, "For today, you are a man, my son."

The men in the great room all echoed, "For today, you are a man."

Everyone swept forward to congratulate Gideon and his parents. There was an outpouring of love and affection that exceeded anything Gideon—for all of his experience of great privilege—had ever known. Tahmineh and Leila held his hands and looked up at him with a gaze that was nothing short of adoration. It was the best day of his life.

Next came the grandest dinner of his life. For all of the over-the-top excesses modern Orthodox families expend on the Bar Mitzvahs of their cherished sons, the *seudat mitzvah* celebratory banquet feast at the Rothsberger mansion that night outshone them all. The family and guests were treated to Covenant kosher wine made from carefully hand-harvested Cabernet Sauvignon grapes in Napa Valley and Kedem kosher apple juice for the children. The food was flown in that afternoon from Olga's on Smith Street in Brooklyn and Tierra Del Sur in Oxnard, California. Salads were as fresh as the day, and there were tubs of watercress, romaine, jicama, and avocado salad with caramelized orange vinaigrette, marinated artichokes, chili rellenos stuffed with potato and taramasalata, authentic Caesar salad, and hearts of romaine with lemon, garlic, and anchovy dressing.

The separate table for appetizers held chicken liver pâté, chorizo lamb sausage and black olive *piadina* flat bread with watercress, cherry tomato salad and zahtar dressing, and huge tureens of lobster bisque. The entrees were hot from the kitchen: eggplant encrusted Alaskan halibut with curry squash agnolotti, tomato concase and an assortment of Italian and Greek olives, oven roasted chili-chocolate rubbed New Zealand rack of lamb, gnocchi, huitlocoche and mushroom sauce, grilled charmoula marinated free-range chicken with squash tajine, chickpeas and three colors of baby bell peppers, veal chop with sorrel-polenta, roasted rapini, and plum sauce, wild Atlantic salmon with sautéed brussel sprout leaves, celery root beignets and crab apple butter, and two-inch thick Texas rib eye steak with endive, fried shoestring potato salad, and grilled grape sauce.

Few had room left in their stomachs for Death-By-Chocolate cake, huge dark chocolate dipped strawberries, an assortment of gelato delivered from Rome, oversized raisin chocolate chip cookies from the original Ghirardelli chocolate store on the San Francisco wharf, peanut butter pareve New York deli cheesecake with chocolate whipped cream, or lemon meringue pie with hazelnut shortbread crust. Gideon did his best to sample them all but had to admit defeat before he made himself sick.

As the evening drew to a close, the guests filed past the Rothsberger butler, Joseph ben Aaron, who collected gift envelopes just as he had done at the *Brit Milah* on the eighth day of G.R. IV's life. The envelopes contained sums ranging from $100 to $200,000—the latter generosities from G.R. II and Rebecca Hershowitz, his grandparents on both sides of the family. There were savings bonds, gift certificates, religious, educational, and biographical books, and more than a dozen expensive pens engraved with "G.R. IV" in 22-carat gold.

The presents of money—as would be expected among the Orthodox— were given in multiples of 18—*chai*, the word for life, a most auspicious lucky number. Ever the rebel, his grandmother Rebecca gave him the keys to a Harley motorcycle that Chava promptly confiscated.

Gideon was almost unconscious by the time he could be led away to bed. His last thought for that day was that life could not be better, and his future had no limits. He was going to be a fabulously wealthy banker, a theoretical mathematician, a nuclear scientist, and a spy. He wanted to remain humble, but he drifted into deep sleep with a prideful smile on his young face.

# CHAPTER NINETEEN

## Lansing, Michigan, September, 1993

Chava cried, and G.R. III had to turn his head aside as they put Gideon on the plane for Lansing, Michigan the first week in September. Although he was still only thirteen, Gideon was familiar with fundamentals of finding his courses online and had already arranged his schedule for the first year in graduate school. Just as Berkeley had done, the University of Michigan saw no problem with him working on a double master's degree and to complete his work in two years if he could do the work. The admissions department had been emphatic that the University of Michigan, Ann Arbor, was a good deal more stringent and expected more from its students than did "that California school."

Ann Arbor is a beautiful city in a lush setting at any time of year, but Gideon had been wise to come a week early to enjoy the beginning of a resplendent autumn. For five days he conducted his own tour of the natural assets of the huge campus located in the northeast quadrant of Ann Arbor. He spent an entire day in the Matthaei Botanical Gardens and Nichols Arboretum and enjoyed it enough to sign on for two hours a week working for free through the next two semesters. The project to which he was assigned was to work with botany department graduate students to convert the landscaping of prominent Ann Arbor mansions to one hundred percent native rocks, plants, and trees. As their trademark, each mansion was to have a backyard prairie and a pond, rain grass, and indigenous buffalo grass growing wild in the front yard. He knew he would need an outlet from his didactic university work, and he looked forward to being part of something good and working with good people.

He drove around Peach Mountain in Stinchfield Woods—which is owned by the University of Michigan—for most of a morning with an accommodating taxi driver. Because the semester had not yet officially begun, a staff astronomer gave him his own tour of the magnificent twenty-four-inch McMath Telescope operated by the astronomy department. He took some time to look at the projects underway by the school of natural resources and environment. Gideon did his best to see as many of the city's 157 parks as he could in two days he allotted for that part of his tour, but barely scratched the surface. In the evenings, he e-mailed his parents and his two sisters—who continued to gush over him. He had to laugh at their exuberant affection for him, and he reciprocated in his messages. His last free day before starting the grind of academics was to rent a one-man kayak for a trip downriver from Barton to Gallup Park. He was in a great mood when he walked into his first class.

As he had been the first few days when he started his undergraduate career at U.C. Berkeley, Gideon was the object of some curiosity as he walked into his first postgraduate class—computers and nuclear physics—a strong mathematical discipline, and known to be a make-or-break course for students interested in either computer science or nuclear physics. Gideon's course of study was tailored for him to obtain a midlevel understanding of nuclear physics and an integration with the economics and business of nuclear energy production.

Walter Duffy was the first man he met. "Hey, little man so spic and span, I think your mom missed a turn. You should have gotten off at Scarlett Middle School on Lorraine Street."

Duffy had a good laugh at his own clever humor. He was not illogical; Gideon knew, since Duffy was six-foot-three and weighed two hundred ten pounds compared to Gideon's five three, 106-pound presentation. Duffy had red hair, a freckled cherubic face, and did not seem to be conveying any menace. He was just a tiresome boor, and Gideon did not take offense.

"No, this is the place for me. What is your major area of study?"

Duffy looked at the boy's face and saw no disrespect; so, he said, "Nuclear engineering. I am not all that great with computers, and it is high time I learned. If you don't mind me asking, you seem pretty young to be taking a graduate level computer course. I hear it is a tough one. I have had several computer engineering classes, but my prof wanted me to have a taste of the nuclear end; so, I am going to start here. You some kind of child genius or something?"

"Maybe, but I haven't had much computer science training or nuclear physics other than what I got in high school. Maybe one of these days you could give me a little help."

That was twist for Walter Duffy. He had been prepared to dislike and to make life a bit tough for the little twerp. The boy's obvious earnestness and humility touched a cord.

"If you're serious, let me know, I would be glad to give you any help I can. It'll take me a while to get over the fact that you are younger than my little brother who is in the eighth grade."

"Thanks."

Dr. Henry Applegate—dual professor of nuclear physics and engineering—walked to the front of the amphitheater shaped room and took his place behind the lectern.

"Welcome," he said. "I won't waste time with any housekeeping details. You can get hold of my T.A. for what you need to know. I have his phone number and e-mail address on the board.

"Now, let's get right to work. First, to be simplistic, computer science, as opposed to gaining proficiency in the use of a computer—a valuable skill—deals with both a scientific and a practical approach to computation and the applications of computer technology for the present and the future. At least at a master's level, those of you who get a thesis done and obtain a postgraduate degree will be a specialist in the theory of computation, systems design, and will be sought after to make business, scientific endeavor, and research decisions from the grade school education and the Ph.D. level to help them reach heights never before dreamt of. I have lived in the industrial age, the space age, and the information age, and now the information revolution. Who knows what you will see? The University of Michigan and the departments of physics, engineering, economics, and mathematics are determined that each of you will come out of here standing at the top of your fields. I am determined that you will be able to use every bit of power possible from the marvelous machine we will study this year—the computer. You will discover that it is the most important purveyor of information, of research—and of war, for that matter—yet discovered.

"You will have to learn how to cope with invasions of privacy by governmental and law enforcement agencies; they are coming. You will have to learn how to protect your own and everyone else's computer function and privacy. It will be a difficult and hostile world. You will have to be the warriors. Learn not only to use this great tool, but to develop a set of ethics about its use before the tigers come in the night. Terrorists, despots, corrupt politicians, adventurous militarists, and probably even avaricious pornographers will soon discover this amoral tool to do injury to the people of the world. Be prepared.

"In the time left in these three hours, we will begin our study of programming language theory and the more mundane activities of computer programming, programming language, and will finish up the morning with an introduction to complex systems. In the syllabus, you will find three chapters that cover these subjects. Master them by Wednesday—a word to the wise."

Walter Duffy let his tongue loll out of his mouth to indicate exhaustion just at the description. Gideon smiled his agreement. It was going to be a mountain to climb, and he was beginning to wonder if he was enough of a climber.

The concept of a computer has a history that goes back as far as the Chinese abacus. The first machine calculator was conceived in 1623 but not practical until 1642. Four arithmetic operations could be done by a calculator built by Leibniz in 1694. The Victorians came up with the idea of, and then a general-purpose, analytical engine; and the manual for its operation was the first programmer's guide. Near the turn of the twentieth century, punch card machines were invented. During the 1940s, true and powerful computing machines were developed. In rapid succession, experts realized that computers had wider applications than just for mathematical computations. The field of computer science broadened and deepened and became a study of its own and became recognized as "computer science." When practical computers became widely available, the study of computers, as well as the use of computers, became an unstoppable phenomenon worldwide.

During the three semesters of the 1993-1994 academic year, Dr. Applegate introduced Gideon and his new friend, Walter Duffy, into the computer world of programming language, a tool to cope with the need to understand the precise expression of methodological information even at complicated and interwoven levels of abstraction, cryptography, the nascent genetic field of mapping of the human genome, computer graphics and computer-generated imagery for advertising and modern entertainment, digital functions for cameras, process simulation, and science. The scientific tools of computation included fluid dynamics and development of physical, electronic, and circuit systems. During that academic year, Gideon developed a proficiency in the application of computer science for the aviation industry and automobile manufacturing and how they enable optimization of design, circuitry, monitoring of in-flight pathways and metal fatigue. Finally, on a sobering note, Dr. Applegate introduced his students—with inescapable proof—that there are unsolvable and intractable problems that are mathematically impossible for computers.

By May, Gideon had selected his master's thesis goal, one that was the perfect wedding of his computer and business aspirations. Dr. Applegate introduced Gideon and his fellow postgraduate degree aspirants to a dramatic new understanding of the business world. Gideon learned about algorithmic trading and how it enhanced the efficiency and liquidity of financial markets, the status of research into artificial intelligence, machines that learn large scale statistical and numerical technique, and application of computer science to television, cinema, advertising, animation, and video games, all highly likely to bring untold wealth to an educated entrepreneur and his banker who got in on the ground floor of the burgeoning industries that were then only in their youth. Gideon decided to write his thesis on high frequency algorithmic trading that exacerbates volatility in the market.

As a sideline, Gideon joined a math club that had a focus on the use of computers for solving extremely time consuming calculus equations. They were allowed to use the university's supercomputer and selected as their project the identification of the largest prime number known thus far. Gideon got his name on the final paper when they finally discovered the historical 15 million-plus digit long number. At spring break, he enjoyed explaining to his mother what a prime number is: any number that is divisible only by itself and by 1 without leaving a remainder. She had questioned why anyone really wanted to know that, and Gideon did not have a ready answer.

Gideon knew that he had to have a master's degree in economics, and had to tailor his work to his foremost aptitude—higher mathematics. His goal through the year was to decide about a problem he could work on and complete during his second year of postgraduate master's work. He sought the advice of his major professor in economics, Dr. Yousef Tavaazo, a native of Tehran trained at the London School of Economics. Dr. Tavaazo was the first person Gideon had ever had close contact with who was a devout Muslim.

During their first meeting, Dr. Tavaazo gave his young student a piece of important advice.

"Mr. Rothsberger, you are young and an obvious follower of Judaism. I emphasize the word 'obvious.' It is all well and good to be a true believer of one's religion, but often; an overt outward demonstration of one's characteristic traditions is off-putting to others with whom you will work. Modern people educated with a wide general perspective may or may not be religious; but they find such expressions in clothing, hairstyles, and activities to be suggestive of extreme dedication, even radicalization, at times. This may be inaccurate, but it is nonetheless important for you—appearance and perception may well be as significant as objective reality. Perhaps you might consider cutting your hair more like the other American men and leave your yarmulke off except for religious services. I have had to do that so people's attention is on me as a person and not a Persian, and especially as a Muslim. We all have to adapt some.

"Oh, as to your choice of a thesis for your master's project, I like the algorithmic trading question. I will get you in touch with some professors in the economics department to help."

On his own, Gideon contacted his father and Levi Schmuel, who arranged for him to meet with a very successful New York Stock Exchange trader, Israel Siegel, to learn about the practical applications of the university theories. Over the course of the next thirteen months, Gideon and Mr. Siegel became mutual students and friends exploring the algorithmic trading concepts and establishing what would become an important future relationship.

Israel agreed with Dr. Tavaazo's suggestion that he tone down his outwardly overt Jewishness, and Gideon took their advice. It was rather liberating, and the boy had to remind himself to put his yarmulke and *tefillin* back on when he went home for visits.

Mr. Schmuel called Zwi Rosenstein to bring the Mossad officer up to date about Gideon's choices.

"They sound solid, Zwi. I think his expertise after he gets these degrees will probably be just what you guys are after."

"I think so, too. I would like to have him tweak the directions he takes a bit. Could you get his father, and I'll get Admiral Daastrup for another face-to-face with Gideon—say in the next couple of months?"

"No problem. Nice to talk with you, Zwi. We'll be in touch.

The second meeting between Gideon and his spymasters-to-be took place three miles from the main university complex in the Holiday Inn Hotel Ann Arbor. The hotel was an average priced, average looking, average Holiday Inn, in Anywhere Average, USA; and that was exactly what the two governmental officers wanted. They wore average grey suits, and nothing about the two of them stood out. G.R. III had been forewarned and—as much as it was possible for one of the richest bankers in the world—he had striven to look nondescript and average as well.

The two Gideon Emmanuels embraced, and there were handshakes all around.

"We haven't a lot of time, Gideon," Adm. Daastrup said without preliminaries, as was his usual efficient mode of operation. "Give us the rundown on your studies and decisions so far."

Gideon gave a brief summary and waited for comments.

G.R. III spoke first, "That certainly seems like an excellent career path for everything you want to do in business."

G.R. IV nodded.

"And it gives you a better base for your math studies. We told you before how much we like the serious involvement in computers. I am pleased with your choices and the advice you have been given."

"I have a few suggestions," Adm. Daastrup said. "Mr. Rothsberger, for your own protection, I would appreciate it if you would give us some time alone with your son. You know this meeting never took place, and the mysterious spy stuff we're going to discuss with Gideon is better you don't know about."

G.R. III nodded at the two officers—smiled affectionately at his son—and made his exit.

*"Indeed, my boy has become a man,"* he mused as he waited on a couch in the hallway.

The meeting took half an hour. Gideon's course of study and choice of masters' theses made some small but important deviations as a result. G.R. III had only enough time to have a nice dinner with G.R. IV at the Northern Lakes Seafood Company about twenty miles outside of Ann Arbor in Bloomfield Hills before he had to get back to San Francisco. The government agents left by a back stairway and through the utility rooms without further encountering either Rothsberger.

Walter Duffy approved of Gideon's new look and told him so.

"I don't have anything against Jews, Gideon, but I think you will fit in easier without the get-up."

Gideon accepted the observation for what it was—well-intentioned and not anti-Semitic. The Mutt and Jeff pair became an odd couple as they worked together for the better part of Gideon's two years at the University of Michigan. Walter helped Gideon with the mysterious quirks inherent in the practical use of computers.

"Everybody hates computers, Gideon. There is even a special junkyard in New Jersey where they let you bring your old computer and destroy it in any of a dozen fiendish ways—sledgehammer, dropping it from a high-rise crane, burning it to a crisp in a blast furnace, grinding it up in a metal shredder; or, my personal favorite, driving over and over it with a huge truck."

Gideon laughed, knowing how Walter and every other computer user felt at times.

Gideon introduced Walter to Jiu Jitsu and Krav Maga; and the larger, older graduate student marveled at Gideon's proficiency in martial arts. He was chagrined that the much smaller and much younger boy could make him tap on a regular basis. Walter got Gideon into a swimming and life-saving class and found him a tennis pro to get Gideon interested in one of the gentlemanly sports. They shared a love of chess, and split the win-loss record straight down the middle.

Gideon helped Walter muddle through the labyrinthine complexities of calculus and three-dimensional geometry. By the end of May 1995, both men had their master's degrees in hand—Walter with his computer graphics theory that he intended to turn into his entrance into the billion-dollar technological industry serving Hollywood, and Gideon with a double masters in computer science and statistics in economics. Not unexpectedly, Gideon received both of his degrees *magna cum laude*. Once again, the Rothsberger clan gathered to celebrate a success. This time, they found that Gideon had an inseparable friend; and Walter was accepted as a near family member despite being one of the *goyim* [gentiles] and as almost as close a friend of the family as Levi and Aaron Schmuel.

# CHAPTER TWENTY

## Israel, summer, 1995

The Rothsbergers and the Schmuels decided to have joint family trips to Israel for the summer of 1995 as a graduation present to their sons—Aaron from Saint Francis Woods Hebrew Academy with honors, and G.R. IV from the University of Michigan with two master's degrees. The two fourteen-year-old boys ignored their accomplishments or lack of them and got along famously wrestling and practicing their Krav Maga every chance they could. Levi Schmuel had elected himself tour arranger, and found a set of tour guides from mixed sources. Unknown to anyone but himself and G.R. III, they were squired around by two Zeev Rosenkranz Tel Aviv syndicate notables, Moise Levinsky and Jacob "The Greaser" Cohen, and by a "government employee," André Lansky. Chava found the two friends of Levi's to be a bit on the rough-cut side for her taste, and the "government employee," Andre Lansky, not to be as forthcoming and informative as she would have liked; but they were ingratiating and interesting characters and, in time, put her at ease.

Both boys were initiated into the realities of who their guides really were, and the part their organizations would likely play in the boys' futures during their first night's stay in the stately pink quartz stone King David Hotel in Jerusalem, built in the 1920s. Levi came to the Rothsbergers suite of rooms and—after a few hushed words with G.R. III—left with both G.R.s and Aaron for a boys' night out. They stepped out to the front of the hotel and took in the panorama of the ancient capital city from the mount on which the hotel sat. Moments later, a black Mercedes Benz limousine stopped; and Major General Zwi Rosenstein stepped out and held the door for the four Americans. Inside the limo were two men the Rothsbergers did not know, but Levi gave the two a small nod of recognition. Neither of those men spoke during the short trip.

They drove down Eliyahu Shama and through the Shabbat traffic to the Mount Scopus campus of the Hebrew University. From the mount, it was possible to see the lights of the city of Jerusalem twinkling below them, the temple mount; and on the other side of Mount Scopus, they could see blackness where the Judean desert lay. In the distance, the building lights around the edge of the Dead Sea were visible. The driver spoke to General Rosenstein, and he spoke back briefly.

They pulled up to the Belgium House Faculty Club, and the driver—a very fit, martial appearing young man—stepped out and opened the doors on both sides. Rosenstein led his guests through the club to a set of stairs blocked off by a velvet rope. He unlatched the rope and signaled to the men and boys to walk upstairs, then relatched the rope's brass hook to the ring on the bannister post.

They entered a luxurious dining room. Only one table was occupied, a large oval cherrywood conference table. Gen. Rosenstein motioned everyone to sit, and they all took their chairs except for their bodyguards. Each of the senior men had two guards standing close by behind him. Moise Levinsky and Jacob "The Greaser" Cohen stood behind the man they had all met the previous day, André Lansky, and a fearsome man dressed all in black.

Rosenstein made cursory introductions.

"Gideon Rothsberger and Levi Schmuel, please permit me to introduce André Lansky, a senior government official, and my superior. And this is my maternal uncle, Zeev Rosenkranz, who heads a major business conglomerate in Tel Aviv."

The man in black nodded, and Gen. Rosenstein took his seat.

The pecking order in the room was immediately apparent.

André Lansky spoke first, "Thank you for coming to meet us on such short notice. Please forgive us for the secrecy and security. Unfortunately, we are men in positions where mistakes cannot be made and still survive. Although Mr. Rosenkranz and I have our differences, we are completely united in the preservation of our homeland for which we must act defensively on a regular basis. We are prepared to work with you in Israel's defense and for the best interests of the United States, our foremost and almost only real ally and friend. You have extensive contacts, influence, and resources as do Mr. Rosenkranz and I. We are prepared to share information with you that you must agree never to divulge. I don't wish to sound threatening, but betrayal of either of the two of us would have ... shall we say, grave consequences."

His heavy lidded eyes made a brief but meaningful glance at the Rothsbergers and Schmuels.

"If you agree to abide by our requirements for secrecy and security, and to help when it is requested of you, we believe you will find our reciprocal help to be most beneficial. We can get into details another time; but for today, let us consider a first step—that of bringing your two fine sons into the fold and to introduce them to their heritage."

He paused for a response from the fathers, who both nodded their acquiescence. He looked at the two boys, and they followed the example of their fathers.

"Good," Lansky said. "Have you anything to add, Zeev?"

"A bit. I know Levi well. We have cooperated in business to our mutual benefit. I understand that you have invested a substantial sum in Mr. Rothsberger's bank and that already you are cooperating in some highly successful business ventures. Our organization stands ready to open doors for you. In return, I ask two things: you keep any business you do with my organization strictly confidential, and that you become our partners in preserving Israel and the *k'lal Yisrael* to the best of your abilities—even to the point of sacrifice. Do we have an understanding, gentlemen? No one is forcing you or putting pressure on you; but if you do agree to join us, you may not walk away with impunity."

"It is clear, Zeev, and I accept. I am in to the death," said Levi.

"For *k'lal Yisrael*, anything," said G.R. III.

"Excellent," said André Lansky. "Now let us turn our attention to these two fine young men. You come from rather different backgrounds, but I am pleased to learn that you are genuine friends. That will be a useful alliance over the years. You may from time to time learn secrets. Sometimes you will be able to share with one another, and sometimes not. As time passes, we will become formal about the requirements to which you will have to agree; but, for now, we ask only that you never discuss the fact that this meeting ever happened except among yourselves and your fathers. This is not even for other members of your families or your closest friends, do you understand?"

"Yes, Sir," both boys said in clear, confident voices.

"Then, I will tell you a first secret. Our arrangement has the blessing of the United States Defense Intelligence Agency. I think you have met Rear Admiral Neal Daastrup. He will be the U.S. officer in charge of all of your activities, and we will act as his confidants and assistants. We will provide training and assistance to you boys as you go about your regular lives. You—like your fathers—will find doors opening for you that might not have seemed likely on your own. In return, we ask that you return once a year to Israel for two weeks of some special instruction that will remain off any records. When the time comes, the DIA, the IDF, the United States, Israel, and, indeed, the *k'lal Yisrael*, will ask that you wholeheartedly join with us for our mutual benefit and to put our many enemies to a disadvantage. Do you agree, so far?"

The boys nodded their assent. If being a Bar Mitzvah meant that they were men, then this was certainly a beginning test of their manhood; and both boys took everything they were being told as altogether serious.

"Tomorrow, the two of you will have a very special tour of our holy land, and you will begin your education. It will be just a taste; but in the months and years to come, you will become first rate members of an elite and very effective organization."

After they arrived back at the King David, the two fathers took the two boys aside before returning to their hotel rooms.

"Do you realize who André Lansky is?" asked Levi.

"Not exactly," said Aaron, "but I don't think he works for Uncle Zeev."

"He most certainly does not, Son. But they do have an understanding. General Lansky is the head of the Mossad. You are two of the very few people in the world who have ever seen him or that even know his name. He seems pretty benign, but don't ever forget how seriously the man takes his commitment to secrecy and to Israel. He is not a man to cross."

"You two seem to know who Mr. Rosenkranz is, but all I got out of the conversation was that he is a businessman. I have met a lot of businessmen—men like my father—but I don't remember having met anyone in my life who made me feel as uncomfortable as he does. How about telling me who he really is," asked Gideon.

G.R. III answered, "Gideon, that man is the head of one of the largest crime syndicates in the world. He controls tens of thousands of people and thousands of different businesses. He has tentacles in every industry you ever heard of. As you might imagine, I don't fully approve of everything he does or is involved in; but I have taken great pains to keep my business with him strictly legal; and, thus far, at least, our legitimate business has been profitable beyond my greatest imaginations. We will profit from our association with him; we won't cross him; we won't betray him; but we won't become criminals. We apparently are going to be spies; but it will be for our own people and against those individuals, companies, organizations, and countries who are our enemies who wish us to be dead just because we are Jews or Americans."

G.R. IV took a couple of seconds to reply then told his father and the Schmuels that he understood and would never forget the lessons of the day.

The next morning, Zwi Rosenstein took the elder Rothsbergers and Schmuels on a whirlwind tour of Haifa, Tel Megiddo, and to the Nof Ginosar Kibbutz Hotel near Tiberias for lunch. In the afternoon, they traveled south to the Dead Sea and Masada. The next day, the boys were still off with the Israeli men; and the adults saw Elah Valley where David killed the giant, Goliath, the ruins of Herod's Palace, the Beit She'an National Park to see the best Roman ruins in Israel, and Armon HaNatziv [or Talpiot HaMizrach, according to Jewish tradition], which includes the place where Abraham and his firstborn, Isaac, first saw Mount Moriah, and Abraham nearly stabbed his full-grown son to death. They paused for lunch in the wandering Mahane Yehuda *Shuk* [Hebrew - market] in Jerusalem that turned out to be an hour and a half meandering, tasting, and shopping spree.

Aaron Schmuel and G.R. IV were fetched by Moise Levinsky and Jacob Cohen in a nondescript Range Rover. Ten minutes later, they were driven to a run-down neighborhood where Moise stopped the vehicle.

"You need to wear a hood from here until we get to our destination. Nobody can know where we are going; you can't know where it is; or one day someone may be able to force it out of you. You can't tell what you don't know. Okay?"

The boys nodded their agreement, although not without a trepidation or two. The two men drove the boys in circles—it seemed to them—for the better part of an hour until they pulled into a walled sandstone residence overlooking the Mediterranean. Moises and Jacob helped Gideon and Aaron out of the Range Rover and removed their hoods. The sudden blast of bright desert sunshine was a momentary shock, and the boys took a while to adjust.

"Let's go inside," said Moises.

The interior of the fortresslike structure was cool, but otherwise not par-ticularly inviting. There were old Arab carpets here and there on the slate tile floors, a few old black and white and sepia photographs in frames on the largely unadorned stone walls, and metal utilitarian military furniture and cabinets. They were ushered into an office which bore a simple sign: No. 2.

General Zwi Rosenstein greeted them and dismissed Moises and Jacob.

"Take a seat. Sorry about the cloak and dagger stuff—security, you know. Sometimes it gets tedious. Today and tomorrow, we want to introduce you what us spies call tradecraft. I think you will find it kind of interesting—better than the movies."

Without wasting any more time, Gideon and Aaron were introduced to more gadgets, weapons, computer arrays, and coded printouts than they could have imagined possible. It was obvious that what they were seeing had taken years to accumulate and billions to fund. For an hour, Zwi arranged for them to have new

U.S. passports made that were entirely authentic due to the full cooperation of the U.S. DIA and the State Department. The only difference between the new passports and the original ones was that there was no entry or exit stamp for Israel to protect them from the future vicious prejudice of Muslim customs agents at Islamic borders. It was an obvious benefit, and the boys were suitably grateful.

In the afternoon, they were spectators at a Krav Maga lesson in the building's training section. Both boys had imagined themselves to be tough and to have had a thorough bruising from their training with Lt. Col. Shai Avitan back home, but the level of brutality and reality of what the IDF soldiers were learning was well beyond the experience of the boys. One man broke his arm, and General Rosenstein told them it was not all that unusual.

"Do you want to give it a try?"

"Sure," answered the boys, but they were not at all sure they did.

Zwi spoke to the instructor and told him that the boys had had several years of training in the United States with Lt. Col. Avitan, and were considered to be pretty good as boys or Americans go.

"But, take it easy, all right, Avri. Let's don't break anything. There'll be a day for that in a few years for these guys. We are expecting good things from them, and we don't want to spook them just yet."

It was evident to the boys that the instructor was pulling his punches and their sparring partners were not nearly as harsh with them as they had been with each other; but still, it was the roughest workout either had ever experienced. Once they lost their butterflies, the boys began to give as good as they got; but the disadvantages of their inexperience and their smaller size was evident. Aaron lost his temper and received a good hard kick to his left thigh, which raised a substantial bump as a result.

In his last match, Gideon was paired with the smallest soldier, David Henderson—strangely enough, not an uncommon name in Israel—in the class. He was a dark-skinned short man with powerful arm and leg muscles. Gideon knew he was in for a fight, but determined not to back down. David was overconfident and sure that he would make quick work of the fourteen-year-old. He came at Gideon aggressively and moved into position for the most common throw in Krav Maga. As soon as he felt his opponent's body shift into position for the hip throw, Gideon countered with a bent-leg strike on the back and side of David's knee, causing it to buckle. David fell and Gideon fell across him and went for a cross-neck choke.

That was a mistake, the same one David had made borne of overconfidence. David rolled Gideon over and grabbed his arm for an armlock. Gideon was able to get David's arm instead and rolled him onto his abdomen. He applied a choke from behind and succeeded in locking his two arms in a figure-four hold. He neglected to remember to secure David's leg with his—which gave David some wiggle room—and he was able to bend Gideon's wrist in a flexion pressure hold that forced Gideon to tap in submission.

Zwi clapped and laughed, and David was good-natured about his win.

"Good job. I won't underestimate you again."

"Next time, maybe you won't have to hold back. I am determined that I will be able to be as good as you. Good moves."

Gideon and David shook hands, and a bit of a comradeship was established.

The rest of the two families went home in the middle of August, and Aaron and Gideon stayed on for a full month of indoctrination. Aaron did better in Krav Maga training, and Gideon was able to exercise his genius in learning cryptography. He covered a two-year course in a month, and even the veterans were impressed. Zwi Rosenstein was pleased with himself for having made such a great discovery. He was sure that Gideon would be an important asset and that Aaron would always have his back.

Back home before Gideon left for Cambridge, he looked up Walter Duffy and they had a two-day backpacking trip to renew their acquaintanceship. Gideon was tempted, but did not yield, to tell Walter about his adventures. They had enough to talk about anyway, and the grueling hike was good for Gideon. He was toughening up.

Pursuing his usual pattern, Gideon took the train to Boston and a bus to Cambridge to get himself established in a new apartment where he would live and work for as long as it would take to get his Ph.D. from the Massachusetts Institute of Technology. He was now comfortable in his new hair and clothing style; he looked every bit as much a goy as anyone there.

At MIT—for Gideon and his professors—formal classwork took a second seat to research. Gideon had been coached by the Israelis and by some computer experts from the DIA while he was in Jerusalem and Tel Aviv about what they needed, and they pointed him at several burning research questions that would be fully acceptable to the departmental professors when it came time to submit his proposal for a dissertation.

Gideon was impassioned about his work, and launched into an intense course of nuclear physics. He targeted structural engineering for the building and maintenance of nuclear energy facilities. He was determined to know everything there was to know about finance, building laboratories, security, electronics, safety, and computer management of the nuclear industry. It was obvious that he had selected a tough nut to chew, and he went at the project with all the zeal he could muster.

# CHAPTER TWENTY-ONE

"Woman is fragile like glass, and men should therefore treat women with delicacy and tenderness as they would handle an article made of glass."

-Muslim (15:19) hadith about the Farewell Pilgrimage
address, p. 801, *8500 Precious Gems*,
Allahdin Publications

"Husbands should take full care of their wives, with [the bounties] God has given to some more than others and with what they spend out of their own money. Righteous wives are devout and guard what God would have them guard in the husbands' absence. If you fear high-handedness from your wives, remind them [of the teaching of God], then ignore them when you go to bed, then hit them. If they obey you, you have no right to act against them. God is most high and great."

-*Qur'an* sura 4:34, quoted and interpreted
by Egyptian-born Abdel Haleem, professor of
Islamic Studies at the School of Oriental and African
Studies, University of London. Oxford University Press, 2004

Aisha, Muhammad's favorite young wife, whom he married when he was in his fifties and she age nine or ten years and to whom he was betrothed when she was six—reported in the hadith: Muhammad sneaked out of the house to visit a graveyard and pray over the dead. Aisha followed him. She returned just before he did, but he noticed she was out of breath, and he asked her why. She told him, and apparently fearing for his life

as he saw her in the shadows, he punished her. Aisha stated:
"He struck me on the chest which caused me pain."
*-Hadith, Muslim*, 2: 2127

## Piranshahr, West Azerbaijan Province, Iran, February, 1993

Afsoon lay unconscious on the floor of the police van the entire distance to Piranshahr, the capital of the county of the same name. Beside her lay a mature woman in Western clothing. She had been savagely beaten; and, like Afsoon, was unconscious. Her breathing was labored and irregular. There were four other girls—the oldest age nineteen—and one elderly woman sitting on hinge-down steel benches on the sides of the van. From time to time, they took turns checking to see if Afsoon and the Western looking woman were still breathing. Somehow, despite the frightening wounds and all of that blood loss, both were hanging on to a thread of life.

The cold winter sun was on its way toward the western horizon—beyond which lay Iraq—when the van approached the Piranshahr County Jail in Piranshahre Mokrian, the largest of the two cities in the county. Those of the girls who could see out; and the two who could read, reported seeing illegal posters nailed to hundreds of trees and telephone poles along the route to the jail. The signs screamed out the protests of the Education Committee of the National Council of Resistance of Iran decrying the "inhuman regime of the Mullahs, who are responsible for loss of lives of two innocent schoolgirls and the severe burning of thirty-six other fourth-grade elementary school girls in a terrible fire in the Shane-Abad village school."

One of the girls who had completed enough elementary school to be able to read Farsi reported to the others everything she could see when the van stopped in front of the gates to the jail compound. The gist of the long posters and graffiti on the jail's outer walls was that the regime of the mullahs had wasted all the assets of the Iranian people in dangerous nuclear bomb projects, warmongering, and the export of terrorism around the world. Each of the messages carried the name of Soheila Sadeq, Chairwoman of the Education Committee.

The prisoner's only comment to her listeners was, "That brave Sadeq woman is a dead person who just doesn't know it yet."

In response to a call to the jail administration office, the twenty-foot tall steel gates swung open, and the van drove in and parked on the north side of the main building. The two burly police officers stepped out and stretched their legs, then opened the rear doors. One of them unlocked the shackles on

140

their ankles and directed the women to get out. Taking cursory note of the two prisoners lying on the van's floor, the officer inside the van kicked each of them to see if they could be roused. When it was apparent that neither even felt the kick, he ordered two of the older girls to drag them out. The guards and the young girls and the older woman walked slowly across the frozen ground dragging Afsoon and the Western woman inside.

The arrest records and internment documents were studied by the admissions officers, and the police guards and their prisoners were led to a row of holding cells on the first floor. The place was dank and filthy. There were patches of blood and other bodily fluids on the narrow hallway floors, and a stench of urine and feces emanated from the cagelike cells. Every holding cell was filled beyond capacity with chador-clad women who watched the procession in silence with heads bowed. It was as if the shades of hell were watching the march of the damned.

The jail guards stopped at the third cage and unlocked the chain-link gate.

"Get back, you *kundes*," he snarled as the prisoners were dragged or pushed into the chilly enclosure.

One prisoner was lying on the wet floor and did not move quickly enough and the guard shouted at her, "Hurry up, *jendeh*!"

The five women who could stand were crammed in among the other fifteen prisoners, and Afsoon and the Western woman were dropped in the middle of the floor. After a few more insults, the guards and the police officers left.

A mature woman stepped over to the two hapless inmates lying on the floor and said, "And I thought it could not get any worse here. I take back everything I said about how bad it is for us. Look at these poor wretches."

"They need help. Bring some water and clean clothes," another woman said.

One of the younger girls laughed at the suggestion that there might be something clean in that place; but clothes, a thin bar of soap, and a pail of grey water appeared from some corner of the cell. Several women began to strip the Western woman, who only moaned in feeble protest as her blood-soaked blouse and Western style denim trousers were removed, revealing deep untreated cuts and spreading bruises that covered almost her entire body. Her face was almost unrecognizable as belonging to a human being, let alone bearing any resemblance to the woman she was before the beatings. The bruises were of different colors, obviously having been inflicted over several days. They did the best they could to clean her up, and one older woman was able to produce a semi-clean old chador to cover her battered nakedness.

"I know who this one is," the old woman announced somberly. "She is the Western newspaper reporter who was arrested while she was talking to the families of female prisoners in front of Orumiyeh Prison last week. She has been gang-raped; you could see that when we cleaned her up."

"She won't make it, and no one will ever know except us what happened to her. Her poor family. No one will ever hear from us or care about what we say; we're not people."

The other women—working on Afsoon—were hardened to every brutality that men could inflict on women and girls, they thought, until they removed the thirteen-year-old's clothes.

"Sweet Allah in heaven!" gasped one of the younger ones. "Her privates are torn to pieces. Look at those awful cuts from a whip. And she has the stink. The monster who raped her tore open her female part and her bowel part so they leak. Someone hated her, hated her more than can be imagined; and she is just a child."

"She is in here for the same crime that most of us are; she was raped. Her rapist or his family did the beating and whipping. I am almost certain that her rapist was not even charged."

There was a sad nodding of heads by every woman in the cage. They set to work removing the tattered remnants of cloth from her chador that were embedded in the dozens of crisscross lacerations on Afsoon's back. The level of pain occasioned by those gentle ministrations aroused Afsoon, and she began to moan involuntarily. She opened her eyes and looked at the ghostlike figures surrounding her.

"Where am I? What happened to me?"

"This is Piranshahr Jail, sweet girl. You were raped, and that got you arrested. Do you remember any of that?"

"Just the rape part. It was awful. I think someone hit me, and I was unconscious. I don't remember the rest."

"Try not to think about it, dear," the old woman said. "There is nothing you can do but try to get better. We'll do our best to keep you from getting infected, but you must be brave. What we are doing is necessary, but you will suffer the pains of the damned before you finally heal up. We are sorry to hurt you, but it is out of love."

The Western woman reporter died in the night while the inmates ate a watery porridge made of wheat meal. The guards ate *khoresht e gheimeh* [split pea and lamb stew]. Her corpse was not removed for two days when she began to emit a sweet-sick stench. Afsoon was aware of her death; it brought to her memory the smell of her beloved Yasmin from a lifetime ago.

With nothing else to talk about for the three months Afsoon was in the jail, she and her sister inmates shared their stories. One woman and her husband had been put in the Piranshahr Jail six months ago after they were found printing a book in a basement room of their house that criticized the ruling regime's interpretation of Islam as encouraging terrorism and murder. She was no stranger to beatings, and had been raped repeatedly at the jail when she was first admitted. She had not seen her husband since her arrest. Two of the women—including the older woman who had sympathized with Afsoon—were in jail for having committed crimes recognized even by Westerners; one was a thief, and the other—the older woman—had assisted her husband in a series of murders that were part of a burglary spree. She had been in the jail for a year awaiting transfer to Evin Jail in the northern suburbs of Tehran. She had not yet had a trial. One young girl had assaulted a policeman who was arresting her for wearing indecent Western attire in a public gathering. For that, she had her teeth knocked out, and was raped before being jailed two months ago. She had not had a trial either.

The remaining eighteen women had been arrested for the crime of having been raped—the theory under Sharia law being that she had willingly enticed a man (or men) to commit rape on her. That she was raped was prima facie evidence of her willingness to engage in illicit sex and to entice a man to commit sin. It is the most common reason for the imprisonment of women in Iran even though it completely defies Western logic. *Zina-be-onf* [rape] is related to adultery, which is a very serious crime in Iran. The evidentiary requirements of the *Qur'an* and Sharia law are almost impossible for a woman to surmount; so, despite a judge's acceptance that she was raped, the woman usually was considered to be a complicit adulterer or fornicator. In the case of several of the inmates, their rapist had even confessed. Some of the women had received *diyyeh* [compensation for injuries sustained equal to a woman's dowry] from a lenient judge who exercised his prerogatives under *tazir* "judge's knowledge evidence" judicial principles and saw to it that she—as the victim—settled the case by accepting *jirah* [compensation] in exchange for withdrawing the charges or forgiving her rapist before she was jailed. The *jirah* settlement usually condemned the woman by being considered a formal confession of complicity in the crime of sexual contact outside of marriage or temporary marriage—which is permitted under *Qur'anic* law [legitimated by *Qur'an* 4:24], according to Shi'i tradition but considered *haram* [evil and forbidden] by the Sunnis. Some of the rapists received harsh *tazir* penalties, such as a 100-lash beating. None of them to that point, however, received the harsh condemnation prescribed by the *Qur'an*—death by hanging. And none of the women was excused for her crime—having been raped. Afsoon was in good company by being imprisoned on the same charge.

Nassir finally found out where Afsoon had been taken and—with an appropriate bribe of a corrections officer—he was able to learn that the girl was still alive. By Iranian law, a woman is allowed one collect telephone call a month—in some cases even one a week—and one visit from one person per month. Nassir submitted all the necessary paperwork and was allowed a fifteen-minute visit with Afsoon in late February. He was allowed to bring a little food and a gift—if that gift passed inspection by the penal authorities—before being handed over to the inmate.

"How are you doing, Afsoon?" he asked as soon as they were seated across a metal table from each other.

Afsoon's wrists were shackled on eighteen-inch long chains attached to the top of the steel table, and her right ankle was attached to the floor. She looked at him sadly.

"How do you think? For one thing, it is terribly boring. There is nothing to do but work, work, work, and listen to all the stupid religious talk on the local Chiches radio station. This is a terrible place. You can't even imagine. I am sorry for how bad I smell, but ever since I was raped, my bowels pass matter into my female parts without my control. It mixes with my yellow water, and many others have the same problem. Yesterday, one of my friends was taken out into the exercise yard. Two men held her down, and another one chopped off her right hand with an axe. Then they torched the bleeding stump and dragged her back into our cell and dumped her on the floor. The day before that, one of the women in the cage next to us was given 100 lashes, just like the *Qur'an* says to do. She died. Do you know why?"

"No," Nassir said in a subdued tone. "Why?"

"She went on a date with a Christian. Her father said that they almost did sex. She said it was not true. But in our wonderful religion, a woman's testimony is only worth half—less than half—of a man's. He won; she lost; and now, she's dead. Something like that goes on here every day. It is called justice."

"Surely, when you get to present your case before the judge...."

"The mullah?... That's a laugh. There will be no lawyers and no presenting cases. We are supposed to have our so-called trial in two months when the mullah comes through. Then, he will sentence every one of us to hang. The next day they will haul us the Evin prison in Tehran, and that will be the last anyone hears about Afsoon."

She hung her head and fought back tears.

"I have heard those terrible things. I at least half believe them. I can't let anymore happen to you. You remember the nomads who used to come to Kandovan Village while we lived there?" he said conspiratorily, looking around for prying ears.

"Yes, why?"

"The Bakhtiaris came down from the Zagros Mountains to go to their winter range along the coast."

There are about two million nomads from a number of different ethnic groups that still live the nomadic life traveling with their sheep, goats, and horses in spring and autumn in search of pastures. Many have been persecuted by the Khomeini and Rahimi regimes and have met disruption of their ancestral nomadic travel routes.

"They stopped at Shakibaie's tents two weeks ago to trade, and I got a chance to talk to some of them. Seems that a couple of their women were kidnapped in Qushchu by Rahimi's police. They charged them with theft and sent them to the Piranshahr Jail. You might even have seen them. The nomads said they were innocent. When they got to the jail, the guards raped them and got them charged for inciting lust in a pure Muslim man. Maybe you have heard of such a charge."

"Not maybe. But what does that have to do with me?"

"The nomads are angry. Very, very angry. They already hate the Rahimi regime," now Nassir was almost whispering, "and this is the last coffin nail. They are going to get their women back. They think that the jailers in Piranshahr will let the hand amputations wait until they can get everything done at Evin. It's a famous place, you know.

"All of the women in Piranshahr Jail will have their trial at the same time as you. The next morning, you will all be put on a bus and transported to Tehran, to Evin Prison. It is a long trip. Anything can happen."

He gave Afsoon a meaningful look. She returned his glance, but hers was quizzical.

"Trust me, little sister, and be ready. I brought you a present, maybe two."

He reached behind his back on the metal chair and produced Afsoon's beloved, *Fereshte*, now somewhat the worse for wear.

The light of life came back into Afsoon's eyes for the first time in a month.

"My angel, my baby."

She gave Nassir one of her most winning smiles.

"Thank you, big brother. A million thanks."

She made a quick grab for the doll, afraid that this might be happening in a dream.

"Not so fast. There's something else. Don't let any of them see this."

He gave a quick serious look to see if a guard was paying attention. None were.

Nassir pushed the doll across the table and under it, a man's folding straight razor.

It would be fatal to be caught with the weapon; so, Afsoon gave her own quick look around the room before the guards took notice of her. She snatched the doll and held it to her chest and deftly let the razor drop into the folds of her chador. She looked around once more, then folded her wrist under and slipped the contraband blade into the fold of her chador's cuff. No one paid the two young people any heed.

"You will be on the bus when the nomads come. Do whatever you have to do to get off and to go with them. I gave them all the money I had to get you a horse. They told me that you could ride away with them, but they would not wait for you. And, Afsoon, I know you have come to care for the women who are going to their deaths; but you cannot help any of them or let any of them get to your horse before you do. Do you understand?"

"Yes. I will do whatever I have to do. This is a chance to live."

"It is. They are signaling that it is time to leave, but I'll be back in a month and in two months and then I can give you more details. Good-bye, little sister. I love you."

"And I love you. Thank you again for bringing *Fereshte*."

One day before the mass trial was scheduled, Afsoon and the women in her cage worked breaking rocks for the macadam surface of the road leading to the jail. It was backbreaking labor and very exacting. Every stone fragment had to be no larger than 2.5 inches across and no smaller than 1.5 inches. Girls who were careless or got tired and did not produce received a lash stroke or worse. Afsoon had toughened as she healed during the five months she had been in the jail, one of the blessings of her youth, but also a gift of genetics that gave her both the strength and the will to get over severe trials. The worse fate was quite obvious. One of the cruelest of the guards selected one girl every day to drag off into the ditch along the road. When the girl returned to work, she could hardly walk, let alone work. Afsoon fingered her razor when she saw him coming towards her.

"Come with me," he peremptorily ordered her.

She kept her gaze on the ground and walked ahead of him as he directed her to do. She was aware of him pausing to look around to avoid being seen by witnesses.

He stopped at a point in the road that was higher above the ditch below. Afsoon could see that the tall grass there had been pressed down as if deer had used it as a bedding ground.

"Get down there," he commanded.

She ignored him and walked ahead about twenty yards to where the road made a fairly acute angle and was considerably higher than the ground below. At the curve, there was a culvert where one branch of the dry streambed passed under the road, and the other continued alongside the roadway where she and the guard had come.

He shouted, "Stop, *jendeh*!!"

She moved her folding single-edged razor out of the sleeve cuff of her chador. Her heart was pounding, and she broke into a cold sweat. She kept her gaze down but used her peripheral vision to monitor the brute's progress as he came up behind her. She had known that her turn would come, and she practiced flicking open the clasp knife hinge of the razor over and over again in her cell when no one was watching. She had practiced endlessly her next move.

He put his powerful left hand on her left shoulder and gave her a strong push towards the downslope of the road. She let herself be moved by his contact; but she moved more than he had anticipated, which put him off balance. She swiftly bent her knees and pirouetted around so that she faced him in a three-quarters turn. She fixed her eyes on his, and he was startled. He did not see her right arm make an oblique swing at full strength and full extension in a semi-circular arc.

He was scarcely aware of the clean razor slash that nearly decapitated him. He was staring at her with a surprised look as he died and toppled backward down the incline and into the ditch in front of the open culvert. He landed head down and exsanguinated into the culvert. Afsoon shuddered in revulsion and looked all around her to be sure she had not been seen. Satisfied that no one was aware, she scuffed dirt over the areas of blood on the roadside and nimbly trotted down to where the man lay, his head canted unnaturally on his neck.

Afsoon was considerably stronger than her size, age, and gender would suggest, owing in large part to the heavy labor that she had done for four months. She gingerly avoided stepping in the large pool of blood that encircled the guard's head and neck and pulled, twisted, and pushed him into the culvert until his corpse could not be seen from the road. She was pouring sweat and breathing as hard as if she had just run a mile sprint. She maintained sufficient presence of mind to cut the straps to his canteen and drank nearly three-quarters of the precious liquid in a couple of gulping swallows. Then she used the rest of the water and the man's uniform blouse to wash off her razor. She inspected it and could see no blood. She had gotten a little blood on her right hand, and she finished the rest of the water washing it. Finally, she found some deadfall branches and tore up handfuls of tall grass and stuffed them into the culvert to cover her would-be rapist.

She inspected the scene of the crime and was content that she was safe.

"Never again. *Never* again!" she muttered with a hiss.

She moved quickly back up onto the macadam road and hurried back to where the girls were chopping rocks. She thought she might faint from excitement and exhaustion; but when no one paid her any attention, she calmed down and resumed bashing her share of rocks with the eight-pound sledgehammer. There were two guards remaining who made periodic checks on the girls to be sure they were working hard enough and suffering enough to satisfy the requirements of their superiors. They did not seem to be aware that one of the guards was missing, and neither did any of the girls.

Their neck collars were reattached, and the chain of linked slaves was marched back to the jail.

When they were shoved back into their cages, the oldest of the guards gave a hollow gallows laugh and said, "Eat hearty, girlies. Get some rest. Big day tomorrow."

Every girl and woman in all six cages knew it was going to be a big day. Tomorrow they would make their appearance before the mullah/judge and then get on a prison bus for transport to Evin Prison and execution. No one in any of the cages spoke that night.

# CHAPTER TWENTY-TWO

**"Women make up one half of society. Our society will remain back-ward and in chains unless its women are liberated, enlightened and educated."**
**-Saddam Hussein,** *The Revolution and Woman in Iraq*

The courtroom of mullah Haji Zamaani Fard was tiny in comparison to the courts of major Iranian cities. It served to adjudicate simple cases such as offenses against the religion, offenses against morality, minor nonviolent felonies, and crimes by women—none of which required attorneys or the presentation of evidence. The most common offenses handled by Haji Zamaani Fard were tazir crimes that only required "judge's knowledge" and therefore only the Haji's opinion. Piranshahr—indeed the whole West Azerbaijan Province—was an exercise in tedium for the learned and traveled cleric and self-styled lawyer and judge because of the banality of the cases he had to see and the travel required of him as a circuit judge.

Although she had more or less become accustomed to her rank body odor, Afsoon was now very much aware of it. Washing did not help more than a few minutes because the offensive odor came from inside her, and she had no control over it. She was well aware that the same pungent scent of feces and urine came from several other girls and women. Afsoon was very much attuned to her surroundings and looked furtively about the room to see if anyone was paying attention to her. Any minute, she expected to be arrested and beaten savagely. She had not heard even a rumor that the guard's body had been found or even that he was missing. That gave her scant comfort. The current threat was enough.

The courtroom had no seats except for the judge and a court recorder. The prisoners—defendants—stood at a low rail; and behind them were arrayed a phalanx of guards, witnesses, and prosecutors. No spectators or reporters were allowed. Afsoon presumed that the trial would be very long, and she was already tired and feeling weak before the first words were uttered.

She was wrong about the length of time it would take to go through the separate trials of forty-three women. Haji Zamaani Fard was nothing if not efficient. Operating under the simplicities of the Sharia law—especially as it applied to crimes by women—he adopted an especially efficient procedure. The process was all the more efficient because in Iran, ninety-nine percent of accused women in these cases receive no legal representation. In Haji Zamaani Fard's court, that number was 100 percent. He did not have to bear the tedium and delay of hearing witness or defense testimony, attorneys' arguments, or objections.

Eyes down and not moving, the women heard the judge present their cases, mostly in aggregate, since the charges were very similar for most of the defendants.

"Criminals," he began. "I have studied your cases, and you are hereby found guilty. Those of you—most of you—have been charged with very serious moral crimes that I choose to equate with adultery. You are enticers of men; you have committed lustful, carnal acts; and your shame shall accompany you to hell. The Prophet, may Allah's blessings be upon his Rasul, described it so; and the *Qur'an* leaves no doubt about such sins and crimes. Many of you have confessed; and for those who have been stubborn in your lack of repentance, my judge's knowledge is sufficient. Your crimes are *tazir* crimes as much as if a man were facing me on a charge of rape."

Haji Zamaani Fard then read each prisoner's name so charged, convicted, and condemned. Afsoon was numb with fear and despair as the names and fates of the women were quickly passed by. She became aware of herself when her name was read.

"Afsoon," he stated, then paused. "I see no family name. Is there a clerical error?"

"No, your honor, this one is not a citizen, not a person. Apparently, the circumstances of her birth were such that her name has never been recorded in the *shenas nameh* [the official Iranian document issued at birth that serves as identification for the rest of the person's life.]."

The judge nodded then intoned his now monotonous judgment, "Afsoon, you are unrepentant; you could not produce the required four pure Islamic male witnesses to verify that a crime of *zina bil Jabar* [rape] has occurred."

He spoke in Urdu, presuming that the ignorant country girl standing before him would only be able to speak the guttural language of her inconsequential village.

"This is your sentence: you shall be taken to the women's section of Evin Prison in the north of Tehran where you shall be hanged by the neck until you are dead. Before that sentence is carried out, the good corrections officers shall rape you repeatedly to satisfy the demands of the *Qur'an* that you are certainly not a virgin. A virgin—by the mercy of Allah, may his holy name be praised—goes automatically to heaven. And you—a temptress and seducer of innocent men—shall go to hell. The rapes will guarantee that fate. Our foremost religious lawyers have declared it to be just. Of course, it is understood that the men must wash first, lest they be guilty of a moral sin. You will be transported immediately after *Fajr*."

So went all of the judicial procedures for every woman but four. They were guilty of crimes of murder, stealing, and blasphemy—in this particular instance for having criticized the government regime. The murderer and the blasphemer were sentenced to death by stoning, and the two thieves were sentenced to public amputation of their right hands.

Had Afsoon had an attorney and had Haji Zamaani Fard been inclined to care about such things, the argument might have been made that Iran had signed the Convention on the Rights of the Child along with almost every other nation in the world. That convention expressly prohibits the execution for child offenders under the age of eighteen. The prosecuting attorney could—and regularly did—counter with the argument that Iran must claim special dispensation in cases where the Convention on the Rights of the Child—a Western invention, after all—was deemed to be "incompatible with Islamic jurisprudence." That argument almost always carried sway in Iran where half of all girls in rural areas—where most of the population resided—were married by age thirteen. The issue never came up in thirteen-year-old Afsoon's case.

Afsoon shuffled silently out of the courtroom under close guard. Many of the women and girls were softly crying or moaning in terror. In her reading about Italy, she had learned of a famous bridge in Venice that led from the courts to the prison where executions took place. Crossing that bridge was a walk to one's death, and it became aptly referred to as "the bridge of sighs." The walk back to the jail could be similarly designated. Each girl awaited the morrow with the darkest of thoughts—the loss of all hope for eternity. Afsoon could not sleep for fear that the guard's body would be discovered, and she would be caught. She would not have been able to sleep anyway because she shared the dread of what the next day would bring.

She clutched *Fereshte* and cooed, "*Shab be khey Nazanin* [good night, sweetheart]."

> **The Prophet (peace be upon him) said: A man will not be asked as to why he beat his wife.**
>
> *-Hadith, Abu Dawud,* **11:2142 9+**

# CHAPTER TWENTY-THREE

## Shinabad, Iran, June 12, 1994

The three convict buses got a late start after *Fajr* prayers because one bus broke down and there was a wait to bring in another one. The vehicles were twenty-passenger Russian-made middle-sized public route marshrutka buses that were a hold over from a large purchase made by the government in 1984. The prisoners had to be shackled by one leg to their seats and, with the change of a bus, the tedious process had to be repeated. The sun was sitting just over the eastern horizon by the time they left Piranshahr Jail to start the nearly fourteen and a half hour 358-mile trip southeast to Tehran. The late start meant that they would go only two or three miles before having to stop to get the guards some breakfast.

Lacking air-conditioning or fans, the buses were already stifling, and the pungent aromas of women with untreated post-traumatic recto-vaginal fistulae, old sweat on their infrequently washed bodies, and their fetid clothing approached the unbearable point before they had cleared the last street in Piranshahr. Afsoon was embarrassed by her body odor, but was resigned to it being a permanent part of her as it was to the other unfortunate female prisoners. She recognized that some of her sweat smell came from the anxiety she felt from her fear of being discovered as the killer of the rapist guard. The guards and drivers were disgusted by the heat and odors from the women and the exhaust from the benzene-burning buses and were anxious to be able to make their first stop.

The Valfajr highway was straight and narrow and passed through open farmland. The caravan of prison buses was headed to the edge of Shinabad in Ostan-e Azerbaijan-e Gharbi where the son of the jail commander ran a small restaurant that prospered from trade with the jail guards and occasional transport caravans of prisoners. It was tedious going with the usual ancient tractors, donkey carts, and cattle herders, all of whom owned the road. The worst block to the traffic occurred almost exactly midway between Piranshahr city and the village.

A clan of Bakhtiari nomads with dozens of black shrouded men, nearly a hundred of their women, and a herd of several hundred goats and sheep were being driven to a new summer pasture near the border with Iraq. Their numbers clogged the road to the degree that it was impassable by the buses. The dress code among the Bakhtiari was the opposite of the usual seen among the Muslims of Iran. The men were dressed in black flowing robes with nothing but an eye slit to identify them as human. They all carried rifles, bandoliers of ammunition crisscrossing their chests, and swords. The women were bareheaded and all wore brilliant dresses of multilayered and multicolored cloth. Mixed with the colors of their fine horses and the white of their goats and sheep, the Bakhtiari presence was dramatic.

Exasperated, the driver and guards of the lead prisoner bus stopped completely and got out. The chief corrections officer approached a Bakhtiari man who seemed to be in charge.

"We are on government business, get those animals off the highway; so, we can pass," he demanded officiously in Farsi.

The nomad said something in a language that the officer could not understand. The nomads speak a Bakhtiari dialect belonging to the Luri language that they brought with them when they were driven northward from their ancestral southwestern Iranian homelands into the Zagros Mountains by the intolerant Khomeini Islamic regime soon after the revolutionaries took control in 1979. What the corrections officer did not understand was a string of insults from a man who hated the totalitarian regime in Tehran. The Bakhtiari had been trading in Shinabad and had listened to the villagers' tales of the fire that occurred in the Enghelab Elementary Girls' School that killed several girls and burned nearly forty of them. The cause of the fire was an exploding oil heater, part of the school's cheap and hazardous heating system. The root cause—every villager believed—was the callous disregard for the children of the village by Rahimi's government. The Bakhtiari were spoiling for a fight.

The head guard walked back to each of the other two buses and asked the drivers and guards if any of them could speak the childish tongue of the nomads. One of the nomads rode up behind him and politely waited until he had finished his insulting description. Then, he spoke to the guard in clear educated Farsi.

"I speak both Farsi and Luri. I will translate if you wish."

"Get those dirty *kaffirs* off the road. You can tell them that."

"It would be best if you and the other guards came as a group to convey your wishes to the men of the clan. It is the courtesy that our people require."

The guard rolled his eyes towards the heavens in exasperation, but he ordered the other guards and drivers to follow him to meet with the "polytheists." The nomad ignored the severe insult to the Muslim nomad clan and brought up the rear of the group. When the guards, drivers, and their translator were assembled in a tight group in front of the buses, a dozen Bakhtiari men rode their horses up and surrounded the guards. It was a tense moment for them; but the translator reassured them that this was just the Bakhtiari way; and the men on horseback should be humored.

He spoke to the assemblage of black-clad and heavily armed men telling them word for word what the guard had said, including the characterization of the Luri language as being "a childish tongue," that the clan members were "dirty," and that they were considered to be *kaffirs* [unbelievers] and "polytheists." The Bakhtiari men were silent. The malevolence in their eyes was the only thing that betrayed their fury.

"Tell them how we regard the criminal regime in Tehran. Tell them about our men they have killed and our women they have raped and put into prison. Tell them this is their last day on earth," said the Bakhtiari head man.

The translator turned his horse around and faced the guards. He gave a verbatim translation of his leader's accusations. The guards looked at him then at the surrounding horsemen in offended shock. Then, several of them reached for their guns.

The Bakhtiari were ready and were much faster than the guards. A one-minute fusillade poured out of the nomad's guns. Caught in the deadly crossfire, every prison official was dead and lying on the ground before they could fire a single shot.

"Clear that garbage from the road and get the women off the buses. Find our women and put them on horses. Nassir, find your woman and bring her to me," the headman ordered.

Nomad men and women dragged the bodies off the road and dumped them into the ditch and set them on fire. Three men entered each of the buses carrying the guard's keys to the chains that held the cowering female prisoners in their seats. Nassir took off his head covering and marched boldly into each bus and demanded to have Afsoon identify herself. As the women moved slowly out of the buses because of their cramped hips and legs, Afsoon hurried up to embrace Nassir.

"You did save me. You promised, and you came. I love you, big brother!"

He gave her a bear hug and said, "You are safe for now. We have to talk to the headman, and he will tell what we have to do next."

The headman explained to his people, to the liberated women, and separately to Nassir and Afsoon what his plan was for each of them. The Bakhtiari would herd their goats and sheep to the border crossing at Piranshahr and with them, the men and women of the clan would pass through customs into Iraq. It would be chaotic, as that crossing station always was; and that chaos would work in their favor. The other prisoners were on their own, but he had the clan women load the buses with food and weapons.

"Can any of you women drive a bus?" he asked the prisoners.

Ten of the women raised their hands.

"Drive back through Piranshahr and turn onto route 26. Go about ten miles then turn left onto an old dirt road and go about two miles to where you will be going on a narrow dirt track with a deep valley below. Get out of the buses and put them into gear and push on the gas pedal and jump out. The buses will fall down the cliff and be lost to sight. Then walk as quickly as you can the six or seven miles to the border crossing. The jail people will not miss you for two or three days because they expect the buses to be going to Tehran and back. Don't hurry. You all have your papers. Wait until there is a crowd crossing into Iraq and join them in small groups. Don't panic. You will be safe in southern Iraq where most of the people are Shi'ites. But you must remember not to criticize the Rahimi regime or let them know that you have been prisoners. Tell anyone who asks that you are refugees from Baghdad who were driven out by Saddam Hussein. It happens all of the time, and they will believe you. God speed."

The women, like free people everywhere, exhibited a renewal of their energy and sprang into action. None of them were strangers to hard work or to danger. They drove to a side road and turned around and headed back towards freedom. Miraculously, the hordes of animals and people parted to let them through without delay.

Afsoon and Nassir climbed the mountainous off-road trails with the Bakhtiari clan people and crossed the border into Iraq three weeks later. The mountains were cool; and the nomads, ignoring borders, herded their animals into meadows and pastures to feed. Their women set up a temporary tent city. The headman summoned Afsoon and Nassir to his tent on the day the camp preparations were finished.

"We have gone as far as we can, and it is time for you to leave us, brother and little sister. I pray to Allah, may his name be praised, that you will find a safe place and that you never have anything more to do with the evil monsters in Tehran. You will be safe in Basrah, and one of our men will guide you to the road that takes you there. Go with God, my friends."

"Muhammad, we cannot thank you enough. We are forever in your debt. Who knows, life is long; and one day one or the other of us may be able to return the favor."

"No thanks is necessary. It was a good day to be able to rid the world of a few of Grand Ayatollah Ali ibn Abi Rahimi's creatures. Consider us even."

With their guide, Nassir and Afsoon rode along highway 3 from Piranshahr towards Al Basrah, Iraq, glad to be free at last from the terrors of their native country. Afsoon held onto her horse's reins and her only worldly possession, her battered rag doll, *Fereshte*.

# CHAPTER TWENTY-FOUR

## Boston and Cambridge, Massachusetts, September, 1995

G.R. III called his son and informed him that his friend, Seth ben Joseph Avotaynu—president of the Boston Federal Reserve Bank on Atlantic Avenue—would be expecting a call. Mr. Avotaynu arranged for Gideon to be an intern at the bank. He was selected to assist the economists and bankers as they conducted research into the economy and prepared Boston's portion of the *Beige Book*, which the Federal Open Market Committee issues two weeks before each of its eight annual Federal Open Market Committee meetings. It is formally the *Summary of Commentary on Current Economic Conditions*, a report published by the United States Federal Reserve Board. Gideon's job was to assist one of the directors in his effort to gather anecdotal information on current economic conditions. The education was valuable and cost only a few hours a week. The opportunity to have acquaintanceship with the most powerful people in the world of finance was invaluable, and Gideon made a careful effort to cultivate relationships with them over the years after his internship and formal education was completed.

One of the bankers he met during a Reserve Board meeting at the bank was an Israeli Orthodox Jewish woman named Miriam bat Ezekiel. She approached the boy at the close of one of the last meetings he was scheduled to attend.

"Hello, Mr. Rothsberger," she said.

She was friendly but kept a distance of four feet between them and did not proffer her hand. He knew better than to try and shake the hand of a married Orthodox woman.

"Why don't you just call me Gideon? In this gathering of important people, I am a bit young to be regarded with such formality."

"You do yourself credit to be humble, Gideon. I am aware of your many quite remarkable accomplishments. I have watched you in the committee meetings. You know when to keep quiet and when to speak. Then, what you have to say is well researched and well delivered."

"Thank you."

"I didn't come to flatter you, Gideon. Rather, certain of our mutual friends have asked me to offer you an invitation to visit with us in Tel Aviv. We will be extending an invitation to your friend, Aaron Schmuel, as well. Would your university work permit you to spend the month of June with us?"

Without much of a pause, Gideon said, "Yes."

"Excellent. Ostensibly, you will be enrolled in an advanced course in banking economics at Tel Aviv University. You will actually attend some classes and functions that will verify your attendance, and you will receive graduation accreditation that will transfer to your doctoral program at MIT. I know that you have had conversations with some people in our government, and I do not have to emphasize the need to be discreet about what I am going to say next."

"I will not betray confidential information."

"Good. You will be spending a majority of your time in Israel with people from the governmental agency with whom you have had an association on a previous visit, and they will begin your education in their special technical areas of expertise. By the way, your parents, the American officer you met, and your MIT major professor, Dr. Kristina Shimazaki, and department co-chairs, Drs. Leif Erik Nielson and Karl L. Nielson—I think I have their names correct and that they are not related—have all agreed to this plan, each on a need-to-know basis."

"I will get everything in order for the trip in June."

"Make sure you bring both of your passports."

Gideon nodded.

Gideon was impassioned about his work at the university, and launched into an intense course of nuclear physics and targeted structural engineering for the building and maintenance of nuclear energy facilities. He was determined to know everything there was to know about finance, building laboratories, security, electronics, safety, and computer management of the nuclear industry. It was obvious that he had selected a tough nut to chew, and he went at the project with all the zeal he could muster. Much of his work in advanced mathematics took place at the Clay Mathematics Institute (CMI) on the fourth floor of their building on Bow Street in Cambridge. At the

CMI, Gideon accepted one of the major challenges of all mathematics as the problem for his doctoral dissertation—the P vs NP problem.

After an extensive study of what appeared to be unsolvable mathematical problems, the directors of the CMI established what they termed the "seven millennial prize problems." The program was designed to alert the general public to the frontiers of unsolved mathematical problems and to honor the "heroes" of math. A prize of $1 million was offered to anyone who could provide a solution to any of the seven problems that would satisfy the very astute directors of the institute.

The problems that had vexed the best minds in mathematics for years, even generations, were: the Birch and Swinnerton-Dyer Conjecture, the Hodge Conjecture, the Navier-Stokes Equations, the P vs NP problem, the Poincaré Conjecture, the Riemann Hypothesis, and the Yang-Mills Theory. Of those, only one had been solved—the Poincaré Conjecture. The prize was awarded to a Russian, and his career was enhanced to the level of a Nobel Prize Laureate with that award.

Gideon chose the P vs NP problem because it dealt with a core mathematical issue of computer science. The problem came to the attention of the mathematical and computer science intelligentsia in a remarkable work—Stephen Cook and Leonid Levin, *The Complexity of Theorem Proving Procedures*, 1971. Gideon's choice, at the suggestion of the two Drs. Nielson—co-chairmen of the mathematics department at MIT—of that problem to study was a very serious calculated risk, since there were a great many of the best brains in the world already working on the problem and had been doing so long before the CMI prize cast light on the need for its solution.

The problem would seem to be deceptively simple to the uninitiated. In brief, it asks a question: Can every problem whose solution can be quickly verified by a computer also be quickly solved by a computer? A major part of the quandary has to do with practicality; can a computer or any bank of computers solve every problem if enough computer power is applied over enough time? Of course, pragmatically, the question comes down to this: Is the problem solvable in a time period that makes the effort useful and not one that approaches infinity? And, this problem coincided with every one of Gideon Emmanuel Rothsberger IV's needs. It would provide the expertise he needed in mathematics, computer science, and engineering, and would yield the young man incontestable prestige, a million dollars, and a doctorate from MIT that would be the envy of the elite in all of those fields worlwide. The risk was that the effort was an all-or-nothing proposition—a colossal gamble. If he failed to solve the riddle, he would have wasted his time at MIT and would not get his doctorate and would have to start over again. That was unacceptable to the ambitious and fully self-confident young man. Failure would deprive him of the fame and the prize, which were not inconsequential factors either.

Gideon had to start work—and work it was—on the fundamental issue for which the prize was being offered. What the computer science world needed was whether a problem could be solved quickly, efficiently, and cost effectively. In this mathematical and computer science problem, "quickly" implies the existence of an algorithm—a step-by-step procedure for making complicated calculations. In computer function, algorithms are used for calculation, data processing, and automated reasoning. Algorithms were Gideon's specialty.

Polynomial time is the reasonable time period sought by computer scientists and operators. It is the length of time required to perform some operation where there are repetitive steps, and the overall time required is a function of the number of steps to the power—exponent—of some value. Importantly, polynomial time algorithms are reasonable to compute—not a lifetime or greater endeavor. For the other type of algorithms—exponential—the time to run them grows too rapidly to be able to compute exact solutions in all cases and are therefore impractical. The general class of questions for which some algorithm can provide an answer in polynomial time is termed "class P" or simply "P." For some questions, there is no known way to find an answer quickly; but if one is provided with information showing what the answer is, it may be possible to verify the answer quickly. The class of questions for which an answer can be verified in polynomial time is called "NP."

Many mathematical calculations involve checking such a large number of possible solutions that they are beyond the current capability of any computer or network of computers however massive or costly. However, the answers to some calculations are quick and easy to verify as being correct. Gideon's task was to determine which situation is true: P=NP or P≠NP. Does P=NP or not? If Gideon determined that P≠NP, it would mean that there are problems in NP—the class of questions for which an answer can be verified in polynomial time—that are more difficult to compute than to verify. While such computer problems cannot be *solved* in polynomial time, the answer can be *verified* in polynomial time. Aside from being an important problem in computational theory and for real world computer function, a proof either way would have profound implications for mathematics, cryptography, algorithm research, artificial intelligence, game theory, multimedia processing, cryptography, cryptanalysis, and several other fields.

NP problems for a computer are presented in a myriad of ways every day to businesses or any other entity that must winnow down choices from many to a few. An example would be the use of a hyper-computer to determine which of a thousand applicants for two hundred jobs available in a new automotive plant in Canada should be chosen and how they would be distributed into the one hundred new satellite branches of the company. Once the computer begins to consider the total number of ways of choosing the people who will be hired and placed from the total number of applicants, it will become apparent that the number of ways to make the choice is greater than the number of atoms in the entire known universe. Not even in the most fertile imagination can a supersupercomputer be conceived of whereby every possible combination and permutation of choice can be employed in the process of making the choices. Many mathematical calculations involve checking such a large number of possible solutions that they are beyond the current capability of *any* computer. However, the answers to some questions are quick and easy to verify as being correct. P vs NP considers if there is a way of arriving at the answers to the calculations more quickly in the first place, or at worst, if reasonable approximations are available.

Gideon started his doctoral work by whetting his appetite on a series of apparently unsolvable problems supplied by Dr. Shimazaki:

-The Collatz conjecture ($3n + 1$ conjecture)
-Create a cubic formula for solving cubic equations.
-Create a quartic—fourth degree—formula.
-Solve the Happy Ending problem for arbitrary n.
-Catalan's Mersenne conjecture
-Determine whether the series $1/2 + 1/3 + 1/4 + \ldots$ converges or diverges.
-Find two irrational square roots, the sum of which is an integer.
-Goldbach's conjecture
-Generate a formula that will provide all the pythagorean triples.
-Are there infinitely many Fibonacci primes?

In June, Gideon and Aaron traveled on separate flights to Tel Aviv Sde Dov airport. They met the transport service in the main terminal immediately outside the security area. Aaron's father, Levi, had arranged for a private minibus. The driver was holding a sign that read, LOWENSTEIN BROTHERS, a phony name for the two young men. He drove them to two different hotels, the Arlozorov Suites Hotel and the Gordon Inn. The following morning, they took taxis to the university and registered for the meetings, taking care to avoid each other as per the instructions given them by Zwi Rosenstein.

Gideon sat in the back on the right and Aaron on the left. Just before the first speaker took the podium, Gen. Rosenstein walked behind Gideon and unobtrusively tapped him on the shoulder and continued on towards the meeting hall's left exit without even glancing at Aaron. As the general and Gideon left the hall, Aaron got up and followed them out. The three walked separately until they came to a black Suburban, then they joined up and quickly got in.

"Sorry for all of the cloak and dagger, boys; but from now on, it will be best if the three of us are not seen together. We are headed to one of the Institute's offices where you will spend the day. Gideon will start getting immersed in cryptanalysis, and Aaron will get to watch and learn from the best hackers in the world—imported from Russia."

The drive took half an hour. The Suburban pulled into the garage of a nondescript apartment building, and the driver activated the garage door button that closed the door behind them.

Gideon said, "Thanks for the opportunity to be here, Gen. Rosenstein. I have been looking forward to this all year."

Zwi smiled and said, "Gideon, here is your first lesson. In the Mossad, the commanders of our little army are called 'champions,' not 'generals.'"

He laughed, and Gideon smiled.

"Seems appropriate to me," Gideon said.

A *katsa* [case officer] met the three at the exit of the garage. He was one of the largest men Gideon had ever seen. The man had a deep scar from a cut on his right cheek and was missing two fingers on his left hand. He walked with a slight limp favoring his left leg, but nothing about these apparent old injuries took anything away from the security or menace his presence represented—depending on whether or not one was in the man's favor.

"Hello, Zwi," he said. "I'll take good care of them. They need to be back to the university at four?"

"It's their cover; so, we can't have them appearing not to have attended."

General Rosenstein gestured to Gideon and Aaron to follow the case officer, then he turned around and got back into the Suburban. The two boys entered the interior of the building from the shabby cluttered garage. The exterior looked no different from several dozen cheap concrete block buildings around it. The interior was a strikingly modern facility. It was immaculate. The floors and walls were covered with sound proofing materials that—to the untrained eye—looked like a designer's space-age motif. Every office door was closed with steel doors, and none of them bore a sign indicating who was in the office or what the function of the office was.

They stopped in front of one of the unassuming doors, and the security guard motioned to Gideon.

"This is your room for most of the time this summer. It is called the Research Department and is responsible for analysis. You will be assigned to a desk, but my clearance is not high enough to know which one. Enjoy your stay."

He placed his thumb on a sensor, and a green light came on. Then, he put his eye to what looked like a hotel door peep-hole for a moment; and a second green light came on. There was a click on the door latch followed by five more, and the door slid open. The guard pointed into the bustling room, and Gideon walked in.

An attractive, all-business, red-haired, freckle-faced, young woman stepped up to him and said, "You are Gideon, I presume?"

"Yes, Ma'am."

"I am not Ma'am. I am Sergeant McGuire. You can call me Ruth. Save the Ma'am for officers, I work for a living."

"Okay, but I'm curious, if it is not too personal. Where did you get the last name of McGuire. It sounds Irish."

"Nope," she said. "I am a sabra—a native-born Israeli—and a fourth generation one at that. Have any idea what a sabra is, Gideon?"

"No ... Ruth. Please tell me."

"A sabra—pronounced "tsalar"—besides being a native-born Israeli—is a thorny old prickly pear. We're known for being prickly."

"I guess you need to be."

"We do, but the other quality of prickly pears is that they are soft and sweet on the inside—like me," she laughed.

"I think I will like the sabras. I always liked Jews, and I like the Israelis I've met."

"Very diplomatic. Now let's get to your place before people begin to talk, young man."

She had him sign the Official Secrets Act, then led him to a conference room where a dozen tired-looking people dressed very casually were seated around a long conference table in comfortable swivel chairs facing computer screens and each other. They were arguing vociferously.

Gideon looked quizzically at Ruth.

She laughed, "They're not mad, just tense and in earnest. Some might say, 'prickly.'"

Gideon nodded.

Ruth announced to the prickly Israelis that the youngster with her was a Ph.D. student from MIT who was going to spend the summer in an internship.

"You are commanded from those in authority to be nice to him."

There was a generalized theatrical groan; and then everybody, including Gideon, laughed.

Gideon was given the names of each of the analysts in their turn around the table. He looked at their eyes carefully as he heard their names, then he paused for just a moment. He nodded to each person and repeated each one's name before moving to the next person. When he came to the last person—a late middle-aged woman who reminded him of Frau Miller back at Saint Francis Woods Hebrew Academy—she gave him a doubtful look, apparently appraising his very tender youth.

She said, not unkindly, "You are the youngest person by far ever to set foot in here, Gideon. Your family must have some real juice."

He smiled, then turned to the occupants of the table and said, looking into the eyes of each person, starting from the first man he had met, "Thank you Levi, Miriam, Rebecca, Alice, Abraham, Constance, Michael, Harry, Daniel, Avril, Julius, and last but not least, Elsie."

Nobody had ever remembered their names before, and the analysts were not entirely sure they liked it since they lived and worked in the utmost anonymity.

"Impressive," said Michael. "I guess you will fit in with these hot-tempered brainiacs. Can I help you with your computer?" he asked sweetly.

Before Gideon could answer, Miriam, asked—in an equally sweet and condescending tone—"Like how to turn it on and how to use your password?"

"I'll manage," he said without elaborating that his Ph.D. work involving computer science was coming along very nicely, thank you. "How do I get a password?"

"Make one up," replied Avril. "Make it exotic, non-Israeli, and involving letters, numbers, and symbols—up to thirty of them total, and nothing that can trace you to yourself or to this holy place. And you can't write them down."

Gideon took his seat and entered his assigned login—"Number One," and without batting an eye, entered a password he made up then memorized on the spot—"SLHAN1__@#%@*trickmagicphantom. The computer screen opened and indicated that his login and passwords were accepted.

Elsie was the senior analyst, and she sat with him to see how well he could navigate. He did well, and she was satisfied. Then she gave him a task.

"Hack the Libyan Defense Ministry Intelligence network. We have been having a little difficulty gaining entrance today."

"Do I have to speak Arabic?" Gideon asked.

"English is fine. The computer can translate as you go. It is a nifty feature."

It was indeed. The other twelve left him alone, and Gideon cracked the code that yielded the password. It took him half an hour, which made him feel like he was not up to par with the rest.

"I'm in," he announced.

Twelve heads turned to him, and they all stopped their arguing.

"Let me see that," Elsie said with a dubious look on her face.

She sat in Gideon's chair, and her fingers tapped rapidly on the keys. In a few moments, she was able to use the mouse. Evidently, the young American had gained full-access entry, and the Libyan computer network had accepted him as an old family member.

"I have to admit, Gideon, we have never gotten in before. This is amazing, and you have done Israel a real service. How did you do it?"

"Math," he answered.

"I was never that good at math. I'd say it is pretty useful after all the nasty things I've spent a lifetime saying about the discipline that was for old men who can't make, change or tie their own shoes."

"Like me," Gideon said with a grin.

Elsie shook her head and laughed, "You're in, boy. Welcome to the club."

Gideon printed off literally reams of documents from the Libyan Defense Ministry. He had to be shown how to reload the paper into the printer, having skipped that class at MIT.

Late in the afternoon, he was given a fascinating tutorial on the disinformation unit in the Mossad, called LAP [Hebrew—Lohamah Psichlogit—psychological warfare]. He learned that a Trojan—a special communication device that could be planted by naval commandos deep inside enemy territory—was in need of some fundamental improvements that required someone sophisticated in very much higher math than the run-of-the-mill analyst, and Gideon was expected to be of help. Once improved, the device was expected to act as a relay station for sending out misleading transmissions to the intelligence agencies of the Muslim counties and to ad hoc terrorist groups. The messages were being made by the disinformation unit in the Mossad—the LAP—and were intended to be received by American and British listening stations. Originating from an IDF navy ship out at sea, the prerecorded digital transmissions could be picked up only by the Trojan device that would then rebroadcast the transmission on another frequency—one used for official business in the enemy country—at which point the transmission would finally be picked up by American ears in Britain. The LAP and the Trojan were already of considerable benefit; and if Gideon and the other mathematicians and signal corps experts were successful, it was hoped that subtle misguiding information could sow confusion for their enemies for years to come. Gideon was convinced that he was not there to have a school tour and thereafter to be ignored by his elders.

At the end of the day, he stood up with the others and started to walk out. Elsie stopped him.

"Gideon, after today, I think it would be good for you to spend half your time at the Nuclear Desk next door, and the other half with the crypto spooks across the hall. Okay with you?"

"Yes, Ma'am...." She gave him a look.

"Elsie."

"Better. It should be fun. I'll warn you: Both rooms are full of crazy, smart people—and I mean both words literally—who are all prickly pears. I know I don't have to tell you, but it is serious business in those rooms. Don't even think of disobeying a rule. That could be interpreted as treason, and believe you me, even the hint of the T word can ruin you."

Gideon nodded.

When the security guard—who did not volunteer his name—deposited Gideon at the Research Department and into Sergeant McGuire's care and keeping, he took Aaron to a room located nearly a city block away from the Research Desk.

"This is the Collections Department," he said. "Espionage."

The guard again showed his thumb and his retina, and like the Research Department, a heavy steel door slid open. Aaron was met by a thin, scraggly-haired man, small in stature, and dressed in an entirely nondescript and rather seedy gray suit, half a size too large for him. He wore incongruous hiking shoes. His face was pale, and he made almost no facial muscle movements. That he was alive was attested to by his intense silver-blue eyes. Something about them made one feel that this was a formidable opponent despite his small and weak appearing demeanor and body.

"Follow me, please, Aaron," the officer said. "I am Antal Disraeli, no relation to the late, great, and lamented prime minister of England, Yahweh rest his soul. I am what is known as a *katsa*—case officer. It may strike you as odd or inadequate that the Institute—which is what we sometimes call the Mossad—has only some thirty or at most forty *katsas* operating in the entire world at any one time. Incidentally, *katsa* means foundation in Hebrew, in case your knowledge of the mother tongue is rusty. I can only name three of them besides myself. We are all compartmentalized and operate on a strict need-to-know basis. You have been given a very high clearance level, only a little short of my own; and you must not betray the trust that has been given you. Any questions?"

"A couple," Aaron said. "How on earth is it possible for thirty or forty of you to run the whole Mossad operation around the world, and how do I fit in? I hope you are not just doing my father a favor and trying to make him happy by showing me around and ignoring the possibility that I can be useful."

"We *katsas* do not run the whole show by a very long shot. Remember Proverbs 11:14 'Where there is no guidance, a nation falls, but in an abundance of counselors there is safety.' That is the current formal motto of our Mossad—The Institute. The *katsas* and their agents prefer the older one, "By way of deception, thou shalt do war." Each of us has multiple agents that we run and a small army of behind-the-scenes helpers who feed us information and point us in the right direction. And, don't forget the *Sayanim*, our unique system of dedicated loyal Jewish helpers. Your father, and Gideon's father, rank high on the scale of people we owe. You are here to learn how to be an agent, probably one of mine. You will have a deep cover, and will learn to be the best liar, thief, con artist, fighter, and betrayer of our enemies that the Academy can produce."

"It's a privilege, Sir."

"We are not very formal here, Aaron. But we are very strict. The first thing we must have you do is to sign the Official Secrets Act. You are a young man, Aaron, but you are a man—remember your bar mitzvah?"

"Yes. Yes, I do."

"You are responsible for your actions. I have to tell you before we go any further; we are good friends and terrible enemies. Do not betray us. Do not talk about what you see here, or hear here, or learn here. You will not have to fear a policeman or a court. You will have to fear me. Understood?"

"Yes."

"Sign here, my boy; and you are a member of the club. We are brothers, friends, and family. You will have our backs, and we will have yours. This is a lifelong commitment."

Aaron signed the form at about that same time Gideon had signed his. They were agents of the Mossad. Gideon was fifteen years old, and Aaron was eighteen.

Aaron spent his day learning how to send and receive codes, how to create disinformation, and how to avoid being caught by the many enemies of the Jewish state. That involved walking around in a stage-set town and trying to avoid being caught by a surveillance team. He failed ten times out of twelve and was told that he was doing better than average. He would accompany a team the next day on a field day in downtown Tel Aviv. He was admonished to think about his failures of the day and to improve his hiding and evasion skills.

At dusk, Gideon and Aaron met the burly guard who had escorted them to their respective departments.

"You have one more stop before you get to head back to your hotels. Follow me, please."

"I'm pooped," said Aaron.

"Me, too," said Gideon, "but I'm really pumped up. I had a great time and learned a lot. I'm beginning to think the Israelis are pretty much invincible. I am a convert."

"I am, too, after today; and it is great to think that we're part of it. It will be a test of our resolve to avoid making a mistake and talking to someone accidentally."

"Well, I, for one, got the message. I'm never going to make that mistake."

The guard stopped at the door of a small office and knocked softly.

"Enter," came a low gravelly voice from inside.

The guard pushed the door open and ushered the two young men inside a Spartan room—metal desk, chairs, and filing cabinets, no pictures, name plates, carpets, or music.

"Sit down," the man behind the desk said, rising to greet them.

The young men recognized the man as André Lansky, one of the men who had been with them in the meeting during their first trip to Israel.

"I am the head here. You do not need to know my name or to remember my face. Welcome to the Mossad. Its full name is *Ha Mossad, le Modiyn ve le Tafkidim Mayuhadim* [the Institute for Intelligence and Special Operations]. Your fathers are distinguished and valued members of the *Sayanim*, and you two will be more deeply and more directly involved than they are. They are proud of you, and we are also. Your academic records and clean social records are both strong pluses. We expect you to live up to the expectations of your families and of the Mossad. You will have a productive summer. Make the best of your time in this building, and look forward to the time when your formal academic training is done; and we will meet again at the Academy. Thank you for your service. The training is tough, but you are strong boys and will one day be as tough as the men and women you meet here. They have been through the crucible, and so will you. Enjoy your stay in Israel."

He stood by way of announcing that the meeting was over, and the boys were escorted from his office and into a small room with two chairs and one table and several medical-appearing devices. They were given polygraph lie detector tests and told they would have at least one repeat each year and more frequently if their handler ordered them to do so. After the test, the guard led them out of the building. General Rothstein's driver was waiting. Both boys were asleep before they stopped at their hotels.

By the end of the summer, both of the newly hatched agents were fairly proficient in their respective areas—Gideon in analysis, and Aaron in espionage craftsmanship. Gideon had provided a calculus-based mathematical blueprint for the improved Trojan, and Aaron had found his lifelong niche as a covert operator and escape artist who could not be tagged by the best IDF or Mossad watchers. He had become a world-class computer hacker, almost as good as the teenage Russian prodigies who ruled the hacker world. They both looked forward with relish to their return in the following summer and their attendance at the Mossad Academy the full year following that.

# CHAPTER TWENTY-FIVE

**Amarah, Iraq, June, 1996.**

The distance from Piranshahr, Iran, to Al Basrah, Iraq is approximately 690 miles depending on the condition of the roads, and the presence of bandits, militias, armies, or sandstorms. In an air-conditioned modern car or truck, travel time is about thirteeen hours, again depending on climatic and sociopolitical conditions. Afsoon and Nassir left Piranshahr June 22, 1994, and Afsoon did not arrive in Al Basrah until October 2 of the same year. They did not have access to an air-conditioned modern vehicle and—in their wildest imaginations—they could not have gotten on an airplane in Erbil for a two-hour flight to their destination.

The two youths rode their horses to the intersection of highway 3 near the Iraqi city of Soran where their Bahtiari guide left them. The time spent near the Iran/Iraq border was frightening to them; and they decided that they had to move away from Piranshahr more rapidly; or they would fall into the hands of Rahimi's agents. Nassir went to the bazaar and was able to trade their two fine nomad horses for 734,500 Iraqi dinar (ID) [about 500 USD]— more money than either of them had ever seen. One problem they faced was the task of keeping it hidden from the prying eyes of traveling companions, national police, and other bandits.

They figured out the system and—after half an hour—were confident enough to board a freshly painted Turkish Ozlem company bus. They computed the costs and determined that with expenses for food and even poor lodging, they could only go as far as Khanaqun. It was a nervous trip because Iraq highway 4 hugs the border with Iran south to Dokan, Sulaymaniyeh, and Darbandikan. At the intersection of highways 4 and 6 near Darbandikan, they ran into trouble.

It had been a good trip to that point, taking only three days to go the first 100 miles. They shared a yogurt, a bag of coarse bread, a plate of beans, a plate of rice, a bowl of cucumber and tomato salad with olives, and a flask of clean water each for 7,345 ID (5 USD). They bought a bag of fried grain for 73 ID to eat for their second meal of the day. After the long hard ride and all of the pressure of the jail escape and the stress of the constant fear, they felt like they could rest. Afsoon was napping, and Nassir was trying to read the *Abrar-e Varzeshi* (Persian) newspaper he found in the bus terminal to see if they had been named as fugitives.

Suddenly, a small roadside improvised explosive device blew out the driver's side front tire and nearly caused the old bus to fall on its side. From across the poorly marked and totally unguarded western Iran border, three Toyota Ranger pickup trucks roared across the road and planted themselves in front, in back, and on the side of the exit door of the bus. Six men piled out of each truck and surrounded the bus, screaming in Armenian for everyone to get out. Most of the passengers and the driver did not understand the language and sat frozen to their seats not knowing what to do. Afsoon understood some of the words and phrases that she had picked up from the bandits who had raped Kandovan Village while she and Nassir had been living there with the Jamshidis.

"They want us to get off the bus, or they will kill us," she told the driver and the other passengers.

Happy to have someone who seemed to know what to do, everyone followed Afsoon off the bus, even though she had had to sit in a far rear seat because of her bodily odor. As the driver and each passenger alighted from the bus steps, one of the bandits struck them a blow with a baseball bat, which hurried them along.

"Dashnaksutyuns. Armenian terrorists," Nassir whispered and received a second blow for trying to communicate.

Afsoon had not forgotten them. She especially had not forgotten the Dashnaksutyun man who had attempted to rape her in Kandovan, and whom she had stabbed in the eye with a skinning knife and killed. She fingered her straight-edge razor now, knowing the murderous reputation of the terrorists through personal experience.

"*Never again,*" she said to herself. "*I will die first. Never again.*"

While a line of EIGHTEEN terrorists held Kalashnikovs on the defenseless bus passengers and the driver, two of them, starting at opposite ends of the line of victims, began to strip them of their valuables. Women were crying. Men were clubbed when they were not fast enough. Three passengers from Afsoon, an old woman resisted when a thug began to pull her valuables bag off her shoulder. Afsoon presumed it was everything the peasant woman valued in her life, and she could not bear to have it taken from her. The terrorist jerked on the bag, and the woman held on with all of her strength. That infuriated the young man. He stepped back, raised his Kalashnikov, and shot her dead center in her bony chest. She crumpled to the ground without so much as a whimper or a groan. The rest of the passengers gave a chorus of frightened groans. The thug smiled and went to the next passenger and the next.

He stood in front of Afsoon and leered.

"A young one," he snarled.

Afsoon held her razor in the palm of her right hand.

He reached up and took hold of the front of her chador with his filthy left hand, both to begin an attack and to communicate his utter disdain for her by using his left hand. Afsoon was strong, and the cloth of her chador did not tear. He set his submachine gun on the ground and took hold of her covering with both hands.

The other Dashnaksutyuns were bored with it all and stood talking, smoking, and checking their guns.

"*Never again*," she thought. "*I will die first.*"

She looked him directly in the eyes. It was unsettling to a man who was used to quick submission by his victims. He blinked. She struck. She whipped the razor up and across his face. His head was bent enough that she could not hit his neck. A slash opened almost from ear to ear baring bone all across showing his upper gums in the middle. It was done with so little movement on Afsoon's part that at first the man scarcely flinched. Blood erupted from dozens of small facial arteries. He leapt back, throwing both hands to his face and began to scream.

In the chaos that ensued, Nassir swiftly bent down and picked up the Kalashnikov, flicked the lever to fully automatic, and swept the barrel in a chest-high arc along the column of killers who were caught totally unawares. They dropped like rag dolls. Fifteen men were dead in three seconds, and the rest were thrown into benumbed and agitated confusion. The passengers screamed and ran in a dozen different directions—anywhere to escape. Nassir exhausted the remaining fourteen rounds into the flailing, confused bandits who could not regroup. The two bandits remaining alive dropped their guns and fled to one of the Toyota Rangers. They sped away back to Iran before Nassir could find another thirty-round magazine and fire off more shots.

Nassir shouted at the driver and the other passengers, "Hurry up. We have to get out of here before they come back. It's safe now. Run!"

Grateful to be alive and taking courage in Nassir's leadership, the terror-stricken occupants of the bus scrambled back on board. Nassir and Afsoon hurriedly collected fifteen of the AK-47s and passed them out to the male passengers. Afsoon entered the bus last, having paused just long enough to collect a dozen extra ammunition magazines.

The driver needed no prodding or instruction. The bus's engine roared into life. The driver put it into gear and floored the accelerator. The bus wheels spun in the gravel at the margin of the highway throwing gravel in a cloud as they took off. There were bodies lying in haphazard disarray on the asphalt, and the driver swerved in a serpentine course to run over as many of them as he could before they hurtled down the highway towards relative safety. He had to stop 100 yards down the road to put a new left front tire, which he accomplished in world record time—only putting on three of the five lug nuts. He did not stop for toilet or lunch breaks until they had gone nearly 300 miles, and the petrol gauge was showing empty. They were able to find the last petrol station for 50 miles, and every passenger knew as well as the driver that running out of fuel would be a death notice. The Dashnaksutyuns would be beside themselves with fury and would be coming for them.

He jumped out of the bus and began filling the tanks of his vehicle. Once they were full, he put the remaining two lug nuts on the front wheel and gave a little *"Alhamdulillah"* that it had not fallen off since they raced away from the crime scene. Passengers crowded into the tiny station to relieve themselves in the only toilet available. Men and women who dared not wait their turn ran off behind bushes, heedless of any proprieties or false modesty. One of the more affluent passengers bought every bottle of water from the proprietor and shared them with the rest once they were back on board. There was almost no talking during the trip through Qasrshirin, then a turnoff onto Highway 48 to Kahanaqin, Mandali, and Amarrh. They filled the bus's tanks again at Amarah, and those who had money bought simple lunches of packages of nuts and grape jelly, 500 gram packages of fried corn, and half liter containers of unflavored Aryan yogurt that could be taken with them on the bus.

Afsoon had been thinking about the danger they were in. She took Nassir aside before they were about to get back on the bus.

"Nassir, the Dashnaksutyuns are coming, you know that. They know the bus, and they will be after it and will stop at nothing to kill everyone. We have been looking at the border with Iran ever since we passed Sulaymaniyeh. There is nothing to stop the bandits from driving along the Iranian side until they catch sight of the bus, then they can make a quick exit, stop the bus, and kill us all."

"What should we do?"

"Get off here and walk into the city. We can hide here for a while, maybe even find some work and let this all calm down. What do you think?"

Nassir thought for about a minute. He scanned the highway in both directions. It was empty of traffic; so, the bus stood out dramatically as a lone target. He shrugged.

"All right. Get your things. Let's see what Amarah has to offer."

The bus left them behind. Afsoon had her *Fereshte* and her razor, and Nassir had all of their food. Both of them had an AK-47 and two extra magazines of ammunition—donations from Dashnaksutyuns who would no longer need them. They were determined not to be ambushed again.

The choice of Amarah was a good one as it turned out. The city is located in southeastern Iraq on a low ridge next to the Tigris River waterway south of Baghdad about 50 km from the border with Iran. It is situated at the northern tip of the marshlands between the Tigris and Euphrates rivers. The population of over 300,000 is predominantly Shi'i, which allowed Afsoon and Nassir to fit in without being noticed as different. Amarah is the busy administrative capital of the Maysan province and a major trading center for the surrounding agricultural area. It is known for handsome cotton and wool woven goods and decorative silverware.

After the American-led Persian Gulf War, Amarah was involved in the 1991 uprisings in Iraq against the dictator Saddam Hussein, a Sunni Muslim. Many Shi'i insurgents throughout Iraq retreated to safe havens in the Amarah area, bringing war with them. Many fighters and civilians were killed and crudely buried in a bulldozed mass grave outside the city limits. Saddam also resorted to a cruel tactic of draining the marshes surrounding Amarah, and had a number of dams constructed to cut off the water supply to the area. As a result, the population was prickly and defensive. They were also accepting of new Shi'i immigrants—Afsoon and Nassir—who were heavily armed and presumably able to defend themselves and the city.

The city was founded in the 1860s by the Ottoman Turks as a military outpost, and it remained a city under military control to one degree or another ever since. It was captured by the British in 1915, and they established a Hashemite monarchy under King Faisal I. The feudalistic society that was present a thousand years earlier persisted throughout these upheavals. In 1958, the people of Iraq overthrew the British in a bloody rebellion and ousted King Faisal II and his crown prince, 'Abd al-Ilah, and Prime Minister Nuri al-Said, who were cooperating with the hated British. The Iraqi Republic was established, and a series of military dictators took power—the most recent one being Saddam Hussein—when Afsoon and Nassir walked into the city. In response to Saddam's despotic treatment of the Shi'i and all of southern Iraq, the stubborn Shi'ites made Amarah the stronghold of the opposition to Saddam's government. The city became the fiefdom of Moqtada al-Sadr, whose father died in the fighting against Saddam. He established a strict Shi'i Islamic autocracy with order maintained by al-Sadr's militiamen. Almost every young man and many young women in the area were part of the militia.

The two newcomers fit in well enough that it took less than an hour for Afsoon to find work in Shafiqah Kadivar's wool carpet factory. She had had ample experience in Astera's tent and at the Jamshidi's in Kandovan with weaving complicated patterns; so, Shafiqah was happy to take her on. She was set to work copying a geometric pattern from the 1920s of a Persian Heriz Serapi rug. In a few weeks, she made friends and began to enjoy her simple life. She missed the opportunity to learn anything except household duties and the weaving that were permitted under al Sadr's iron-fisted religious rule. Reading or learning mathematics was out of the question. Her bodily odor was offensive; but among women, it was not so uncommon to have such a problem, and for the same reasons as Afsoon; so, she was accepted.

Nassir found part-time work as a journeyman silver smith, but he spent most of his time training with the militia and going on episodic commando raids against government facilities. Al-Sadr's provocations did not go unnoticed by Saddam and—eventually—the dictator retaliated in force. The Baghdad-Basrah highway cut through the Maysan province and was vital to the governments and bazaaris of both the Sunni north and the Shi'i south. Being located just west of the border with Iran, Iran had targeted the area during the Iran/Iraq War of 1980-1988 because of its strategic significance to the Iraqis.

In September, two months after Afsoon and Nassir found a new life in al-Sadr's Amarah, Saddam's army stuck. They cut off the highway between Baghdad and Amarah, drove the peasant farmers out of the marshes and up to Amarah, and began a siege intent on barring al-Sadr access to the Amarah-Basrah portion of the highway.

In a few days, Afsoon's peaceful existence ended; and, of necessity, she had to take up arms and hide in the swamps to help repel the invaders. She killed men, and saw men killed around her. Saddam's forces were on the verge of overrunning the city, and Afsoon knew what her fate would be. It was another of her "never again" moments. Shafiqah Kadivar fought alongside her. She was an ultimate pragmatist, which trumped her bazaari sympathies for the al-Sadr regime.

"Afsoon, my dear. It is time for us to escape. I think I do not need to tell you what will happen to a pretty young girl like you if you are still here when the *kaffir* army enters the city. I have friends in Al Basrah. We need to go there tonight."

"I can't leave Nassir. He is all I have," Afsoon said with profound sadness.

"I doubt that he will survive. He is on the front lines—Kalashnikovs against tanks. They don't stand a chance. He would want you to live. I have a fierce desire to live and to find a place where I can be at peace to run my business. That is not much to ask. Come with me."

Emotionally, Afsoon was torn, but her pragmatic side was every bit as powerful a driving force as was Shafiqah's.

"Maybe I can see Nassir sometime, somewhere, somehow," she said mournfully, "but I know you are right. I will leave with you tonight. I will collect a few things first."

She packed a canvas suitcase with two sets of clothes, all of the money she and Nassir had saved, her precious ragdoll, *Fereshte*, a double-edged combat knife she had been issued by the militia, and six 30-round magazines of 7.62x39 ammunition for her AK-47. The two women rode in the back of a pickup truck with a friend of Shafiqah's over rutted dirt back roads to Al-Kabir where highway 6 was still open. There, they booked a ride on a Kuwait Public Transport Company minibus all the way through to Al Bashrah.

A firefight erupted between the Saddam and al-Sadr forces between Mijar and Al Shafi, and the minibus had to pull off onto a side road. A government army unit came menacingly close; and the minibus driver and its six passengers had to scatter into the underbrush to hide, leaving all of their belongings on the bus. Afsoon kept her combat knife and her razor in her hands ready to fight to the death rather than to be captured. The army unit fired a few desultory shots into the darkness, but no one was hit. The unit proceeded north towards Amarah; and as soon as it was out of sight and hearing range, the bus driver sprinted for the bus.

"Get on the bus. I am leaving in the next five minutes with or without you. Hurry up!"

Afsoon had hidden near the bus and close enough to hear the announcement. Unfortunately for her, Shafiqah and an older woman had hidden nearly half a mile away and were unable to hear the command to board the bus.

The driver started the engine.

"I am leaving. I know we are two short, but we cannot wait. I will give one last call, and then we have to leave. We will all be killed if we don't take advantage of this small opportunity."

He was emphatic. He yelled at the top of his lungs out the open minibus doors. No reply came, and neither of the missing women made it to the bus. The Kuwait Public Transport minibus left in the direction of its home country as fast as the little engine's power could move it. Once again, Afsoon had to mourn the separation from a friend. She knew that she would never see Nassir or Shafiqah or Astera or Yasmin or Elaheh again. She was sad, but she was determined to live. All of her suffering thus far in her brief existence on earth could not be for nothing. She set her eyes straight ahead.

# CHAPTER TWENTY-SIX

## Al Basrah, Iraq, October 2, 1996

It was the middle of the night when the Kuwait Public Transport minibus stopped in the depot in the center of the largest city Afsoon had ever seen. The bus driver was anxious to get home to his wives and six children. They had not seen him for well over a month; and he had not had a good meal or a safe, peaceful day since he had started his bus route that led him to a war zone. He had no further responsibility to his passengers; and he walked away from them without so much as a good-bye, leaving sixteen-year-old, inexperienced Afsoon on her own. Shortly, she was alone in the bus station on the intersection of Baghdad and Saad Streets. As if she did not have fears enough, she found a newspaper carrying a front-page story of a terrorist bombing of a bus carrying elementary school children and their teachers a few blocks from the station.

It was hot, and her oppressive black chador held the heat in like an oven. She was extremely tired, afraid, and bewildered in her new surroundings and knew that she was vulnerable. She put the lever of her AK-47 off safety, and looked about for a direction to walk. She heard footsteps behind her and began to walk faster. The footsteps grew rapidly closer. She was too tired to run, and was sure she could not outrun her pursuer. She swung her submachine gun to her shoulder and tripped the lever so that each pull of the trigger would release three shots in rapid succession.

"Put down the gun, young lady. I wish you no harm. Perhaps I can be of assistance."

The voice was gentle, even kindly. Afsoon strained her eyes to be able to discern the man's face. It was a uniformed policeman, and that struck fear into the girl.

"I won't let you hurt me," she announced defiantly.

"I am a policeman. You look lost, and this is not a place for a girl—not at this time of night. Where are you going?"

Afsoon was inclined to lie, but the policeman's demeanor was so nonthreatening that she decided to give him the benefit of the doubt for the moment.

"I don't know. I just got off a bus from Amarah where there is a war on. I am trying to find a place to stay."

Her words were calm and nonthreatening just like those of the policeman but; unlike him, her eyes were intensely wary.

"I know just the place. Would you please come with me? The police station is just around the next corner. You can feel safe there. I will arrange for you to be taken to a place owned by the Americans. You will be riding with a few other girls who have no one. Does that sound all right to you?"

"Maybe. I will walk behind you and will keep my gun."

"That is all right with me. Just don't make a mistake and accidentally shoot me in the back."

"I'll be careful. But you remember that I can defend myself."

"You are safe. Before morning, you will not have to worry anymore. Trust me."

Afsoon was not much for trusting, especially for trusting men; but this man seemed to present no immediate threat; so, she followed him at a safe distance to the promised police station. She waited outside while he went in, promising to bring back a woman.

In five minutes, the policeman returned with a powerfully built and well-armed female in uniform.

"Hello," she said, "I am Sergeant Nikahd of the municipal police. You can call me Naomeh, if you like."

Like the male police officer, her voice was calming and nonthreatening. Afsoon began to relax a little.

"I'm sure you are hungry and thirsty. Won't you come into the station and have something to eat and drink with me?"

Afsoon cautiously agreed and started to follow the police officer.

As they started up the front steps, Sergeant Nikahd turned to Afsoon and said courteously but firmly, "I'm sorry, but we cannot take a loaded weapon into the station. Please take out the magazine and any chambered rounds."

Afsoon did not want to do that; but it seemed the lesser of evils to being out on the street; so, she did as she was asked. She kept one hand on her knife, holding it in the folds of her chador, ready, but out of sight.

No one menaced her. The station was busy and; generally, she was ignored except by Sergeant Nikahd, who brought her chai and a small plate of fresh fruit and crackers that Afsoon wolfed down.

"Take it easy, there is more where that came from."

Afsoon smiled sheepishly.

"I forgot my manners," she said.

Sergeant Nikahd returned her smile.

It took an hour, but with proper papers in hand—selectively saved from her trip on the prison bus—Afsoon joined four other girls and were helped aboard a minibus. Three serious female police officers accompanied them. Even the bus driver was a female. It was comforting to the refugee girls. It was still pitch dark out. Afsoon knew she was headed into the great unknown, and she hugged *Fereshte* for comfort and fingered her razor for security.

The drive was an hour long and led Afsoon and the others to the southern edge of the city. The bus stopped at the gates of a well-fortified compound, and the driver radioed in for permission to enter. Two armed guards stepped out of the shadows and checked the driver's credentials and gave a cursory look at the police officers and their young charges.

"Enter," one of the gate guards said.

The girls and their meager belongings alighted and stood nervously in front of the heavy doors of what appeared to be an old palace. The doors opened, and a lone woman dressed in clothes entirely foreign to Afsoon stepped out and walked to the girls. In an act that totally took the girls unawares, the woman gave each of them a strong welcoming hug. Several of the girls began to cry, such was their relief. Afsoon liked the hug, but remained impassive and wary.

"Come in, my new young friends," the woman said to them. To the officers, she said, "I'll take good care of them. Thank you so much for saving them from the mean streets."

The officers nodded, got back into the bus, and left the compound.

Little more was said. The woman summoned three helpers; together, they settled the girls into Spartan but clean and inviting bed rooms. Afsoon had a room of her own, the first one of her life. They were helped into showers, the first modern shower Afsoon had ever seen. She was highly reluctant to take off her clothing, but the knowing and kindly senior woman nudged her forward.

"I know something of what you have been through, my dear girl. We can help you, and you can trust us. You will not come to any harm here. Believe me, we have seen everything that you can show us, and we do not get shocked. I can tell by your smell that you have suffered some unspeakable things. We have sympathy for you; but more than that, I am sure we can make things better. Now let me get rid of those clothes."

Afsoon shyly and reluctantly shed her clothes, looking down at the floor all the while. Mrs. Toshkhani—the woman in charge—gave a small involuntary gasp as she saw the terrible scars covering Afsoon's back, buttocks, and legs. It was evident that the child had been brutally whipped by what amounted to a cat-o-nine-tails. It was the worst such scarring she had seen, and she had seen a great deal. Despite her resolve not to do so, she again gasped as she saw Afsoon's ruined and soiled genitalia.

"I'm sorry, good lady, I am not clean. I cannot keep myself clean. You will not want to see me or to be by me. I will try not to be any trouble to you."

"Oh, God, my angel. I can only imagine what hell you have known. You are welcome here. You will be loved and protected. Your suffering is over. Please let me hold you."

Afsoon gave in completely and let the heavyset woman embrace and hold her. Mrs. Toshkhani kissed her forehead and soothed her hair. Afsoon fought back tears; but she could not resist, giving herself completely to the beautiful rotund brown lady. It did not occur to her to hold on to fears that she would be betrayed. Aisha Toskhani washed Afsoon gently and thoroughly, talking to her all the while.

"I am a Kashmiri Pandit from north India. Do you know where that is, dear?"

"No, I only know Iran and Iraq and have read about America, wherever that is."

Mrs. Toshkhani explained her clothing and the red mark on her forehead.

"I am a Hindu," she began. "That is a different religion to yours, Afsoon. I hope you are not offended by me touching you. To your religion I am a *kaffir*, a polytheist."

She was speaking English, and readily detected that Afsoon was not understanding everything she said.

"My native language is Persian, as it is for most of the people where I come from. Would you rather we used that language?"

"No, my English is not so good, but I want to learn it better. I understood most of what you said, but what does 'polytheist' mean?"

"It means 'one who believes in many gods.'"

"Not just Allah?"

"That's right. Do you dislike me because I am a polytheist and a *kaffir*, Afsoon?"

"I do not believe in any god, and I hate Allah and everything about Islam. You are very kind, and I certainly have no reason to dislike you," Afsoon said in deep earnest.

"I can't blame you after what you have been through. Try to let hate go, child. You have a long and good life to lead; hating will only slow you down and block your progress."

Afsoon nodded. She was becoming tranquil and sleepy under the kind woman's ministrations.

"Let me explain my clothing that is so different from yours. In the place where I lived until a few years ago, we did not fear the female body and did not cover it severely. We lived among Muslims and got along well; but my friends and I had sympathy for the poor women who had to wear such ugly, hot, and awkward clothing, if you will forgive me for describing them so."

"I have always had the same opinion, but I have never known a woman who dared speak as you just did. She would get a beating from both men and women."

Mrs. Toshkhani smiled, and, having finished bathing Afsoon, handed her a luxurious heavy, spotlessly white towel. The girl dried herself off, enjoying immensely the sensation of rubbing the soft material all over her body. She had never even seen a fine towel before.

"I was telling you about my clothing. It is the way most of my friends dress, although in Kashmir where I come from, the clothing is heavier because it is so cold there so much of the time."

She demonstrated the articles of her clothing and gave a brief explanation of them as she went.

"This is called a *pheran-pravarna*," referring to her long flowing silk dress that was colored in a brilliant rainbow of oranges, reds, and yellows and had wide flowing sleeves fringed with brocaded stripes.

Around her chest she wore long stripes making red borders that were attached to an open collar that extended from the shoulder all the way along her skirt. Some of her ample bosom showed, and Afsoon was surprised at the fact that the large woman was not even aware of her lack of modesty. It was refreshing to Afsoon who had never seen a woman's neck out of doors, let alone having seen a glimpse of bare breasts, however slight.

"We like to wear a pair of these dresses—an underlayer we call a *potosh*, which is made of heavy cotton in north India and very light cotton here in Iraq where it is almost always hot. My sash is called a *loongy*. Do you like it?"

Afsoon nodded.

The *loongy* was wide and even more brilliantly colored than the rest of her clothing. It was made of a shimmering blue patterned silk that stood out in high contrast to the hot colors of her *pheran*.

"On my head, I always wear a *Taranga*. It symbolizes the decorative hood of the celestial serpent we call a *nag*. You can see that it has a decoration of a flowing serpent's body that tapers into a double tail."

The tail almost reached Mrs. Toshkhani's heels. She went on to explain the other parts of her headgear: the *Kalaposh*, a conical hat, the *Zoojy*, a network cloth topped by embroidered motifs that flowed down to the small of her ample back, the *Taranga* itself, which was made of three narrow, continuous wraps over and around the head, with the final round having *moharlath*—starched and glazed over with a soft giant shell, and finally *Poots*—two long lengths of fine white muslin hemmed together longitudinally with a fish spine pattern. The whole piece constituting the *Poots* was rolled and wrapped inwards from both sides to form long bodies of a pair of snakes with tapering tails at the lower end and a hood at the other top, where it opened and covered the top of the headgear and flowed down over the back, almost touching her heels.

After a lifetime of drab female clothing that made the women look like ghostly specters to keep them from being attractive to men, it was wonderful to Afsoon to see such vibrant colors and to feel the radiation of the new and strange foreign woman. She fell asleep holding *Fereshte* and dreaming of the sun, of brilliant flowers, and of the kind woman.

When she awakened, she was famished. A bell sounded and all of the girls dressed and hurried down to communal tables filled with foods that were unfamiliar—a fact that was not at all surprising in this new, wonderful, and strange place. Spread before the girls and the staff was an abundance of eggs—fried, scrambled, poached, and basted; American breakfast meats—bacon, ham, and sausage; fresh fruits—grapefruit, seedless red grapes, and kiwi; pastries—croissants, bagels, and cheese; fruit, elephant ear, and bear Danishes. Afsoon had never seen any of the food except eggs, and never prepared in such enticing ways. She felt like she had died and gone to the heaven she did not believe in.

Mrs. Toshkhani appeared half an hour late wearing morning clothes—a long silk tunic and fine woolen trousers. Her black hair was braided in a different style, and she was wearing an assortment of varied color tassels. She clanked from multiple bracelets, anklets, and necklaces made of gold and pearls. She wore a blue-colored stone pendant on her forehead.

"Hello, girls," she said in Farsi, Iraqi Arabic, Kurdish, French, then finally in British accented English.

She gave a slight bow and joined them in the feast. When they were finished, Mrs. Toshkhani gave the girls their assignments for the day.

She saved Afsoon for last, "Afsoon, my dear, I have two important people for you to see today. Please come with me."

Afsoon followed the Indian woman to a white stucco building with a red cross on its front. She thought it might be a church. They went inside and took a seat in the small waiting room. In a few minutes, an Iraqi woman in a gleaming, stiffly starched, spotless, white cotton uniform and cap directed them to come with her.

"The doctor can see you now," she said.

Mrs. Toshkhani had Afsoon sit on an examination table. The room smelled faintly of antiseptics and medicinal alcohol. It was immaculate.

The examination door opened and a woman in a business suit entered.

"Hello," she said, offering her hand, "I am Dr. Sylvia Asad. I am one of three physicians in the compound, and my specialty is obstetrics and gynecology. Do you know what that means, Afsoon?"

Afsoon was impressed that everyone knew her name.

"No," she said.

Dr. Asad explained in simple layman's terms and then went on, "Afsoon, Mrs. Toshkhani has told me about your problem with odor and poor control of your solid wastes. We are familiar with that here. You do not need to be ashamed, and you do not need to be afraid. We are here to help you. I can give you some medicine and help you to keep as clean as possible. Tomorrow, an important American lady will come to Al Basrah to our compound. She can help you have surgery to make the problem of your female parts go away. Would you like that?"

"What is surgery?"

This was asked by a girl who scarcely knew what a doctor was and had never been inside a medical facility.

Dr. Asad explained surgery in simple terms and spent some time informing Afsoon about the repair of female genital mutilation injuries, paying particular attention to having the girl understand the repair of recto-vaginal tears and fistulae.

"Do you understand? Do you have any questions?"

It was all rather overwhelming, but Afsoon thought she understood the basics; so, she shyly answered, "No, Doctor. Thank you."

The concept that a surgeon could cut her and sew her back up to make the terrible problems of her female injuries better was rather overwhelming—both wonderful and frightening.

"Oh, I do have one question: will the pain be very terrible when the surgery is being done?"

It was asked so matter-of-factly that both the doctor and the compound director had to clench their teeth to keep from reacting with tears to the innocent question of a girl who had endured so much for so long that she expected only suffering.

"No, my dear, no. You will be given medicine to put you to sleep, and you will not feel anything. You will have some pain in the area for a few days after the surgery, but it will not be terrible; and it will go away."

"Thank you."

Due to renewed unrest in southern Iraq between the Sunni and the Shi'i, the American visitor was unable to land in the small airport near the compound; so, her arrival was delayed a week. Afsoon was assigned to clean the dormitory barracks floor where her bed was located, which took less than two hours each day.

Mrs. Toshkhani introduced her to an elderly man—Haji NaazemZadeh Harandi—in his office in the library. Although she had never actually seen such a place, Afsoon was familiar with the concept from her reading. The librarian was a scholar in Sharia law and Islamic history. In addition, he had studied a wide range of historical, geographical, economic, and sociopolitical subjects in his long and scholarly life. He was wizened and had long white hair and a beard. His body was frail; but his face was animated; and his eyes were keen and observant. He was dressed in a light beige *dishdasha*—a flowing ankle-length garment with long sleeves. Underneath, he wore an *izaar*—an undergarment like a kilt. On his head, he wore a crocheted Pakistani *taqiyah*. He began asking Afsoon questions.

"Have you been to school, Afsoon? Can you read? Do you know English? How about other languages? Do you have a knowledge of history or about the world outside Iran and Iraq? Can you do arithmetic?"

Her answers seemed improbable to the old man, but he was too polite to tell her so. She was only sixteen years old and a girl. She had never been to school, yet she could read and write at least some in six languages, including English, and spoke seven, knew the general geography of the world, and was proficient in mathematics beyond the level of the average male high school student in Iraq.

He was gentle in his questioning, but could not accept what she was saying until he had her write short paragraphs in each of her languages about history, politics in Iran, and had her solve some simple story-problems in math. His usually impassive face became animated, and he became excited about the prospects of being part of the remarkable girl's further education.

Haji Harandi lived in the American compound because he had fallen into strong disfavor with his fellow Shi'ites over questions of interpretation of the *Qur'an*, the Hadith, and the law. He would not accept the common sense applications that dictated maltreatment of females, the maintenance of slaves, the prejudicial attitudes towards Sunnis—similar in nature to the reciprocal prejudice of the Sunnis towards the Shi'i. In a Christian or Buddhist nation, such differences of opinion might have resulted in the haji being labeled an eccentric or even a distasteful heretic at worst; but among the rabid Shi'i of Iran and southern Iraq, such idiosyncrasies were capital crimes. During the declining months of the first American Gulf War in Iraq—Desert Storm— the haji and a number of other condemned men and women were given sanctuary in the guarded American compound, which was a vestige of the American invasion. The place became a haven for orphans who were abandoned and neglected, for girls who had suffered gross maltreatment in the name of the dominant religion, and for dissidents against the Saddam regime who had nowhere else to hide.

He knew that he had little time before the American contingent returned and would learn of the prodigy that had happened into the compound and would exploit her. He decided to test her and to help her learn as much as he could in the short week he would have her for company.

"Afsoon, I would like you to go to school. I will be the teacher, and you will be the only student. Would you like that?" he asked hopefully.

"Oh, Haji Harandi, I would love that. I have wanted to go to school all of my life. I even told my adopted brother, Nassir, that I would dress as a boy and sneak in. He told me that I would be killed if I was caught, and I had to give up."

"My girl, this is a little piece of America. Forget all of what you have been told about America being the Great Satan. Shaytan has control of the leaders of Iran and Iraq and probably of the other Islamic governments. Here, you will know freedom. You will be able to learn and not be told that it is not allowed for girls. When would you like to start?"

"Now."

The answer was simple, truthful, and heartfelt. Her face radiated her earnest desire—enthusiasm for learning that he had never seen in his lazy, inattentive boy students when he taught in the Al Basrah Madrassah.

"Now it will be."

Haji Harandi told Mrs. Toshkhani that Afsoon would no longer be able to do chores. She had too much to learn. That very day, he had native speakers come to the library classroom and begin to converse with her in Urdu, Farsi, Kurmanji, Azerbaijani, Turkish, and English—with a bias towards English. There were no Aramaic speakers; so, Haji Harandi had to accept her at her word that she was facile with that esoteric old language. In the days to come, they covered Iranian, Iraqi, and American history, sociopolitical and economic issues as rapidly as he could talk. She soaked up his output like an inexhaustible sponge.

He told her about the precious library where they were sitting and the sacrifices that had gone into obtaining and saving the treasures within the walls of the building in which they were now sitting. Alia Muhammad Baker was a librarian still living in the city. For fourteen years, her library had been the meeting place for those who love books. When the Gulf War descended upon the country, Alia feared that the library building and collection of thirty thousand books within it would be destroyed by the ignorant hyper-religious zealots forever if she did not act. In a war-stricken country where civilians—especially women—have little power, this intrepid librarian struggled against what appeared to be insuperable odds to save the priceless collection.

At Afsoon's request, Haji Harandi and several of the other scholar-residents of the compound told her about the native city they loved. Al Baṣrah is the capital of Basrah Governorate, situated in southern Iraq near Kuwait and Iran, which made it a prime target of attack by the Islamic Republic of Iran during the Iran/Iraq War. At the time of Afsoon's tutorial, it had an estimated population of 800,000. Basrah contains a significant proportion of Iraq's oil reserves and is also Iraq's main shipping hub, although it does not have deep water access, which is handled at the port of Umm Qasr. Because of urbanization, the high employment rate in the city, and the abundance of jobs in the oil industry, there is a low level of importance of agriculture in the governate.

The city is part of the historic location of ancient Sumer, the putative home of Sinbad the Sailor, and a proposed location of the Garden of Eden by many Muslims and some Jewish scholars. It was built in 636 BC and is Iraq's second largest and most populous city after Baghdad. In 1949–50, the city served as a center for the flight of Jews to Iran, on their way to Israel and safety. Thousands were helped by smugglers to cross the Shatt al-'Arab to the Iranian shore. It is consistently one of the hottest places in the world, with summer temperatures regularly of 45-48-plus degrees Celsius [113-119 degrees Farenheit]. The city was too close to the Iranian border for Afsoon's comfort.

They stopped only for short breaks for the bathroom and Spartan meals. The days began early, and the haji did not even pause for the five daily prayers. They quit at night only when both of them fell asleep in their chairs. Afsoon was blissfully happy during those seven days. She had found herself in the arcane languages and difficult subject material. Learning was life for her, and her life had taken on meaning devoid of the terrors that surrounded women in Iran. She was free and looked forward to the next week with more anticipation than she had ever felt before. What lay in store for her when the Americans came?

> "The great advantage of an American is that he has arrived at a state of democracy without having to endure a democratic revolution and that he is born free without having to become so."
> -Alexis De Tocqueville, *De la démocratie en Amérique* [*Democracy in America*], 1835-1840

# CHAPTER TWENTY-SEVEN

**"God exists since mathematics is consistent, and the Devil exists since we cannot prove it."**
                    **-Andre Weil, 1906-1998 French Mathematician**

## Boston and Cambridge, Massachusetts, September, 1996

Gideon entered his second year at MIT refreshed from the change of learning institutions during the summer and a conviction of what he was going to do with his life. Late in the fall semester of 1995, he solved the P=NP vs P≠NP problem, and spent the entire winter semester of 1996 in hiding and secrecy lest his coup be learned and the surprise spoiled before he could announce it at the defense of his dissertation in May that year. He had opted for a grueling course of study that excluded the chance of having a social life or friends. He and Walter Duffy seldom saw each other, and he and Aaron Schmuel avoided contact now after receiving Mossad orders to do so.

The sixteen-year-old prodigy made a definite decision early in the fall semester of 1995 not to pursue theoretical math or physics. His time with the Mossad had convinced him that he was more of a reality-based person and wanted to have a hands-on experience of life, albeit at a level of expertise that would allow him to soar above the rest of his competitors, whether it be at his university, in his bank, or analyzing data as a spy. It gave him a small thrill every time he allowed himself to whisper the word "spy."

He therefore sought explorations of issues close to the base of calculus that gave rise to clear and commonsensical analyses of commonplace questions that could be understood not only by "speaking math" but which could be rendered into English and explained to intelligent but non-expert people.

He came to live with the derivative and the integral so as to know and to feel the physical basis of reality and how to express that reality. Despite the voluminous nature of calculus textbooks and the ponderous nature of articles in mathematical journals, it was apparent to Gideon that the differential was simply an expression of how fast things are changing—the "instantaneous change." The integral deals with the static world, providing a dynamic view of that world. Small portions of structures accumulate from fixed structures. Together, the two aspects give definition to otherwise mysterious problems of change and motion.

By altering his ideas about science, math, and the natural world, Gideon found that his sense of religion—his own and others' faiths—was altered. He no longer saw religion as an explanation of creation, of human behavior, of history, or even of morality. He became a practicing Jew who enjoyed the rituals and the camaraderie of the faith but did not concern himself with the supernatural. In his none too frequent or lengthy free time, he began a serious study of the Theory of Evolution. He became knowledgeable enough to make PowerPoint presentations and to give lectures at the university. He no longer looked like the nice Orthodox boy he once was; but for all of his pragmatism and scientific bent, he was still a caring and compassionate young man who was idealistic enough to hope for a better world and to seek ways to make it happen; but he was no longer driven by religious ideology. He maintained his steady correspondence with his sisters and parents who hung on each of his messages as seriously as if he were a Talmudic master.

Mathematics was his foundation. He was convinced that the structures he created to study and model motion such as the trajectory of antiaircraft ordnance or space orbiting vehicles were identical—at least mathematically—to the structures that model the aspects of economics, growth of populations, flow of traffic, fluid dynamics, and even planetary motion. He came to love calculus because of the fact that it was—to him—the most valuable conceptual notion and most effective mental tool ever discovered.

During spring semester, along with his effort to perfect his work on his dissertation, he focused his attention in mathematics on economic issues. He did projects to provide better ways to analyze the stock market, joined a study group to measure the economics of banking trends, and worked with a think tank formed among his contacts at the Boston Federal Reserve Bank. That group evaluated the complex calculus of changes in risk, cost, revenue, and how the complicated interplay of all of those factors could be understood and manipulated. They produced a banking protocol that became known as the "Boston Theorem of Economics," because it applied worldwide to all sorts of business structures. From each of these projects, Gideon got his name on a paper published in a peer-reviewed journal. He was the lead author on the Boston Theorem publication.

Computers were of such inestimable value to his work that papers on the mathematics of computers followed naturally. Gideon made name for himself in computer science before he even received his Ph.D.; and, for fun, he practiced hacking into the computers of large industrial companies and banks and revising their financial structures to their benefit. In so doing, he gained an enormously valuable insight into the companies, especially banks that competed with the Rothsberger Family Bank. He tucked away the information for possible use another day.

His accelerated studies in practical nuclear physics, nuclear engineering, and computers made him one of the world's foremost experts in the field that combined such arcane areas of interest. Gideon began getting job offers from industry early that spring semester. He turned them all down. He was firm about banking at the highest levels of authority and was determined to change the way his bank functioned, to give it the most advantageous insights and results—and him a great deal of money. From his stock market and shopping mall investments, he was already a rich man by almost anyone's calculation, and he had not yet turned sixteen.

Mid-May, he was certain of the solidity of his dissertation. He would announce his conclusion on the "unsolvable problem" on May 23rd at his doctoral defense presentation. He shared the information and the evidence for it with the head of the department of computer science, Dr. Willard Lazar, his major professor at Berkeley, Samson Bernstein, his math tutor, Dr. Stephen Ammon Rhodes, his major professor, Dr. Kristina Shimazaki, and the department co-chairs, Drs. Leif Erik Nielson and Karl L. Nielson, and no one else. Everyone agreed to a vow of secrecy.

By university policy, he was required to invite two prominent mathematicians from other well-recognized math departments at different universities. He selected three world-class minds, each of whom was likely to mount a concerted effort to discredit the thesis of his dissertation—Professor Eli Goldberg from Tel Aviv University, Dr. Harrison Standage Jr. from Harvard, and likely his most powerful critic, Dr. Stanley Protel Thatcher, head of the MIT computer science department. The three experts also agreed not to divulge the conclusion of the thesis, but were free to announce that it was the most controversial doctoral dissertation in math or computer science in the past fifty years. Gideon kept the proofs of his conclusion a guarded secret among his co-authors on the book he had worked on in conjunction with the dissertation itself.

As soon as Gideon sent off the letters to the professors, he and his department heads submitted the dissertation as a book to the University of Chicago Press under the title, *One Unsolvable Problem Down, Five to Go* with Gideon's name first and all the departmental professors' names following. Directly after receiving the announcement letter, the university and the Clay Mathematics Institute scheduled the presentation in the MIT Stata Center, one of the largest and most splendid lecture halls in the world, known for its one-of-a-kind exterior—designed to attract attention all around the world. They booked six floors of rooms in one of the premier hotels in Cambridge, the Charles Hotel, expecting to take full advantage of the hotel's latest technology and its 18,000 square feet of indoor and outdoor banquet space. No expense and no hyperbole were spared.

Immediately upon receiving the announcement, Dr. Thatcher from the CMI wrote an op-ed piece in the *New York Times* in which he excoriated the very idea that one of the unsolvables had been solved and stated in print that it was ludicrous that a mere boy could have done so. He went so far as to announce that the CMI would pay the million-dollar prize, and he—Dr. Thatcher on his own—would pay $500,000 if he was proved wrong by the upstart. That was rather a considerable risk for a man who lived on his none-too-large university professor's salary, and half a million dollars would just about empty his personal accounts.

On that night of nights in the life of Gideon Emmanuel Rothsberger IV's life—sixteen years in total—he was announced to a roomful of people whose average IQ was five points above genius and whose list of credits was likely the highest ever gathered in a single building. And almost every one of them was certain Gideon was dead wrong and was there to see the great fall of the prodigy who was born with a silver spoon in his mouth and whose life had been an endless progression of accolades.

Gideon stood quietly at the lectern for a few moments until the room became silent.

"Ladies and gentlemen, colleagues, and all the brilliant minds of mathematics, I am humble—a mere boy—to present my doctoral dissertation and to answer my critics. The department has distributed a summary of the dissertation and its proofs. I trust that all of you have one and will follow along as I present it and as I answer questions put to me when I am finished.

"The announcement is that I have solved one of the unsolvable mathematical conundrums, the so-called P vs NP problem. The answer is that P≠NP."

He wrote the conclusion in large capital letters on the plastic sheet under the lectern's projector. The letters stood four feet tall on the screens around the room. There was a murmur of protest and doubt and no discernible approval. No one—not even his family—dared clap—even the quietest and most decorous little clap.

Undaunted, Gideon launched into a one-hour long presentation that was unfathomable to most of the audience, but he did it with aplomb and a sense of humor that won over his audience to him, if not to his ideas. At the end of the lecture, the room was silent enough to hear heads turning from one side to another and up and down. There was a sudden dramatic and universal applause. Gideon received one of the few standing ovations ever given to a presenter who was not a beloved retiring professor or a Nobel Laureate.

He turned and faced the table full of tuxedoed challengers, and said quietly, "Ladies and gentlemen, I am ready for your questions."

And he was. For another hour, some of the most arcane and difficult questions ever posed to a mathematics Ph.D. candidate came at Gideon in an unrelenting cross fire. He never glanced at a note, wrote rapidly on the board in the language of calculus, and assured every doubter that he would afford him or her a private meeting to cover anything still in doubt. When they were finished with their queries, even the challengers gave him a standing ovation, knowing that they had met their match. Only Dr. Thatcher hung back.

He said, "Your work is impressive and worthy of your being granted a doctor of philosophy degree; but I am not yet convinced, certainly not a million and a half dollars worth. I, for one, will take you up on that offer to meet privately. I think there is a fatal flaw, but the information is too huge for me to digest in this one short evening."

"I welcome the challenge," Gideon said, and the evening was over.

§§§§§

Afsoon was seated between two men—Haji Harandi and a Sikh named Harpreet Singh—working on trigonometric function problems, when Mrs. Toshkhani and a blond woman walked up and stood behind them.

Afsoon was explaining the concept of inverse functions to the haji, who had not had any formal training in math beyond algebra. Mr. Singh nodded approvingly.

"Excuse me," Mrs. Toshkhani interrupted. "I would like Afsoon to meet our American benefactress. Afsoon, this is Brenda Daastrup. Mrs. Daastrup, I am pleased to introduce our budding mathematician, Afsoon."

"I'm pleased to meet you, Afsoon. Could you tell me your last name ... your Christian name..." and realizing her gaffe, she corrected herself, "your surname?"

"I have only the one name, Ma'am. I have no *shenas nameh*."

Mrs. Daastrup looked to Mrs. Toshkhani for a translation.

"In Iran, every person is issued a *shenas nameh* at birth as their official lifelong document. Without one—and I don't mean that you have been absentminded or careless and lost it—you are not a person. You may well be subject to a great deal of mistreatment without that document, which is increased by the fact of being a female."

Mrs. Daastrup shook her head sadly, "We'll have to remedy that."

"Among other things," Mrs. Toshkhani said quietly.

"Have I offended?" Afsoon asked, concerned.

"Certainly not. We are just concerned about you," Mrs. Daastrup hastened to say.

She turned to the men, "Would you tell me the truth about something I want to know about this girl?"

They nodded.

"Mrs. Toshkhani tells me that she is something of a child prodigy, maybe a budding math genius."

"It is hard to say with such a short time to be with her, but this is a sixteen-year-old girl who has never seen the inside of a school. She was expressly prevented from attending. However—on her own initiative—she used her adopted brother's school books and taught herself to read and has learned seven languages, including English and Aramaic, as you have heard. She tells us that she did every problem in every math book in the county where she lived; and despite not having ever had a proper teacher, she was able to master mathematics from the most basic to trigonometry, which is the highest level book she could find. We were presumptuous enough to think we could teach her, but she has been teaching us," Haji Harandi said.

"And I might add that this girl learns more quickly than any human being I have ever met. She forgets nothing, and she can do math by intuition. I gave her three story problems I remember from advanced algebra, which is as far as I went, and she had only to hear them to be able to figure them out, to intuit them, if I may say that," said Mr. Singh.

"Gentlemen, would you mind if we took her away from you for a bit? I can only be here for two days, and I want to see what we can do to help her."

"Surely, Mrs. Daastrup. We would all be most pleased if this gifted girl could be helped to realize her potential. Outside this compound that you so generously keep going, there is no hope for her."

None of this was lost on Afsoon, who kept a steady gaze on Mrs. Daastrup. For one reason, she was simply the most beautiful human being the young girl had ever seen. Had she ever seen a movie, she would probably have thought of the beautiful Nordic woman as a movie star. Mrs. Daastrup—Brenda, by her own preference—was tall, willowy, and a true Swedish blond. Her hair was tousled from the heat and wind of the summer's day, but it hung to her shoulders in shimmering golden folds. Afsoon had never seen a blond person in her entire life; and Brenda was so different from all the other women with whom she was familiar, that she could have come from a different planet—or from the the *firdaus* of the *jannah* [the highest level of the garden of paradise]. Brenda had a beautiful shape, one not hidden by a formless chador or Burqa, yet she seemed covered and modest, while unable to hide her physical charms. As she watched, Afsoon determined that Brenda's beauty—like that of Mrs. Toshkhani—came from a strong inner glow. Afsoon was strongly drawn to her.

"Would you like to come with us, Afsoon?" she asked.

"Yes."

"We will meet with the doctor first, if that is okay with you."

"I do not know what 'okay' means."

Brenda smiled. "It is the most popular English word in the whole world. It means good or at least fairly good. It is a very useful word."

Afsoon quietly included it into her permanent vocabulary.

The three women walked into the doctor's clinic and waited until the nurse told them that she could see them. Dr. Asad greeted them warmly.

"Afsoon, may we look at your injuries?" Brenda asked softly, "And Dr. Asad can explain things to us; so, we can get you proper help."

"Yes. But I do not want others to see. I am ashamed."

Tears formed in Brenda's eyes. She was momentarily unable to speak.

"There is no shame, dear girl," Mrs. Toshkhani soothed.

Afsoon removed all of her clothing and stood naked. Brenda could not stand it; she began to cry.

"My, God, how terrible. I'm sorry that I cannot control my emotions better, but this is by far the worst thing I have ever seen. I cannot even imagine the suffering this girl has known. This is the product of years of awful abuse. I would like to strangle personally every monster who inflicted such terrible things on this sweet little girl."

Mrs. Toshkhani added, "She was considered a slave when she was born, and worse, a nonperson. Abuse was to be her lifelong lot, and it was not only *her* lot in life. A rural peasant Muslim girl is not even considered as valuable as a true slave. Without help, she will fall back into the hands of the patriarchy here, and eventually they will kill her."

"But why," moaned Brenda, "how could they? I cannot, for the life of me, understand what I am seeing."

Dr. Asad directed Afsoon to put her clothing back on. She stood impassively as the women talked about her as if she was not there. They were kind and meant well, she knew; so, she did not take offense.

The doctor then described the wounds on her back, "This is not rare. She was guilty of a crime."

Brenda raised her eyebrows in protest.

"Yes, the crime of being raped. She was whipped with a knotted multi-tailed rope until bites of her flesh were torn off. You see, she was guilty. She was a female; and because of that, she was targeted by a man. You can bet that the man was considered a victim. You have seen her genitalia. I saw you look away. That represents a double crime. This little girl was probably about ten when her mother figure took her to a filthy back street, helped to hold her down, and a cleric cut her to pieces, all in the name of Islam. She is one of millions. I know that you have heard that, but here is the reality. Perhaps we could save this one girl. She has a recto-vaginal fistula. The smell is obvious. It is fixable, but not in this country. Real experts are required, and I am not at all surgeon enough to make her whole. Please, Mrs. Daastrup, take her with you. You know the surgeons; I have given you the very short list. They are all in Europe or in America. Please."

"I will make it happen," Brenda said with absolute determination.

Afsoon went to dinner, and Brenda and Dr. Asad sat down on at a desk and manned two satellite phones. Brenda's brother-in-law was a naval admiral, and her husband was a CEO of a major software manufacturing company and was very wealthy.

Adm. Daastrup answered after three rings.

"Neal, this is me."

"Hi, me. What's up?"

"I have made a discovery—a diamond in the rough. There is a girl here named Afsoon. I am going to adopt her; so, she can have a last name and a life. She is a child prodigy with an encyclopedic but largely untrained mind. She is a polyglot and is able to learn mathematics at a rate that is astounding. We—and that includes you and your precious DIA—have to get her to

America for the repair of her recto-vaginal injuries from the usual: FGM then rape. She is a tough and resilient little character. I think she can be educated and can make a real contribution. She knows all about Iran and hates the country, its leaders, and its religion with a cold fury. Sound like someone that would interest you?"

"Yes, my dear little sister. I instinctively trust your judgment. I also have a heart. I will help all I can to get her the necessary surgery; and when her health permits, we can work on her education. You wouldn't be shinin' me on about her brains, would you?"

"Just wait until you see her. Your people are coming by tomorrow for just a few hours of inspection. I want to cut my own trip short and take her back with me. Please make that happen."

"Consider it done."

They passed a few pleasantries about their families, then the brother and sister-in-law signed off.

The following day, the DIA plane boarded Brenda and Afsoon for the next adventure for the young girl who was seeing her first airplane on the ground. The hardened navy men took to Afsoon immediately, and made her trip as comfortable and as much fun as only lonely men can do. Aside from Nassir, the navy men were the first males she had encountered who were genuinely nice to her—even affectionate without being sexually threatening. She astounded them with phenomenal feats of memory and found it fun when they tested her with number lists, navigational math problems, and made her laugh with American tongue twisters. Brenda knew that she had picked a winner who would yield benefits that far exceeded any costs that would be incurred in her health care and education. Afsoon Daastrup—as everyone came to know her on the plane—was as excited and thrilled to be on that plane as any sixteen-year-old girl could be at her sweet-sixteen birthday celebration.

# THE STATUS AND TREATMENT OF WOMEN UNDER ISLAMIC LAW AND PRACTICE

**"Barber-surgeons: 'If this is established, then circumcision for a man consists of cutting off the foreskin, and for a woman in clitoral excision. So it is obligatory for men and women to do this for themselves and their children, and if they neglect it, the Imam may force them do it for it is right and necessary.'"**
**-Egyptian Shafk'i lawyer Ibn al-Ukhuwa (died 1329 A.D.)**
**Edited by R. Levy, Gibb Memorial Series, 1918, pp. 163-164**
***Manual of Instruction for Muhtasibs—***
***Custodians of Public Morals and Inspectors of Markets***

The *Qur'an* and the *Hadith*—taken at face value and with some artful interpretations and omissions—can be used to support the argument that Islam provides equality in treatment of men and women, and even protections for women from men. Believers point to the *Qur'an's*—Muhammad's— emphatic defense of women, especially to the *nisa* [women's rights], chapter 4, one of the longest in the *Qur'an* with 176 verses:

- Men and women are moral and spiritual equals in the sight of Allah.
- They are expected to fulfill the same duties of worship, prayer, faith, almsgiving, fasting, and pilgrimage to Mecca.
- Allah recognizes the full personhood of women.
- Islamic law states the contractual nature of marriage, requiring that a dowry be paid by the man to the woman rather than to her family, guar-

antees women's rights of inheritance, and guarantees the ownership and management of their own property.

- Women were also granted the right to live in the matrimonial home and receive financial maintenance during marriage and during a waiting period following death of the providing spouse and after divorce.
- Women have the same rights in relation to their husbands as are expected from the men. [Sura 2:228]
- Approval and consent of a girl to marriage is a prerequisite for the validity of marriage in Islam. She has the right to say yes or no, and may not be forced into marriage for any reason.
- Men are commanded from the *Qur'an* ["I command you to be kind to women."] and under Islamic law to render kindness to women, especially their wives, "Dwell with your wives in kindness for even if you hate them, you might be hating someone in whom God has placed so much good." [*Qur'an* 4:19]. In another hadith, he said, "It is only the generous in character who is good to women, and only the evil one who insults them." In one of his last commands in his farewell pilgrimage before his death, he kept repeating, "I command you to be kind and considerate to women."
- The same admonition applies to mothers, in a Hadith, "The Prophet Muhammad (peace and blessings be upon him) said, 'Paradise is at the feet of mothers.'" Once a man came to him and asked, "O, Messenger, who among mankind is worthy of my kindness and love?" The Prophet answered, "Your mother." "Who next?" "Your mother." "Who next?" "Your mother." Only after the third time he said, "And your father."
- "Whatever men earn, they have a share of that and whatever women earn, they have a share in that." [*Qur'an* 4:32]

However, apologists for the religion seldom mention other less sanguine, but equally holy statements in the holy writings:

- "Women have the same rights (in relation to their husbands) as are expected in all decency from them, while men stand a step above them."[*Qur'an* 2:228]
- It is clear that Islamic laws pertaining to inheritance give men a higher share—twice that of females in most instances. "Allah commands you regarding your children. For the male a share equivalent to that of two females." [*Qur'an* 4:11]. Apologists argue that this entrenched discriminatory religious policy derives from women having been granted certain

listed securities—most particularly in the condemnation of the barbaric practice of infanticide of female infants by burying them alive—not a common practice in the Middle-East of today—and in the interest of family unity and preservation. "This is because of the deficiency of a woman's mind." [*Qur'an* Sura 2:282]. Islamic inheritance laws still favor men. Another security is more nebulous—the *Qur'an* admonishes families to greet the birth of a girl with the same enthusiasm as they would for a boy.

- Although a few remarkable women have held high political, governmental, and even military rank, no woman has ever held a religious title in Islam.

- Women are disparaged and objectified with respect to sexuality. A husband, by right, has sex with his wife, "as a plow goes into a field," which can be with or without her consent. "Your wives are a place of sowing of seed for you, so come to your place of cultivation however you wish and put forth righteousness for yourselves. And fear Allah and know that you will meet Him. And give good tidings to the believers...." "Jews used to say: "If one has sexual intercourse with his wife from the back, then she will deliver a squint-eyed child." So this verse was revealed: "Your wives are a tilth unto you; so go to your tilth when or how you will" [2.223, Bukhari]. "Your women are your fields, so go into your fields whichever way you like..." [*Qur'an* Sura, Al-Baqarah—The Cow—2:223]. To be indelicate, this refers to sexual positions and that women are for men to use in whatever sexual manner the men choose, again with or without the consent of the woman or the age of the female.

- The *Qur'an* is unequivocal about the privilege of men to have sex even with prepubescent females. In the context of divorcement from wives: "O Prophet, when you (and the believers) divorce women, divorce them for their prescribed waiting period and count the waiting period accurately.... And if you are in doubt about those of your women who have despaired of menstruation (you should know that), their waiting period is three months, and the same applies to those who have not menstruated as yet. As for pregnant women, their period ends when they have delivered their burden." [*Qur'an* Sura 65:1,4].

- The *Hadith* are the verified sayings of Muhammad, the Prophet. The most reliable collector was Bukhari, who died in 870. The Hadith are not strictly scripture per se, but they are held to be sacred second only to the *Qur'an*, and are studied and regularly quoted as being definitive statements of the religion of Islam since the words are those of Allah's Messenger.

- There are multiple examples of the attitude throughout Islam of the sexual function of women to give pleasure to the husband, irrespective of her own choice or preferences. "If a man invites his wife to sleep with him and she refuses to come to him, then the angels send their curses on her till morning' [Bukhari]. It is clear from the context of this hadith that the fathers of prepubescent girls may give them away, and their new husbands may consummate their marriage with them. Important Islamic scholars who hold that the *Qur'an* is universal, unchangeable, forever rebuke Muslims who deny that this verse is valid. Muhammad is the great and perfect example for Muslims to emulate. "[T]hen he [Muhammad] wrote the marriage (wedding) contract with Aishah when she was a girl of six years of age, and he consummated that marriage when she was nine years old." [Bukhari]. "The Prophet asked Abu Bakr [Muhammad's foremost companion] for Aisha's hand in marriage. Abu Bakr said "But I am your brother." The Prophet said, "You are my brother in Allah's religion and His Book, but she (Aisha) is lawful for me to marry." [Bukhari]. And for Muslim men everywhere, "When I got married, Allah's Apostle said to me, 'What type of lady have you married?' I replied, 'I have married a matron.' He said, 'Why, don't you have a liking for the virgins and for fondling them?'" Jabir also said: Allah's Apostle said, 'Why didn't you marry a young girl so that you might play with her and she with you?'" [Bukhari].

- It is clear that, from the beginning, the leaders of Islam considered women to be weaker and wickeder. "The Prophet said, 'I looked at Paradise and found poor people forming the majority of its inhabitants; and I looked at Hell and saw that the majority of its inhabitants were women." [Bukhari] The hadith goes on to indicate that the majority of the inhabitants of hell are women because they are ungrateful and harsh towards their husbands. There is no word about the husbands' ingratitude and harshness in that important hadith.

- Slave girls are the sexual property of their male owners [*Qur'an* Sura 4:24].

- A man may be polygamous with up to four wives [*Qur'an* Sura 4:3].

- Husbands may hit their wives even if the husbands merely *fear* high-handedness in their wives (Note from Carl Douglass: quite apart from whether they actually *are* highhanded) [*Qur'an* Sura 4:34].

Scriptural, traditionalist, or superstitious belief aside, most objective observers are well aware of the actual practices of Islam with regards to the treatment of women, especially in Iran—arguably the most benighted and retrograde theocracy in the Middle-East—Pakistan, and Saudi Arabia. In accordance with universal example of the Prophet, Grand Ayatollah Khomeini married a girl ten-years-of-age, and encouraged other men to do the same. He gave a statement of Iranian policy: fathers should give their daughters away before their first period. Shortly after the revolution in Iran—1979—he lowered the marriage age for girls from eighteen-years-old under the Shah's regime downwards to nine-years-of-age. In so doing, devout Muslims will not stray from original Islamic ideals, but their beliefs and practices remain shocking and abhorrent to the vast majority of the nonbelievers throughout the world.

No matter what the Islamic world at large may indicate, there is no evading the reams of evidence that the government of the Islamic Republic of Iran, the supporters of the rabidly strict regime, the police, and the military forces use rape as a weapon of coercion and terror to exact submission to the revolutionary regime. The most common offense for which women are imprisoned is that of having been raped. Floggings of girls deemed to be immoral in some manner are common place, as well as are honor killings for offenses such as smiling at a man, protesting an arranged marriage, wearing Western-style clothing, listening to Western music, or attending American and European movies—especially with male friends of which the father and brothers disapprove.

Sharia law in Iran is draconian and makes girls and women virtual prisoners in their country and to their own ignorance. There is a new Passport and Exit Law bill, which makes it mandatory for girls and women to have the approval of their "guardian" (father, husband, or paternal grandfather) to exit the country—this despite the fact that the law is at odds with the Iranian Constitution. Today, more than 60 percent of all university students in Iran are women, almost back at the level the Shah had provided. Iranian universities recently announced that more than 70 subjects in the liberal arts and sciences are now permanently closed to women, including archaeology, computer science, business management, and civil engineering; and there are restrictions on how many women can be enrolled in such academic pursuits as pediatrics and obstetrics and gynecology.

Within months of the founding of the Islamic Republic of Iran after revolution, the Shah's 1967 Family Protection Law was repealed; female government workers were forced to observe Islamic dress code; women were barred from becoming judges; beaches and sports were segregated by sex; the legal age of marriage for girls was reduced to nine; and married women were barred from attending regular schools. After the revolution, Parliament made it compulsory for all women to observe the veil and—for the first time—rules prescribing the Hijab as proper attire for women were written into law. Following the revolution, the most restrictive and punitive of laws were enacted to control women's clothing. According to the law, women's clothing should meet the following conditions:

- Women must cover their entire body except their faces and hands—from wrist to the base of the fingers.
- Women who choose not to wear a chador must wear a long overcoat called a manteau. The manteau should be thick enough to conceal what is underneath, and should be loose fitting.
- Women should not wear bright-colored clothes or clothes that are adorned so that they may attract men's attention.
- Offenses by women are dealt with by the Morals Police.

"Bad Hijabi" offenses included the wearing of tight clothes such as trousers without an overall over them, clothes bearing foreign words, signs or pictures, nail varnish, brightly colored clothing and improper modes of body movement or talking. The punishment of bad hijabi was 74 lashes in the 1983 Penal Law. In 1996, the Penal Law was reformed and the punishment of bad hijabi was reduced to prison—from ten days to four months) and/or a fine—from 50,000 to 500,000 Rials.

Although the complete covering of the female body when she is outside is described as a safety protection for women, there have been unintended deleterious health consequences. Scientists have long recognized a causal link between failure of exposure of the body to sunshine and multiple sclerosis [MS]. MS is a serious disease of the nervous system more common in females with a first manifestation in the third and fourth decades of life. The disease causes a plethora of neurological signs and symptoms that early on wax and wane but later on become permanent and progressive with devastating loss of function. 0.68 cases per 100,000 population were recorded in Tehran in 1979 just before the commencement of the Islamic Revolution. By 2005, sixteen years after the imposition of restrictive clothing requirements for women, the incidence had risen progressively to 4.58 cases per 100,000. The change in incidence is far more than is statistically required to be significant. It is dramatic. No other change in Iran with respect to women has been discovered by researchers.

Being covered by heavy opaque drapings and being prevented from exposure to life-giving sunlight has done serious harm to the immune systems of innocent women, resulting in an increased incidence of autoimmune diseases: Vitamin D levels in women, reported in 2011, are low and are associated with rickets, osteomalacia and osteoporosis, high blood pressure, Type 1 diabetes, colorectal cancer, Crohn's Disease, chronic lymphocytic leukemia, lupus erythematosis, rheumatoid arthritis, psoriasis, gout, infertility, depression, Alzheimer's disease, and periodontal disease to name only a few conditions that have seen increased incidence in women as a direct cause of the backward requirements placed on women by the Islamic Republic of Iran.

-Sources: *Mayoclinic.com, Wikipedia, WebMD News* (Salynn Boyles), Julia Pakpoor and Sreeram Ramagopalan, Oxford researchers in *Genome Research*, Edel Rodriguez, *Sun Blocked* in *Smithsonian.com*, May, 2013.

Segregation of the sexes for public places such as beaches, swimming pools, schools, libraries, cafes, restaurants, hairdressers, or sport halls was ordered and legally introduced. According to the law, there had to be separate sections for the sexes at political meetings, conferences, weddings and funerals, and even men and women should form different queues. Females caught by revolutionary officials in a mixed-sex situation can be subjected to virginity tests.

The restrictive rules dominate female athletic involvement. Female Iranian athletes are all but prevented from participation in the Olympic Games. In December 2007, the vice president of the Iranian Olympic Committee, Abdolreza Savar, issued a memorandum to all sporting federations about the "proper behavior of male and female athletes" and that "severe punishment will be meted out to those who do not follow Islamic rules during sporting competitions" both local and abroad. Men are not allowed to train or coach women. Iran's female volleyball team was once considered the best in Asia, but due to lack of female coaches, it has been prevented from international competition. Iranian women are allowed to compete in sports that require removal of the *hijab*, but only in arenas that are all female. They are banned from public events if spectators include unrelated men.

Grand Ayatollah Khomeini stated, regarding education, "As the religious leaders have influence and power in this country, they will not permit girls to study in the same school with boys. They will not permit women to teach at boys' schools. They will not permit men to teach at girls' schools. They will not allow corruption in this country." When women protested, as one suffragette observed, "We didn't gain any political freedoms like promised. We also lost our personal freedoms. As early as 1981, there were thousands of teenage political prisoners inside prisons. At the beginning, they attacked us with baseball bats, then tear gas, then live bullets." When she was sixteen years old, she was arrested at a demonstration against Khomeini's new Islamic Republic. She later wrote that, "They took me into a small room in Evin Prison. Two men tried to handcuff me and realized my wrists were too small; so, they put both of my wrists together into one cuff and as it clicked, I heard my right wrist crack. They tied me to the bed and they struck me on the soles of feet so many times with a cable wire that my feet looked like balloons with toes on them." During the time of the Shah, "some 5 or 6 prisoners were in each cell. During my time, there were 50, 60, or 70. There was no room to move, at night we slept like sardines."

"As early as 1981 there were thousands of teenage political prisoners inside prisons. At the beginning they attacked us with baseball bats, then tear gas, then live bullets." She was raped repeatedly by the guards as were many of the women. They never dared to talk about the rapes.

Unfortunately, such maltreatment is not an aberration; it is inculcated in the Penal Code of the Islamic Republic of Iran. For example, Article 102 specifies the manner of execution and types of stones that should be used. Article 102 states that men will be buried up to their waists and women up to their breasts for the purpose of execution by stoning. Article 104 states, with reference to the penalty for adultery, that the stones used should "not be large enough to kill the person by one or two strikes; nor should they be so small that they could not be defined as stones." This makes it clear that the purpose of stoning is to inflict pain in a process leading to slow death. Of women saved from stoning and those who have been granted stays of execution, at least three cases of individuals sentenced to stoning have been executed by hanging.

A summary of the penal code has been translated by Dr. Soheila Vahdati. Some of the interesting laws include—Article 84: An old adulterer or an old adulteress who qualifies as marriage-bound shall be subject to flogging punishment prior to stoning. Article 88: The adultery punishment for a man or woman who does not meet the marriage-bound conditions is one hundred lashes. Article 96: The flogging shall not be carried out in too cold or too hot weather. Article 98: When a person is sentenced to multiple punishments, the order of carrying out the sentences must be such that none of them prevents another; therefore, if someone is sentenced to flogging and stoning, first flogging and then stoning shall be carried out. Article 100: The flogging punishment for an adulterer man shall be carried out as he is standing and wearing no clothing except to cover his genitals. Lashes must forcefully inflict his entire body except for his head, face, and genitals. An adulterer woman shall be flogged in a sitting position with her clothes bound to her body. Article 106: Adultery during the holy times such as religious festivities and Ramadan and Friday and at holy places such as mosques will constitute flogging in addition to the regular punishment.

Attacks on lesbian, gay, bisexual, and transsexual people by authorities in Iran since the Iranian Revolution of 1979 have come into conflict with the penal code, which is itself Mediaeval and barbaric. International human rights groups report floggings and death sentences of lesbian, gay, and bisexual individuals.

Such discriminatory, demeaning, humiliating, and flagrantly anti-female rhetoric, laws, and actions are not limited to Iran, of course. A list of institutional injuries by the Islamic patriarchy against defenseless women over just the just the past ten years would be much longer than this book. A few examples will suffice to illustrate the fact that the forms of discrimination against women are widespread, if not entirely universal:

- According to the official statement of the senior Muslim clerical body of the largest Muslim-majority nation of the world—the Indonesian Ulema Council—"the practice (of FGM) is a religious obligation that should be done to control women's sexual desires."
- No woman has been able to vote in the Pakistani village of Mateela, near Sargodha, for many decades. Mateela is one of 564 of the 64,000 polling places in Pakistan where not a single woman voted in 2008—all because the men of the village—their husbands—decide that the women cannot vote. The prevailing reason given by the men is that women do not have the mental capacity to vote; others cannot vote because they are not allowed to leave the house; others are not allowed to vote because the polling places allow the mixing of genders; and others cannot vote because the man of the house does not consider the nominal cost of the required ID card to be a worthwhile use of the family's money. Restricting the right to vote is a common practice throughout the Muslim world, especially in rural areas where education is limited.

-Source: Rebecca Santana, *Associated Press*

- Islamic Tuareg fighters from the Movement for the Liberation of Azawad (MNLA) seized Haribomo and other parts of northern Mali following a March 2012 military coup that plunged the previously stable West

African state into chaos. But better-armed and wealthier Islamist groups had chased Tuareg fighters out of town. Under the Tuareg occupation, there were cases of gang rape and an increase in forced marriage. The Islamists brought Sharia law with them, with its brutal punishments such as lashing and stoning. They forced the women of Haribomo to cover up from head to toe, and they outlawed sex before marriage. That notwithstanding, Islamist occupiers committed acts of sexual violence against the women themselves on a grand scale. There have been at least 200 documented cases of forced marriage and sexual violence since March 2012, according to the Gao-based nongovernment organization GREFFA, citing a report by the U.N. Special Representative of the Secretary General on Sexual Violence in Conflict. GREFFA saw the report but it has not been made public. Meanwhile, a joint initiative by U.N. Women and GREFFA has collected the testimonies of 52 girls and women who suffered gender-based violence in the towns of Gao and Menaka since April last year.

-Source: Wikipedia

- A fifteen-year-old rape victim has been sentenced to 100 lashes for engaging in premarital sex, court officials said. The charges against the girl were brought against her last year after police investigated accusations that her stepfather had raped her and killed their baby. He is still to face trial.

The legal system of the Maldives, an Islamic archipelago with a population of some 400,000, has elements of Islamic law (Sharia) as well as English common law. Ahmed Faiz, a researcher with Amnesty International, said flogging was "cruel, degrading and inhumane," and urged the authorities to abolish it.

-Source: BBC

- Sudan:

Sudanese security officers in Kadugli the capital of South Kordofan/Nuba mountains state started an arrest campaign against women in Kadugli. The conditions in the Kadugli prison are described to be inhuman by some detainees released. A released detainee from Kadugli, who was detained on

December 14th, 2012, informed the reporter that he had been severely tortured while he was detained in the Army 14th division base in Kadugli, the capital of South Kordofan state. He said that "they take us with our eyes covered to closed rooms and they beat us and put us in big barrels of cold water for hours. The peoples who were torturing us were not Sudanese they were not speaking Arabic." He said this kind of torture had been used on him and many of his colleagues [detainees]—men and women—and the detainees were always taken with their eyes closed to the torture rooms.

The women in Al OBied women prison are detained in a cell of 4×5 meters for 30 women with 6 children at least, and they all use just one bathroom and they are not allowed to use it after the sun set; so, they have to spend 15 hours, from 5:00 PM to 8:00 AM without going to the bath room; and they have plastic basins to go inside the cell. The women are ordered to cook their food—which is lentils—and they have just two meals a day—many days without bread. The detainees are not allowed medical care, family, or lawyers visits.

-Source: BBC

• Afghanistan:

The Women Living Under Muslim Laws (WLUML) international solidarity network and Violence is Not Our Culture Campaign (VNC) strongly condemn the imprisonment of women and girls in Afghanistan (approximately 400 of them) for so-called "moral crimes," including running away from home. The new study released by Human Rights Watch (HRW), *I Had to Run Away: The Imprisonment of Women and Girls for "Moral Crimes" in Afghanistan* documents the phenomenon of these "crimes," which often involve flight from early forced marriages or domestic violence. Some women and girls have been convicted of *zina* (sex outside of marriage) after being raped or forced into prostitution.

Although running away (without permission) is not a crime under the Afghan criminal code, the Afghan Supreme Court has instructed judges to treat women and girls who flee as criminals. According to HRW's report, women and girls were criminalized because they escaped from forced and underage marriage, beatings, stabbings, burnings, being threatened, or after reporting of having been raped, kidnapped and/or having been forced into prostitution. However, when women have gone to the police to report, there is rarely an investigation, let alone prosecution and punishment.

The use of religion and customs to justify the policing of women's behavior including control of her sexuality remains pervasive in Afghan society. "Moral crimes," which these women and girls in prison are accused of, are intertwined with the customary beliefs on 'honor' and 'dignity'. The notion that women are the vessels of familial and communal honor also becomes the justification for patriarchal control over them. 'Honor' is also intimately tied to a woman's economic value. Girls are not viewed as able to generate income for the families and are therefore 'disposable' to men who could support them. Thus, child marriages are practiced widely, particularly as poorer families can get sizeable dowries for their daughters. Criminalization of child marriage has had little impact, in part because real age is difficult to establish when neither births nor marriages are routinely registered.

Girls who are perceived as no longer 'virgins' are not only devalued and ineligible for marriage, they could be criminalized even if they were victims of rape. Girls and women who flee their homes because they are subject to violence or domestic abuse are seen as equally tainted, as no one can vouch for her honor if she was 'unsupervised' outside the reach of her male family members. Police are authorized to arrest these girls if a complaint is lodged by a husband or relative, but will rarely investigate their own complaints. Prosecutors have a tendency to ignore evidence that corroborates their innocence, and judges often convict on the basis of illegally extracted "confessions." All these despite the passage of the Elimination of Violence Against Women (EVAW) Law in 2009, which criminalizes acts of violence against women. The implementation of this law is sorely lacking.

-Source: Human Rights Watch

Islamic apologists have answers and counters to the critics around the world who consider such laws and penalties demeaning and injurious to women and girls and barbaric in their ferocity—even without bringing up accusations of murderous terrorism and bigotry. The most definitive statement came on March 13, 2013 and is presented here, translated from Arabic, in its entirety.

"In the name of God the Merciful"
Statement of the Muslim Brotherhood about The Convention on the Elimination of All Forms of Discrimination Against Women (CEDAW) which violates all principles of the Islamic Sharia and the Islamic community.
The Commission on the Status of Women holds a conference in the period from the 4th to the 15th of March 2013 to approve a document titled (The

Convention on the Elimination of All Forms of Discrimination Against Women), a deceptive headline that includes items collide with the principles of Islam and its basic unanimous elements of *Qur'an* and Sunnah, destroy Islamic ethics, and seek to demolish the institution of the family, which the Egyptian constitution confirmed is the building block of the society, and hence achieve the dismantling of the community, and end to the last step of the intellectual and cultural invasion, and eliminate the privacy that preserve elements of Islamic societies and its cohesion.

It is enough to give a closer reading at these items to realize what is meant to us, and these items are:

1. Grant girls their complete sexual freedom, as well as the freedom to choose their sex and the freedom to choose their sex partners (i.e., choose to have a normal sexual relationship or atypical) with rising the age of marriage.

2. Provide contraception for adolescent girls and train them on how to use it with the legalization of abortion to abort undesirable pregnancy under the name of sexual and reproduction rights.

3. Equality between an adulterous husband and a wife, and equality between adultery children (outside of marriage children) and legitimate sons in all rights.

4. Granting homosexuals all their rights, protection and respect, and grant protection for women in prostitution.

5. Grant wives all the right to sue their husbands with charges of rape or harassment, and the competent authorities should grant same penalties similar to raping or harassing a stranger.

6. Equality in inheritance.

7. Replace guardianship with partnership, and fully share the roles within the family between men and women such as: spending, child care, home affairs.

8. Equal access to the marriage legislations such as: Stop polygamy, *Iddah*, mandate, and the dowry, and stop obligatory spending of man on the family, and to allow Muslim women to marry a non-Muslim and others.

9. Withdraw the authority of divorce from husbands and authorize it to judiciary and share property after divorce.

10. Cancel the obligatory authorization of the husband in: travel, work or going out or use contraception.

These are the destructive means of the institution of the family and community that calls for the return of the first medieval period.

The Muslim Brotherhood call upon rulers of Islamic countries and Foreign Ministers and their representatives in the United Nations to reject this document, and also we invite this organization to live up to the level of the pure family relations prescribed by Islam.

Also Muslim Brotherhood calls al-Azhar to act according to its leading role and to condemn this document and declare the position of Islam towards its articles, as it is the reference for Muslims.

As well we call other Islamic groups and associations to take a decisive stand against this document and the like.

We also call for women's organizations to adhere to their religion and the morals of their communities and the elements of our social life and not to be seduced by the deceptive, misleading and destructive calls for urbanization.

-The Muslim Brotherhood
Cairo: 13 March 2013

-Source: Muslim Brotherhood Facebook Page

# CONCLUSION

The Islamic punishments have encouraged a culture of violence against women—especially within the family—and has spilled into violence against children. This has been commented upon by many within the country [Iran].... The fact that men receive a lighter punishment if they commit violence against women undoubtedly encourages such violence. We saw how women could be killed with impunity during alleged adultery. Stoning to death for adultery, although technically admissible for both sexes, has also been carried out mainly against women.

-Source: Zohreh Arshadi, who was a practicing lawyer in Iran prior to her forced exile to Europe.

-Sources: *Walden University Online—LookLex Encyclopedia*; *OpenCourseWare*, University of Notre Dame. *Faith, Practice, and Law in Sunni and Shi'i Islam. ugu.edu—University of Georgia online*; *Wikipedia.* Michael Axworthy, *A History of Iran: Empire of the Mind;* Ervand Abrahamian, *A History of Modern Iran*; Nikki R. Keddie, *Modern Iran: Roots and Results of Revolution;* Hamid Dabashi, *Iran: A People Interrupted;* Amnesty International, *Iran: Violation of Human Rights, 1991; Pour Mohammadi and the 1988 Prison Massacres, Human Rights Watch Report*, December, 2005. *Iran, Lonely Planet*, Andrew Burke and Mark Elliott, 2008, *Islam*, ed. John Alden Williams, 1961; *Islam*, 5th Ed, Cesar E. Farah, Ph.D.; Dore Gold, *Hatred's Kingdom: How Saudi Arabia Supports the New Global Terrorism*; Milton Viorst, *In the Shadow of the Prophet: The Struggle for the Soul of Islam*, Wilfried Buchta, *Who Rules Iran?* 2000.

The first thing which comes in my mind when I hear "Violence against Women" is injustice, cruelty and an act which will destroy generations. It hurts me badly. To me it is brutality, butchery and barberry (sic) against one of the greatest creation (sic) of the God. A woman is mother, sister, wife, daughter or a girlfriend. How can we go to that extreme level to disrespect all the relations a woman might have and torture her mentally or physically?

-Syed Mahmood Kazmi, *Violence against Women and Human Rights Day*, December 9, 2012

# CAST OF CHARACTERS
[Most important continuing characters—*]

## IRAN

| | |
|---|---|
| Nawsheen Shakibaie | Afsoon's birth mother, fourth wife of Ahriman |
| *Ahriman Shakibaie | Afsoon's birth father, master of a tent hamlet near Qushchu, Kurdestan County, West Azerbaijan Province, Iran |
| *Fereshten Shakibaie | Ahriman's first wife |
| *Azadeh Shakibaie | Ahriman's fourth wife |
| *Afsoon Daastrup— Afsoon Mouradipour | Biological daughter of Nawsheen and Ahriman Shakibaie, adopted daughter of Neal and Brenda Daastrup. Mourapidour is a cover name |
| *Astera Shakibaie | Ahriman's third wife |
| *Yasmin | Wet nurse and surrogate mother to Afsoon |

| | |
|---|---|
| Kamin Shakibaie | Ahriman and Fereshten's third son, Afsoon's half-brother |
| Muhammad Shakibaie | Ahriman and Fereshten's son, Afsoon's half-brother |
| Shokofeh | Astera's servant |
| Farhad Sharifi | Shepherd boy, illicit lover of Astera |
| *Firudin Jamshidi | Afsoon's temporary paternal guardian in rural Kurdestan County, West Azerbaijan Province, Iran |
| *Mariella Jamshidi | Afsoon's temporary maternal guardian in rural Kurdestan village |
| *Nassir Jamshidi | Loving "brother" of Afsoon in rural Kurdestan village |
| *Elaheh Jamshidi | Daughter of Firudin and Mariella Jamshidi |
| Mozaffarian and Gorgani Jamshidi | Elder sons of Firudin and Mariella Jamshidi |
| Dina Jamshidi | Daughter of Firudin and Mariella Jamshidi |
| Fatemah Shakibaie | New—fourth—wife of Ahriman after death of Astera |
| The Dashnaksutyun | Armenian bandits |
| *Fereshte [angel]. | Afsoon's beloved rag doll, made for her by Nassir |
| Imam Ali Abedi | Cleric who preformed FGMs |

| | |
|---|---|
| Imam Zamaani Fard | Cleric in Kandovan who conducted Dina's funeral |
| *Grand Ayatollah Ali ibn Abi Rahimi | Supreme Leader of Iran—the Agha, the SL |
| Saif-al-din and his wife, Parveen | Temporary guardians of Afsoon in Kandovan Village, Kurdestan County, West Azerbaijan Province, Iran |
| *Hassanzadeh Shakibaie | Eldest son of Ahriman and Fereshten Shakibaie |
| Shireen | Shakibaie slave girl |
| *The Bakhtiaris | Bedouin nomads from the Zagros Mountains |
| Mullah Haji Zamaani Fard | Circuit judge at Piranshahr jail |
| Shafiqah Kadivar | Afsoon's employer at a wool carpet factory in Amarrh, Iraq |
| Sergeant Naomeh Nikahd | Municipal police, Al Basrah, Iraq |
| Aisha Toskhani | Kashmiri Pandit woman in charge of humanitarian relief center, Al Basrah, Iraq |
| Dr. Sylvia Asad | Physician at the humanitarian relief center, Al Basrah, Iraq |
| Haji NaazemZadeh Harandi | Scholar, librarian, teacher at the humanitarian relief center, Al Basrah, Iraq |

| | |
|---|---|
| Roshanak Rahimi | Wife of Supreme Leader Grand Ayatollah Ali ibn Abi Rahimi |
| Ali Hosseini Mejazi | Chief of staff of Supreme Leader Grand Ayatollah Ali ibn Abi Rahimi |
| *Mohsen Shahamatdoost and successor Hormoz Okhavat | Presidents of the Republic of Iran |
| Yazid ibn Sarrafzaadeh | Chief of Staff of the Armed Forces of the Republic of Iran |
| *Moqtada al-Benizir and Ayatollah Ali Hossein Golzar his successor after al-Benizir was murdered. Aisha and Khadija | Head of the Atomic Energy Organization Iran (AEOI). His wife and daughter (a singer) |
| *Mullah Ali Salar Omidyar | Director of the Ministry of Intelligence and Security (MOIS) |
| *Behrouz Omidi | Director of the Ministry of Intelligence and National Security of the Islamic Republic of Iran (MISIRI) or VEVAK. |
| Abdul Qadeer (AQ) Khan | Smuggler of uranium enrichment and nuclear weapon technology to Muslim countries |
| *Hamid Hejazi | SL guard, Agent-Ex |
| *Daniel and Brenda Daastrup | Georgetown, Washington, D.C. Daniel is Neal Daastrup's brother, and Brenda, his sister-in-law. They are the adoptive parents of Afsoon |

| | |
|---|---|
| Dr. Nawal El Mubarak | Egyptian feminist physician and surgeon who repaired Afsoon's recto-vaginal fistula |
| *Ali Mohamed Mustaffen | Director of the Central Bank of the Islamic Republic of Iran |
| Ali Muhummad Sharifi, Mahdis and Javaneh, Mojtaba | Iranian Foreign Minister, his wife and 2 children (singers) |
| Col. Dariush Aghdashloo | On-site commander of the Agha's private security force. |

Col. Dariush Aghdashloo

1.  Daron Naderi
2.  Ayatollah Mohammad Esmail Rahmanipour
3.  Ali Hossein Rahnavardand
4.  Bobak Larijani
5.  Col. Darius Aghdashloo

The management of the SL's household and directors of his personal guard [SL Agha Rahimi's oldest friends, if the Supreme Leader of Iran's Muslims could actually have friends in the usual sense]:

1.  Head of amputee war veterans
2.  Currently a member of parliament
3.  Director of IRGC intelligence
4.  Head of the guard corps and member of the Security Council
5.  Second in command to Rahnavard.

*Project *Jahannam Adur* [Hell's Fire]    Iranian project for manufacture of nuclear weapons, placing them in missiles, and delivering the missiles on Israel and the U.S.

219

| | |
|---|---|
| *Elizabeth Dayan | American expatt living in Iran, horse rancher, and spy for The Iran Nuclear Interdiction Project |
| *Elias, Zachariah, Elijah, Kelsey, Leopold, and Pearl Nichols-Dayan | Children of Elizabeth and co-conspirators. Elias is an active agent with Aaron Schmuel in Iran |
| *Rabbi Ya'akov ben Avraham | Persian Jewish rabbi who ostensibly is a loyal citizen of Iran and secretly becomes an agent for the American-run Iran Nuclear Interdiction Project. Member of Neturei Karta—Ultra-Orthodox Jews, a Jewish Sect that opposes both Zionism and Israel. |
| Esfandiari Razizadeh | Deputy of Moqtada al-Benizir, head of the Atomic Energy Organization Iran (AEOI) |
| Razmara Tassoudji | Deputy of Moqtada al-Benizir, head of the Atomic Energy Organization Iran (AEOI) |
| *Amir Vehrahrami | Chief engineer for research and development at the Bushehr nuclear plant |
| *Hormoz Mohammad-Bagher | President of Bank Sepah, Tehran |
| Cantor Avril Azaria | Jewish singer |
| Ali Hassan Zolein | Member of the Majilis who spoke of Israeli Trojan Horse |
| Ayatollah Ali Hossein Golzar | New head of AEOI after al Benizir's murder |

| | |
|---|---|
| Arash Behdad | Finance Minister of Iran |
| Saad ad-Daula Khan | Bakhtiari headman near the Caspian Sea |
| Muhammad | Bakhtiari headman who helped Afsoon escape from jail |
| Shapour Del-anchin, Fereydoon Alipour, Amilie Bakhtiari, and Ali Asghar | Bakhtiari tribespeople killed during Afsoon's escape |
| Dr. Abbas and Mrs. Ahuva Homayoun | Afsoon's doctor aand nurse during the escape |
| Ghurkas Thapa Dhanbahadur and Ghhetri Krishnabahadur | Carter Miller-Partridge's two Indian SAS agents |

## ISRAEL

| | |
|---|---|
| *Major General Zwi Rosenstein | Deputy director Mossad |
| Zeev Rosenkranz | Chief of Tel Aviv Israeli mafia –"Kosher Nostra" |
| *Max Rosenstein | Zwi's brother and second in command of Kosher Nostra |
| *Moise Levinsky | Ranking Kosher Nostra officer |
| *Jacob "The Greaser" Cohen | Ranking Kosher Nostra officer |
| *General André Lansky | Director of the Mossad |

| | |
|---|---|
| David Henderson | Mossad agent and Krav Maga expert |
| Sergeant Ruth McGuire | Mossad analyst |
| *Levi, Miriam, Rebecca, Alice, Abraham, Constance, Michael, Harry, Daniel, Avril, Julius, and Elsie | Mossad Institute analyst group |
| SLHAN1__@# percent@*trickmagicphantom. | G.R. IV's Mossad login code |
| Antal Disraeli | Mossad *katsa*—case officer |
| *Elsie Silberberg | Electronic communications analyst, friend of G.R. IV |
| Gideon Meier and Rudolf Ashensky | Mossad agents active in battles between Bakhtiari and Iranian army. |

## UNITED STATES

| | |
|---|---|
| *Gideon Emmanuel Rothsberger, I, II, III, IV [G.R. I, II, III, IV] | Line of wealthy Orthodox Jewish bankers; G.R. III and IV are members of the *Sayanim*. I is deceased, II is CEO of Gideon Products Universal, III is president of Rothsberger & Company Bankers, and IV is senior vice-president of the bank. Part of the Iran Nuclear Interdiction Project |
| *Chava Dayan-Hershowitz Rothsberger | Mother of G.R. IV |

| | |
|---|---|
| Tahmineh and Leila Rothsberger | Twins daughters of G.R. III and Chava, and sisters of G.R. IV |
| Nathan Rothsberger | Uncle of G.R. IV who opposes him for the position of senior vice-president and president-elect of Rothsberger & Company Bankers |
| *Rebecca Hershowitz | Mother of Chava and grandmother of G.R. IV |
| Dr. ben Schulberg | Chava's obstetrician |
| Joseph ben Aaron, | Rothsberger's butler |
| Ruth Kline | G.R. IV's nannyAbba Cogen |
| Abba Cogen | G.R. IV's *mohel* [circumcisor] |
| Rabbi Bergen | Rothsberger's rabbi |
| *Aaron Schmuel | School bully, later friend of G.R. IV, action agent of the DIA in the Iran Nuclear Interdiction Project |
| *Levi Schmuel | Aaron's father, member of Kosher Nostra |
| Rabbi Pinchas ben Yisroel, ha-Rav | Headmaster, Saint Francis Woods Hebrew Academy |
| Leopold Antal Lavigne | Dean of students, Saint Francis Woods Hebrew Academy |
| *Lt. Col. Shai Avitan | Martial arts instructor, IDF. Krav Maga expert |

| | |
|---|---|
| Professor Samson Bernstein | UC Berkeley Professor and tutor for G.R. IV in elementary and high school |
| Gilda Rogdonavich | Master's thesis *Gifted Child* about G.R. IV |
| President Tate-Waring | President of UC Berkeley |
| Tom Bradshaw | Senate Majority Leader |
| *Ali ibn Massoud | VEVAK contact agent in the Ali and the Twelve Imams mosque |
| Dr. Stephen Ammon Rhodes | UC Berkeley math professor for G.R. IV |
| Dr. Willard Lazar | Head of the department of computer science—G.R. IV's major professor at Berkeley |
| Dr. Stanley Protel Thatcher | Head of the MIT computer science department |
| Miriam bat Ezekiel | Message courier—member of the *Sayanim* |
| Dr. Kristina Shimazaki | G.R. IV's MIT major professor in mathematics |
| Drs. Leif Erik Nielson and Karl L. Nielson | MIT economics department co-chairs |
| *Rear Adm. Martin Torgelson | Assumed the office of DDDIA in 2011 when Neal Daastrup retired. The appellation "3D" stuck with Vice-Adm. Daastrup, so Torgelson became known as the Swede. |

| | |
|---|---|
| Rabbi Pinchas ben Yisroel, ha-Rav | Headmaster, Saint Francis Woods Hebrew Academy |
| Leopold Antal Lavigne | Dean of students, Saint Francis Woods Hebrew Academy |
| Professor Samson Bernstein | UC Berkeley Professor and tutor for G.R. IV in elementary and high school |
| *Howard Ryan, Glen Gabler, Agnes Maxwell Cunningham, Oliver Sandstone, Umberto Gonzales | Presidents of the U.S. |
| *Army Col. Avery Holmes and Navy Captain Victor Raylan | Heads of DARPA and the SSG-CNO respectively. [Defense Advanced Research Projects Agency and Strategic Studies Group for the Chief of Naval Operations] |

## SWEDEN

| | |
|---|---|
| Jonas Zillacus | Ambassador to the United States |
| *Ali Nylander | Consular agent in charge of trade and economic affairs |
| Dr. Arvid Bergström | Counselor for Swedish defense |
| Counselor Ms. Sanna Kullberg | Special Advisor, Homeland Security Affairs |
| Magnus Bielvenstram | Minister-Counselor, Trade and Economic Affairs |

| | |
|---|---|
| *Johannes Hjerdstadt | Ostensibly, the undersecretary for embassy affairs. Actually, an agent of *FMUndSäkC* [Swedish Army Intelligence]. |
| *Marta Olson | Agent of *FMUndSäkC* protecting Afsoon in Sweden |
| *Ingrid Hakkensdatter | Agent of *FMUndSäkC* protecting Afsoon in Sweden |
| Nick Staphanakis | DIA agent protecting Afsoon in Sweden |
| Michael Grodmore | DIA agent protecting Afsoon in Sweden |
| Hassan Tajbakhsh | VEVAK agent following/ protecting Afsson |
| Mohammad Ali Nikookar | VEVAK agent following/ protecting Afsson |
| Ayatollah Mammad Qazwini | Senior VEVAK agent in Sweden |
| Salar Sabeti | VEVAK agent in Sweden who first approached Afsoon at the University |
| Mohammad Ali Nikookar | VEVAK agent in Sweden |
| Ali Hossein | VEVAK agent in Sweden |

## FRANCE

| | |
|---|---|
| *Miriam Shahnameh | Maiden name of Gideon's wife— opera singer |

Elijah and Ruth Shahnameh    French Orthodox Jews, parents
                             of Miriam

Gideon Rothsberger V, and Ruth    G.R IV and Miriam R's children

Marius Duvalier    Elderly French singer

## NORTH KOREA

Gen. Gangjon Chung-a    North Korean General, head of the
                        DRNK Institute of Atomic Energy

Col. Dockko Yong-Jin, and Dr.    Officials of the North Korean
Soung Hong-jik                   [DRNK] Institute of
                                 Atomic Energy

AUTHOR CARL DOUGLASS, a former neurosurgeon turned full time author, writes with gripping realism because in all his books he has been there and done that in some measure. He grew up in a small town where fighting was the rule, not the exception. He was determined to escape the sameness of geography, intellectual outlook, and career prospects of the majority of his contemporaries. In complete naiveté, he applied to only one well-known major university for his undergraduate work, and to everyone's surprise, he was accepted. He found himself out of his league scholastically and had to work like a Hannibal to find a way or make one to succeed in that rarefied atmosphere. His goal of success was to become a neurosurgeon, and he did it. His career in academia and the military as well as his work as a medical humanitarian provided the background to produce the riveting tales that have made their way into his remarkable books.